The Sun and The Moon

Bailey Mckean

MILTON & HUGO L.L.C.
4407-11 Park Ave., Suite 5
Union City, NJ 07087, USA

Website: *www. miltonandhugo.com*
Hotline: *1- 888-778-0033*
Email: *info@miltonandhugo.com*

Ordering Information:
Quantity sales. Special discounts are granted to corporations, associations, and other organizations. For more information on these discounts, please reach out to the publisher using the contact information provided above.

Library of Congress Control Number: 2023924090
ISBN-13: 979-8-89285-004-9 [Paperback Edition]
979-8-89285-005-6 [Digital Edition]

Rev. date: 12/27/2023

ACKNOWLEDGMENTS

*To the haters who didn't believe in me and prayed on my
downfall. Thank you for encouraging me to do nothing but be
better than you and achieve your dreams before you could,
And to my mommy for backing me up and "helping to take a bitch down."*

· 1 ·

MARSHAL

I hadn't slept yet. All I could think about was how she was gone. Winnie was gone. The love of my life, the only girl I swore I'd ever love, was just… gone. I would never be able to hug her again. I'd never be able to breathe the sweet smell of the cherry blossom perfume she wore every day for two years. I would never get to feel the warmth of her face against my neck again when she hugged me or her soft lips on mine. I'd never get to feel the brush of her lips against my sensitive skin again. Her fingers would never interlock with mine again. I'd never get to feel that kind of intimacy again. We had broken up in the past and had our on-and-off-again times, but never like this.

Winnie had called me earlier and asked me to lunch. We met at a diner in town with a 60's retro theme that had the servers wear 60's themed uniforms and serve you on roller skates. Winnie had gotten there before me and ordered my regular order: a double burger, fries, and a strawberry milkshake. We talked like usual, making small talk and laughing about inside jokes. The server brought us our food. Winnie had her diet coke and a salad, and we fell into a content lull eating. I was about halfway through my burger when Winnie put her fork down and looked at me with a pitiful expression, and then she said it;

> *"Marshal, don't you think it's just wild we're going to be juniors in high school this year?! In two months, isn't that wild? It's crazy, Marshal!" she said in her regular bubbly tone, but then she swallowed and shifted in her seat uncomfortably. "And you know Marsh, I've spent so much of my life with you; we've been together forever, right?" I*

1

nodded between bites of burger. She continued on with a sad smile that I didn't quite understand. "Soon, it's going to be over. I mean, we'll be off to college and well..." she paused to clear her thoughts before speaking quietly, "We need to think about our futures and, more importantly, our futures," my stomach dropped when she said that. I knew where this was going.

'*I think we should see other people, and I really found that high school challenges me as a person, you know, Marsh? I just think we're growing up and changing, our individuality is developing, and I need to find my place, Marshal, and well...Right now, I think my place isn't with you...*'

I couldn't speak. I couldn't think. Winnie's lips were moving, and sounds were coming out, but I couldn't hear the words she was saying. Her hand reached for mine, but I pulled away quickly. Too quickly, like her touch was going to burn me. I got up abruptly from our booth, tripping on my untied shoelace, almost smacking my face off the black and white floor tiles. People turned to stare, but I didn't care. I needed to get out. I was suffocating all of a sudden and couldn't breathe; everyone's prying eyes only made it harder. My face was red and hot, and there was a pressure in my throat. I needed to get out of there. I got up and ran. Greedily sucking in fresh air only to choke on it.

It was dark outside now. I didn't know how long I'd been laying in bed, minutes, hours, days? My stomach turned. All I knew was she was gone. Everywhere I looked, there were pieces of her in my room, reminders that she still existed but was no longer in my life. There were photos of us or things she'd gotten me, like little trinkets, even a sweater she'd left at my house before school had gotten out; on my nightstand, there were two purple hair clips and a hair tie. It felt like she was in every part of my room and in every part of my life. There was no escaping it. It was suffocating; I couldn't breathe, and my chest was too tight. It was strangling me, the grief squeezing my lungs and throat so I couldn't breathe.

With each reminder, a fresh pang of hurt rolled through my chest, adding to the sensation of my already rapid and shallow breathing. My eyes burned with the hot heat of tears, but they wouldn't fall. Not yet. I didn't know what to do without her. I was nothing without her. At that moment, I might have started crying, but I wasn't sure. I was numb and couldn't feel anything right then and there; it was like the heartbreak expelled me from my body, and I was floating through space. The only thing reminding me of being here was the flipping of my stomach, the burn crawling up my throat as I heaved.

I sat up and realized I was soaked in sweat, my hair was damp, clinging to my neck and forehead, and my shirt felt too tight, my jeans were too heavy, weighing my legs down, and the denim against my legs felt horrible. I ripped off my clothes and stood in my room in my underwear; the sticky heaviness of the air making my skin stick was a welcome sensation compared to the previous one. Inside, I could feel nothing; I was empty. Nothing seemed real.

The wall space above my bed was occupied by a photo wall shaped like a heart. Winnie had taken a bunch of pictures of us and printed them out. My mom let her in. She arranged all the pictures of us in a heart as a surprise. The images were put up in December as my Christmas gift, and I looked at each individual photo carefully in a way I had never truly done, taking the time to take the scene in full and appreciating them in a way I never had. The pictures ranged over long periods of time, and you could see the change in us both. We both started to look older in the pictures; my hair went from neatly trimmed to shaggy, hers from long to a short bob. Our eyes became duller and our faces thinner, the childish fat melting away.

I loved Winnie since the first day I saw her in third grade. I remember how I was so nervous I couldn't speak to her. I'd start to panic and throw up. Kia always made fun of me and told me how stupid I was for falling so hard for Winnie. We'd been apart before over stupid stuff, and Kia was always there with me, but this time, it was different. Something about what she said to me told me it was for real this time. She had never sat me down like that; 'we should see other people' was all I could think about. Over and over again, I could just hear her words. She was serious about this, a serious I'd never seen in our relationship before. It felt like I'd just been kicked full force in the gut, the realization of everything finally sinking in. The realization hit me, making a burning sensation crawl up my throat. I grabbed at my stomach before eventually expelling the acidic bile, my throat stinging with the burn as it flowed from between my lips.

It was 1 A.M. on a summer night, and I was cleaning up my vomit in my underwear, probably crying.

· II ·

KIA

I woke up to a swift kick in the back.

"Up yours, Thatcher," I responded meekly, my words mumbled as I buried my face into my pillow.

My head hurt, and so did my back from Addison Thatcher's foot being jammed between my shoulder blades. I kept my eyes closed tightly and folded the pillow so I could hold it over my ears as if it would help keep my head from exploding. I didn't remember much from the night before. I wracked my brain for answers that didn't seem to exist, hidden by a thick fog. All I could remember was wanting Marshal. We did something last night, or maybe we were going to, but I just remembered a feeling, Marsh wasn't there. Every part of my body hurt.

"Wrong. Big Fun left hours ago," a different voice than I was expecting said. It was sweeter with more charm than the deep voice of the heavyset boy I'd been expecting.

"Kenneth James! You can't kick people in their sleep!" I yelled into my pillow and groaned. He chuckled softly

"Well, I just did, so what are you gonna do about it?" I could only imagine the smirk that went with it.

"That's not an effective method of waking people up, dude."

"Worked for you? Now get up. It's two o'clock in the afternoon, and we're going to Marshy's house."

I took my face out of my pillow and looked at KJ, squinting with displeasure; my eyes were not entirely focused, but I could still make out his blurry form. He stood directly above me, leaning down so our faces were close enough that I could make out most of his features without my glasses. KJ was pretty tall, the second tallest out of our friend

5

group, myself being the tallest. He was bony, with scrawny limbs and ribs jutting out for being so underweight as he was. His cheeks were hallowed with a defined bone structure no longer hidden by any kind of childish fat he once had. His eyes almost looked sunken in but were still vibrant, giving a much-needed bit of color against his pale skin and blonde hair. His hair used to be much lighter, but it changed to a dirtier blond as we grew up.

"Glasses?" I asked, turning my head from side to side, searching for my glasses, the clear plastic frames lost somewhere, evading my sight. When I first picked them out, I thought the clear plastic was a good idea; they'd go with anything, but when I passed out on my friend's floor, it was hard to find them again.

"I took 'em off you last night. Here," KJ handed them to me, and I blinked a couple of times, truly waking up now that my vision was clear.

His room was small and stuffy; the curtains were drawn, so it was dark, but you could still see the sunlight coming through the holes. KJ was fully dressed; his hair was still a mess, but in a beautiful way. His hair was choppy from his mom's haircuts, and the ends of his hair would sometimes curl, leaving it to stick up like it was now. Even in late June, he still always wore the same muted red zip-up hoodie with what he called a 'cybercore' graphic across the chest that had almost completely faded away. He'd gotten in middle school and still wore it daily without fail despite its raggedy appearance. I couldn't tell if the red was so muted from age, dirt, or perhaps even its original color, but I always imagined it started brighter.

"What did we do last night?" I asked. The little bit of light in the room hurt my eyes, and just looking up at KJ made my head start spinning. He scoffed with a smirk before answering.

"Jesus, man, you really went hard," he said, flashing a full toothy smile now. When KJ smiled, his entire face went into it. His whole face lit up, eyes crinkling up as it stretched ear to ear. He'd proudly showcase the gap in his teeth from a missing canine unashamed. His nose scrunched up and crocked like his smile. He'd broken his nose a couple of years ago, and it had never been the same since now turned noticeably to the left. His smile always reached his eyes, giving a mischievous look to the otherwise innocent set of baby blues he had. Despite all his flaws, he still had that boyish charm.

"What's that supposed to mean?" I plummeted my head back into my pillow, instantly regretting the sudden moment wincing as I sucked in a sharp breath.

KJ kicked me again," We played mini golf, remember?"

"Then why do I feel like my head is being ripped apart and I have ninja stars stuck in my eyeballs?"

"Yeah, okay, we played mini golf, and then we did a shit ton of drinking." he chuckled.

"Why don't you seem like you're dying? And Thatcher? How'd he manage to get up and leave?"

"Because god hates you," KJ chuckled with that shit-eating grin of his. He paused and looked at me thoughtfully. "Oh wait, you like-actually believe in god... because Jesus hates you. Jews don't believe in Jesus, right?" I just scowled.

"We believe he's a real person, you idiot, just not the son of god," I grumbled back, to which he only laughed at himself more.

"He didn't drink anything; he said he wanted to feel better than you in the morning and then rub it in your face how you massively hung over, and he feels great. He went home early, though, so I guess he missed his shot."

"I'm never doing this again," I grumbled from my position on the floor.

"I live in a house of alcoholics, Ki. Don't worry, we have plenty of hangover cures," he grabbed me by the wrist and pulled me over from my stomach onto my back. I scrunched my face up in annoyance. "We're gonna go find out why Marsh ditched us last night. Thatcher said he was just being an asshole, so he didn't care and went home."

I managed to get myself into an upright position. *Did Marshal ditch us? That's why I was missing him?* A groan escaped my throat in favor of a verbal response. KJ left the room, and I folded my knees into my chest. Somehow with everything wrong in KJ's life, he was still this happy-go-lucky guy. I didn't understand how he could be so chipper and almost flaunt that he lived in a house of alcoholics like it was nothing but granted; it was nothing to him. KJ and I had been best friends along with Tatcher and Marshal since pre-K.

When we were younger, he had this all-American boy-next-door look to him, a blue-eyed blonde-haired boy who played baseball, but that was all he had; his home life was the complete opposite. The town always looked at the Conwell family as white trash, good-for-nothing alcoholics, and druggie rednecks. The poor family that lived in a shoebox-sized trailer who were never clean or well-fed and were either something to look down on or pity. And KJ couldn't help but agree to it. His entire life, he'd been the scandal of the town; all the small-town drama always seemed to start with *'Guess what the Conwells did now.'* I couldn't tell if KJ was genuinely unbothered by how everyone treated and looked at him, with sad looks and pitiful smiles or upturned noises, or if he was just good at keeping up his persona that nothing bothered him and he was some untouchable happy-go-lucky guy.

KJ bounced back into the room, humming to himself. He came back in with a bottle of pills and a glass of something. He offered me two round pills from the bottle and then the glass. I gave him a questioning look.

"Aspirin" I gave my head a slight nod to the hand with the glass of mystery liquid. "Just drink it," KJ said. I put the pills in my mouth and swallowed them dry before chasing them with a swig from the glass. I immediately spit out the drink; my eyes burned, tears welling up while I coughed, choking.

"KENNETH JAMES! WHAT THE FUCK IS THAT⁉!" I screamed, still coughing. "Jesus Christ, I think I'm dying!"

"It's watered-down coffee, pickle juice, a little bit of salt, cough syrup, and a smidge of vodka," he said.

"Sick KJ!"

"It works for my parents, so don't knock it till you try it, man." He just shrugged, and I scowled at him before plugging my nose and tossing my head back, guzzling down the contents of the glass, trying not to think about the concoction I was drinking. I sat a minute longer while my stomach turned.

"Okay, KJ. Gimme a minute, and I'll get up," I said, unfolding my legs and stretching out. KJ turned away and closed the door behind him as he left. My body was stiff from sleeping on the floor. I managed to stand up off the floor and started to gather up some clothes to change into. My shirt had KJ's horrible elixir down the front of me, and I didn't even know where my pants were. I couldn't tell if the clothes around me were clean or dirty, but I didn't care. I ran a hand through my thick curls, trying my best to detangle the frizzy knots with my fingers.

I reached around, grabbing random clothing articles, not caring or paying attention to what they were. I had to put all my energy into ensuring they were facing the correct way and on the right side out, as I was still trying to get my barrings. I was dizzy, and my head was swimming. My mouth tasted my death, and my head still throbbed rhythmically. I declared myself good enough to leave KJ's house and exited his room. KJ was leaning against the wall across from his bedroom door. I opened the door.

"Sorry, I didn't expect to stay over, so hope it's okay. I'm borrowing your clothes and stuff," I said, tugging at the shirt before I looked down at myself. I took the time now to inspect the clothes I'd put on. The shirt I picked up off the floor was black and bleach-stained with some band logo I didn't recognize. KJ's jeans were a bit tight, considering his waist was slimmer than mine, and the knees had both been ripped open.

"Yeah, it's cool, now let's go already," KJ said impatiently, rocking back on his heels like a little kid. I checked my neck quickly for the short beaded necklace I always wore, breathing out a reassuring sigh feeling the engraved bead with the letter 'm' on it. The necklace hadn't left my neck since I had gotten it. Marshal had made himself and I matching necklaces at summer camp when we were twelve. His made from an assortment of blue beads with someone and a bead engraved with the letter 'K,' and mine being made up of an array of oranges, yellows, and a couple of shades of pink.

"Oh yeah, I didn't touch that. Figured taking your glasses would have been enough to freak you out, and I didn't think you'd strangle yourself or anything," KJ shrugged, having picked up on my small sigh.

"Thank man, I sleep with it on anyway," I said, following behind him as we left the house.

✦ III ✦

MARSHAL

There was a soft knock on my door, followed by obnoxious banging. I remained silent and didn't move even when the door opened. It was like I was paralyzed, forever stuck on my back staring at the ceiling, my eyes focused on the cracking plaster following it until it ended in the corner.

"Jesus, this is depressing," said a voice I could recognize anywhere after being friends with its owner for over a decade. I tried to say something in response, but instead came out a mix between a groan and a sob. Two sets of footsteps shuffled into my room. I glanced over, straining to turn my head just enough to see the red fire of Kia's hair and the deep red of KJ's hoodie in my prereferral vision. His hair was an unmistakable orangey red with curls he pridefully maintained, but today I noticed they were rather unruly, which was odd for him, typically not leaving the house without doing his twenty million-step long hair routine. His curls set on top of his head, almost illuminating him like some kind of fiery sun. His hair brought out the dark green of his eyes.

Kia walked further in from the doorway he was positioned in, followed by KJ running at me and flinging himself onto my bed and on top of me. The air in my lungs was all pressed out from the impact, and I gasped from under KJ's body weight.

"Fuck'in.. fucking get off my Kenneth!" I struggled

"You missed mini golf lame-wad," KJ said as he sat on the edge of my bed. I propped myself up on my elbows. KJ's face was bright, and he grinned at me, trying to look innocent. Kia stood close to the door, looking down and picking at his fingertips. Skin picking was a nasty habit Kia had always had, even back in elementary school; when he was

10

uncomfortable or anxious, he'd pick at the skin around his fingertips. The habit hadn't gotten better, and he still frequently had bandaids wrapped around his fingertips.

"Oh yeah," I sighed. "Sorry guys, something happened, and I just-"

KJ cut me off with a wave of his arms, "You didn't miss much Addie lost, threw a fit, we went over to Cade's place, and Kia got wasted." I looked over at Kia, tilting my head, trying to imagine what drunk Kia was like.

"Can you please stop staring at me like that!" He snapped, "And put some fucking clothes on, Marsh!"

"Hey, you guys are the ones who barged into *my* room. Not my fault I'm not dressed," I tsked at them, and KJ snorted a laugh while Kia's face grew slightly pinker. I noticed how he wasn't dressed in his regular attire. I stared a bit longer, frowning; those *aren't his clothes. Where'd he get them from?*

"Kia, can you toss me a shirt or something?" I asked moving my body that felt like it was filled with lead so that now I was fully sitting up to face KJ. Kia shuffled around in my dresser and hit me with a T-shirt and basketball shorts.

"Your room is a mess, Marshal," he tutted at me. "How do you live like this? What kind of psychopath doesn't fold or separate his clothes in different drawers." Despite his tone, I could tell by the slight quiver in his voice he was smiling, "And it smells like death in here, Jesus!"

"HoW dO yOu LiVe LiKe ThIs," KJ mocked, waving his hands around, and we both laughed. It felt good to laugh after Winnie broke up with me. I thought I'd never be able to do that again. I felt a pang in my chest, like someone hitting me deep in the bottom of my soul with a sledgehammer.

Winnie.

I started to hear her words over again in my mind. All night I had laid in bed thinking about why now? Why did she break up with me? What happened? At some point, I fell asleep but was still exhausted; it was a restless sleep. Kia still stood awkwardly in the middle of my room. He hadn't looked at me the entire time. His gaze either fell, or he was facing away from me like he was trying to avoid looking at me.

I felt a sob try to jump out my throat, and when I tried to shove it back down, I made a wheezing sort of cough. "Winnie broke up with me," I said in a small broken voice; the effort to get that sentence out was autiable. KJ was sitting next to me, laid out on his back across my bed, scrolling through his phone, cross-legged with my hands in my lap, fidgeting with a ring on my thumb.

"Is that what came up? You bailed on us for another one of your stupid breakups?" Kia asked with a twinge of annoyance and bitterness. KJ stopped scrolling, and both of us looked at Kia's. This was the first time he'd looked at me since entering my room.

"No, dude, it's not a stupid split up this time. She means it. Kia, Winnie, like, actually broke up with me" I met Kia's eyes, and his demeanor changed. The annoyance was gone and had been replaced by a more compassionate look. We stared into each other eyes until Kia snapped his head back down to avoid looking at me anymore.

"Like for real?" He sounded almost hopeful, but I knew it wasn't that.

"She said we should 'see other people, '" I said, looking down.

"Dude, that's like super weak," KJ remarked, "you guys were like together forever. What happened?"

"I don't know, man, and I don't think I can fix it this time. She like sat me down and everything." I realized I was waving my hands around while talking and folding my arms across my chest.

"Oh man," KJ sighed.

"All I can think about is what she said. It's all a blur, but I can't get her words out of my head. All night I couldn't sleep; just kept asking myself why."

"Sometimes chicks just lose interest, same dick for too long type of thing," KJ said, uninterested, with a twinge of mild sympathy before he was back to scrolling.

"Gross KJ!" Kia squealed, and KJ chuckled to himself. "Come on, Marsh, put your goddamn clothes on. Let's get out of this hole of despair."

I looked over at Kia and watched him walk out of my room; *those are KJ's clothes he's wearing*, and for some reason, that didn't sit well with me.

KIA

Marsh kept looking at me and frowning. His eyes were tired, and the bags underneath them had gotten darker. He looked rough, which had become his baseline over the last few years, but this time it looked deeper. His gaze seemed far off, eyes unfocused, and his mind in a whole other world of his own. There'd be some type of jealousy that would wash over his face, but only when he looked at me with his attempts at suitably taking sneaking glances. It was subtle enough that I was probably the only one who would notice, and KJ would tell me I was being overly paranoid if I brought it up.

It was one of those things that I tried to tell myself I was exaggerating, but when you know someone your entire life, you pick up on those looks, no matter how small. I scolded myself internally at least a dozen times, telling myself to knock it off, and in KJ's voice, I heard him say I was just being paranoid; still, the unease tugged at my gut. I tried to act like I didn't notice his staring, and I tried to act like it didn't bother me either, but it did. The intent behind his stare and how long his eyes would follow me, he looked a thousand miles away, but he was here, trailing every movement with his eyes.

It was late in the afternoon now, the sun at its peak in the sky, beating down on us sitting on the shore of the lake. KJ suggested a 'much-needed beach day,' so now, after a quick stop back at KJ's place, KJ, Marsh, and I sat around the rocky man-made beach of the lake in silence. KJ was more sprawled out on top, laying on his back on top of his zip-up rather than sitting. His shirt slightly lifted, and he had pulled out a pair of sunglasses I didn't even notice he had, now wearing them over his eyes and basked in the sun. He had rolled up his pants and taken off his shoes and socks earlier when he had tried to convince Marshal and me to go swimming with him, but after standing in the water up to his mid-calf and kicking at us, he gave up when he realized neither of us was going to give in.

Marshal dug around in the rocks with a stick pushing around pebbles and dirt mindlessly now with his knees tucked into his chest. My head still hurt, and with the brightness of the sun, my eyes started to hurt, making my head hurt more, and it was all a vicious cycle of hurt. I sat with my legs straight out in front of me, a fishing pole in hand. My line started to move, and slowly, I began to reel it in. It was quiet, and I hated sitting there like that, but I didn't know how to break the silence. When I finally got my line fully reeled in, there wasn't anything left on the hook. I huffed out in annoyance, momentarily electing another brief look from Marshal as I got ready to recast. Before I could throw my line back out, the problem of breaking the silence found a solution.

A rock the size of a baseball flew overhead and landed in the lake, making a large splash. Marshal and KJ both snapped their attention to the ripples of where the rock had entered the water, then looked to the direction it came from.

"Goddamn, it missed 'em," Addie huffed, coming out from the brush, his thick frame followed by a boy half his size, who both looked and acted like Addie's shadow.

"Eat shit," I said, not looking back. The sound of Addie's steps grew closer, followed by lighter steps. "Guess I'm definitely not catching anything now, asshole."

"Shut up, ginger!" Addie snapped, "Jesus, it took forever to find you guys. Benji and I had no clue where you losers went, and I guess none of you have ever heard of answering a text before? Huh?" Addie huffed again.

"Hey ya, fellas!" Benji's voice carried out with his subtable southerner accent. Benji moved to West Richer in the fourth grade from somewhere down in the States. When he first opened his mouth, the four of us; KJ, Marsh, Thatcher, and I all looked at him astonished, faces scrunched and contorted with heavy confusion due to the strange way of talking that he'd mostly shaken, but there were still hints of the accent that lingered today along with his word choices.

"Hey, Benji," Marshal, KJ, and I all said together.

"Wow, you fellas seem like you could use some cheering up," Benji smiled. He had taken a seat next to me after I had laid my rod down.

"Not me, little B," KJ replied, still laying out on his back, "Marshal's depressed and Kia's hungover, but me? I'm king of the world."

"*Pfft-* Marshal's always depressed. What's new?" Addie snickered.

"Shut up, Thatcher, you're fat, and no one likes you," Marshal said dully, throwing the stick he was messing with at Addie.

"Well, what's wrong, Marsh?" Benji asked, leaning over towards him.

"Winnie and I broke up. We're over, over now."

"Awe, buck up, Marsh, it'll get better. It always does," Benji chimed in gleefully.

"Thanks, Benji, but you're wrong. She said we should see other people and everything. I can't win her back this time. Some bullshit about her 'individuality' or something."

"Oh well.." Benji trailed off.

"Just drop it," I said. I had focused my gaze out onto the lake's horizon line.

"Hey Kia, I'm sorry you're like on your period or something but don't make that our problem," Thatcher snickered at me.

"For the love of god, Thatcher! You're not fucking funny! Sorry if I just don't want to listen to any more of Marshal's self-loathing and wallowing."

"Kia, what's your damage today?!" Marshal snapped at me. I felt my face flush, heating up, and I turned away, staring at the tips of my shoes.

"Nothing. Never mind, forget it." I muttered.

"No, serious, why are you all of the sudden acting like a girl," he pressed further.

"I'm not acting like a girl!" I scoffed. "I'm just saying what everyone else is thinking, Marshal," bitterness invaded my tone. His eyes narrowed, lips turned into a downward frown giving me a look that said, 'Go on, keep talking, I *dare* you'.

"All day, you've cried about Winnie, and I've sat here with KJ and listened to it but Marsh, this shit happens all the time to you guys!" I raised my voice now despite the protest from the still prescient thumping in my skull. I felt the anger rise in my throat. I hated Winnie.

"She breaks up with you, and then like, three days later, you're back together! You always end up back together, and it's just the same old shit on repeat, so pardon me for getting annoyed at how repetitive this is getting!"

I balled my hands into fists after dramatically waving my hands around. I didn't know why I got so angry, but I meant everything I said. I *was* tired of this same old routine. I was always there for Marshal, and for *his* sake, I hoped it really was over, but I knew it wouldn't be just like all the times before. I just wanted her to go away and stay out of my life entirely but especially stay out of Marshal's life, she was constantly fucking things up between us, but I had it; this was my official last straw.

"You know what? Go fuck yourself," he spat back at me.

"Come on, KJ, let's go!"

"Why'd you bring me into this??" he responded, startled.

"URGH!" I gave them all the finger before I stormed off. I pushed past Addie, who stood near the treeline, and stomped down overgrown plants in the path to get back to the road. My breath hitched, and I felt the red-hot heat of rage building in my chest, my steps falling just as heavy as my breathing. This was all unbelievable.

How many more times was this going to happen, and all the guys are going to keep fawning over Marshal and his 'whoa-is-me routine', before they're sick of it too? How many more times before Marsh finally stayed away from her for good? Before he realizes there are other people who love him? People who he's known his entire life and people who will do anything for him, people who see him as if he hung the moon and the stars. How much longer was this all going to go on until someone got some fucking sense knocked into them. Maybe if that rock Addie threw had his Marshal in the head, he'd see what an idiot he's been his entire life pining after this girl who repeatedly lets him down. I didn't even realize I had my finger in my mouth until I felt the satisfying sting of the skin being ripped away from my nail between my teeth and got the metallic taste of blood on my lips.

"Fuck," I muttered, shoving my other hand into my pocket in search of a band-aid while I continued to suck away the blood pooling where there used to be a flap of skin.

Fuck those dudes, and fuck Winnie! How can she do that to us!... us? Marsh, how could she keep doing this to Marsh?!

· V ·

MARSHAL

I took a long drag of my cigarette as I leaned my head back. With my head against the wall, I let out a deep exhale of smoke, watching it dissipate into the air, getting lost and mixing into the smoky atmosphere above me. While KJ and Craig passed a bong between them, I stuck with cigarettes. I hated weed; I never wanted to try it. I hated even the idea of smoking it ever since my dad started, spending all his time in the basement with his stupid hydroponic weed farm, obsessing over it and making it basically his entire personality that he grew weed in our basement. When he did that, I decided I'd never smoke it; instead, I'd be a strictly cigarette kid. The closest I dealt was weed was supplying it to my friends from my dad's hydroponic farm I only ever provided the weed now.

I sat in KJ's bathtub with Craig and KJ's legs tangled over mine while we all smoked. They were both high at this point, laughing hysterically at each other nonsense like idiots with half-lidded red eyes. I just sat there between them, saying nothing. KJ and Craig had been smoking buddies since sixth grade. Craig's boyfriend, Theo, sometimes would tag along, but he didn't smoke as much, so it was mostly just us. Craig Martinez was always a quiet guy. He could be intimidating at times with his height towering over most people, how little he spoke to anyone but Theo, KJ, and me, along with his resting asshole face, chronically looking bored or annoyed with everything.

He was a very blunt type of person and usually an asshole, but when he smoked, he became a new person. He opened up and dropped his not-giving-a-shit attitude, lowering his guard and overall becoming less of an asshole. Sometimes when he was really out of it, he'd start rambling to KJ about space; the meaning of life, alines, how vast space really was, whether it was infinite, and sometimes he'd his theories on ancient societies. He'd spew numbers and facts, random trivial things he'd memorized, and KJ would rattle back some nonsense. They'd both end up laughing or paranoid, contemplating human existence.

Tonight was a laughing night, for some reason, everything the other said was the most hilarious thing ever said and from his position in the bathtub, KJ reached over and opened a cabinet. He produced a bottle of vodka and, between gasping breaths, handed it to me.

"Craig and I can kill our brain cells while you kill your liver, Marshy," KJ said before taking another hit. I nodded as to say thank you before unscrewing the cap and taking a long slow sip. I let my throat burn a little and held the taste in my mouth before finally swallowing the whole drink. It was warm and familiar, I savored the feeling as warmth spread through my body and my nervous system slowed down. I took another and another. I wanted to just forget about everything. I wanted to become lost in the sensation. I wanted to be floating, I tried to slip out of my mind, but I kept being pulled back as I thought back to the lake and what happened with Kia, how suddenly he blew up at me.

I tried to drown all my thoughts out with the bottle in my hand, taking more and more each time I thought of Kia. The perfect shade of orange his hair was, not obnoxious but not too close to brown, an ideal shade of glowing orange that looked like the sunset. He overtook my thoughts the further I slipped away, letting the warmth take over. My brain fogged over no longer functional as I tried to speak, and all that came out were slurred words with no coherent meaning; still, I couldn't seem to let my mind wander off of Kia. I thought back to how it made me almost angry. That he was wearing KJ's clothes, he borrowed clothes from me all the time, and there was almost a feeling of pride when I saw him in my clothes after a sleepover or something but nothing compared to the unease I felt setting him in KJ's ill-fitting clothes. He was acting so weird, and he had been for a while. We were supposed to be best friends, irrespirable, but he was being a dick. Not much of a best friend.

The more I thought about Kia, the more I became filled with an unknown feeling. Kia and I had been best friends since elementary school when we got to high school. All of a sudden, he started acting weird; we weren't as close as we used to be. Now it was always KJ and me. I looked to KJ and Craig as they devoured a family-sized pack of Oreos. I missed Kia. I missed how we used to be. Maybe that unknown feeling was some sort of nostalgic longing.

My head started to slump to the side. I thought again back to Winnie. Hot rage started to build up in my chest, making its way behind my eyes, and I blinked rapidly, trying to get the room to appear clear and unblurred. How could she do that to me? The other times we'd split up, at least there had been a concrete reason. Sometimes I said or did something stupid and didn't apologize. Most of the time, I never realized I'd done anything wrong until I was being broken up with. Other times it was because of what I didn't say or do, but she always told me. None of this bullshit like this time

"Fuck.. F- uck you, Winnie!" I yelled my words came out from between lips that didn't want to open. I slightly jumped at my own voice, sounding foreign. The words sloppily tumbled out, and Craig and KJ both looked surprised. "Yeah fuck her!" I yelled again. "And you know what!? Fuck you, Dad! That asshole fucked up my entire life!" I yelled. I tried to get up, but my body wouldn't allow the movements I needed to do so.

"Shit, did he drink that whole bottle?"

"Yeah, I think so. Damn, he's wasted, dude."

"Man, I'm tired of having drunk guys crash at my house, fuck. He can't go home like this."

I could hear them both talking, but I couldn't understand which voice was coming from where. Two arms slid into my armpits and struggled to hoist me up. I tried to step out of the bathtub but started falling. A frenzy of hands grabbed at my body, preventing me from smashing down onto the floor.

"Goddamn it, Marshy, c'mon Craig, help me get him to my room I'll put him where I put Kia last night."

I was stumbling along with the support of Craig and KJ until we got down the hallway to KJ's room. They let go of me on top of a pile of blankets and a pillow on the floor at the foot of KJ's bed. I heard them both walk away, and the door clicked shut. I pressed my face into the pillow and inhaled.

The pillow had a comforting smell, and I wrapped my arms around it, holding it close to my chest. I started to cry. I cried about Winnie mostly, how I'd never hold her like this again, how I missed the smell of her hair when I hugged her. I was going to miss how soft her skin was against mine. I cried because it was unfair. Everything in my life was unfair. I hated Winnie right now I hate her for being so cruel, for not giving me a reason. I hated my dad more. I hated his constant fights with my mom, I hated their divorce, and I hated all his stupid ideas. I inhaled, trying to refill my lungs, preparing for another sob.

With each breath, I calmed down a little bit more due to the comforting scent of the pillow. There was something familiar about it that made it so comforting. I tried to think about what the smell was, but before I could come up with it, my eyes were closed, and I was drifting away.

It was 2 a.m. when I woke up. My head was still swimming but I was able to remember drinking in KJ's bathtub and him and Craig dropping me on the floor to sleep it off. I couldn't remember whether or not I had actually started crying or if that was just a dream. The thing I knew was real was how badly I hurt. I missed Winnie, I wanted to call her; I wanted to go see her now. I sat up, still gripping the pillow. The hurt I felt reminded me of how much hate I felt for Winnie. I was so angry at her. I wanted her to know how much it hurt I wanted her to know I hated her now.

KJ didn't live that far from Winnie, but the longest part of the walk was keeping in a straight line since I wasn't quite sober. I stood out in her front yard below her bedroom window. I reached down, found a handful of pebbles, and began pelting her window with them. After about the fifth pebble, a light inside the room flickered on. The window opened, and Winnie stuck her head out, looking down at me. I hate how beautiful she looks. Her hair had grown out to her shoulders now, it was messy, and looking up, I saw that she had on a white tank top that loosely hung around her shoulders, swooping low so I could almost see her entire breast.

"Marshal! What the hell are you doing!" she whispered, yelling angrily down at me.

"I wanted to tell you W-Winnie," I started, "that- that you're a bitch!"

"Oh my god, Marshal," she sighed heavily with disappointment.

"I hate you, Winnie!"

"Stop yelling. You're going to wake up the whole neighborhood!"

"N-no! Because… 'cause you're a bitch!"

"You're drunk, Marshal! Go home!"

"Why Winnie? You didn't give me a reason! I deserve a reason!" I yelled.

"Oh, for fucks sake Marshal!" She slammed the window shut, and a few moments later, she was coming out the front door. There we stood face to face. Her eyes looked caring and compassionate, but her face told a different story. She cupped my face in her hands.

"Go home, Marsh, you're drunk I can smell you from here," she said, sighing heavily. I lowered my eyes and stopped at her bare shoulder. I trailed down to the part of her that was exposed. I put my hands on her hips.

"Wanna taste it too?"

"What?" She tried to pull away, but I held her firmly. I leaned in and sloppily put my lips onto hers, moving my hand to the small of her back. I received a swift smack to the side of my face, and Winnie broke away from me. "Get the fuck away from me, Marshal!" she looked scared.

"Winnie, I love you!" I reached out to try and grab her wrists.

"Marshal, I left you because you need to get your fucking behavior under control! You can't spend every night getting shit-faced with KJ! You're ruining your life and the people around you! You have problems, Marshal, and you need help!" She yelled with tears streaming down her face. We both just stood in the dark, staring at each other, until she turned to go back inside.

"FUCK YOU WINNIE!" I yelled at the now-closed door before dropping down to sit on the sidewalk. I put my head between my knees and started to cry again.

• VI •

KIA

I made my way down the stairs to answer the nonstop ringing of my doorbell. I didn't bother to put on pants or my glasses, planning on just telling whoever it is to fuck off so I could go back to bed. When I opened the door to see Winnie on my porch, it caught me a bit off guard, and I was slightly embarrassed to be standing in front of her in just some boxers with cartoon characters printed on them barely covered by KJ's bleach-stained shirt. She looked tired, and her eyes were puffy, like she had been crying a whole lot. I started to say something, but she just threw herself into a hug, wrapping her arms around me.

"You're his best friend, Kia," she let out in a mumbled cry "I don't know what to do."

"H-hey there, Winnie, uh, good morning, I guess?" I awkwardly stammered out, not being able to think about what to do now. I stood on my front porch frozen until she let go, and I led Winnie inside. Together we sat in awkward silence. She started to tell me about seeing Marshal last night, *great they're getting back together for the thousandth time.. again,* but she went on to tell me about how scared she was for him.

"He was outside my house at 2:30 in the morning yelling at me. He was drunk and angry," she shuttered. " He's changed Kia, he's not who he used to be"

"Yeah, but like, isn't that why you guys broke up? Changing and growing or whatever?"

"No, that's not what I-" she thought carefully before continuing, "he needs help."

"Help?"

"Theapry or rehab, I don't know. He's so angry all the time."

22

"Marshal has a right to be angry he has a lot of shitty stuff happening in his life Winnie!"

"But the drinking Kia! You're his best friend you *have* to see it too." I thought about it. Everyone around here drank; we all had shitty lives and wanted to lighten up. Even if you didn't have a shitty life, you still drank for fun. It was customary for us. So what if Marsh's drinking got heavier the more stuff he had going on? It's not like he was violent, and he wasn't wasted all the time like KJ's parents.

"It was one bad night, Winnie, you have to realize you crushed him. It's not like before, and he knows it."

"And this is why I broke up with him!"

"Winnie, please, he's just blowing off seem. You saying he needs help… it's like saying that KJ and Craig are drug addicts because they get high a lot. They're not hurting anyone, and Marshal isn't either," I stopped putting my head in my hands, rubbing at my eyes, a minor headache forming from not being able to see clearly, "Leave him alone. He doesn't need your help Winnie you've already done enough damage."

"Oh my god- He did hurt someone, Kia! He hurt me! I'm scared for him! And Jesus Christ, I've done enough damage?? " her face was red, and I could see the anger building in her. "Wake up Kia, you need to see him for that he really is."

"I'm sorry that he's changing and growing out of that perfect boyfriend, Winnie, but maybe he's not the problem. It's such a bitch move to break up with someone because you can't deal with their emotional baggage!" I yelled, "Maybe inside of breaking up with him and coming crying to me, you could have talked to him and figured your own shit out!" I had stood up while I was yelling, now towering over her, but Winnie stood up too, matching my stance as she yelled back.

"Kia, you don't know what it's like in a relationship!" I thought Winnie was going to hit me, she looked furious, but instead, she grabbed me by my shirt and pulled me into a kiss. Her fingers snaked around to thread themselves into my hair, and I was overwhelmed by confusion. Her lips were warm and moist against mine. I couldn't react I didn't know how to respond. She bit my bottom lip a little, her lips still working against mine, and I sat there, unable to do anything. She stopped when she realized I wasn't going to kiss her back and gave me a hurt look.

"Winnie! What the actual FUCK!" I shoved her back, and she looked down and wiped her lips with the back of her hand. "You can't go from yelling at me to... to fucking kissing me!" She continued to look down. I could tell she was starting to cry now.

"I'm sorry- I can't even really explain why I did that, but Kia, I tried to talk to him, and he won't talk to me," she raised her hands to her face to try and dry her eyes. "I broke up with him because I don't know him anymore, and he's not letting me in. Clearly, there's someone else he is letting in." she got up and headed for the door. I wanted to ask her what she meant by that last part, but she was already gone.

"Oh my god, this is un-fucking-belivale…. You're- you're fucking- Jesus Christ, Winnie," I stammered, still trying to get a grasp on what just happened.

That was the first time a girl had kissed me, and something inside me felt wrong. I had kissed a girl in the fourth grade, just a little peck, and once under the bleacher at a school dance in middle school. The last time I kissed a girl, I felt the same way *wrong*. Kissing girls was something every guy wanted to do, but I couldn't understand why. My stomach turned, thinking about my awkward kiss under the bleachers. It was so uncomfortable having her lips on mine and her tongue sliding into my mouth. After we had kissed, I ran away. I lied to my friends, saying it was great, assuming that they actually knew it was gross, too, but not wanting to look weird by saying it.

I returned back to myself, the momentary whirlwind of emotions calming down as I took deep breaths. I thought about the last thing she said to me, and I couldn't put any type of meaning to it. I sat alone grappling, trying to figure out who or what she was talking about. The morning was still early and what just happened was too much to think about for the time it was. I went back to what Winnie told me about Marsh's drunken fit in the middle of the night. *Drinking is normal for us, even if it's a little heavy, right?*

The standard for alcoholism in West Richer was pretty low, along with the standards for most things. Maybe Winnie was looking too far into it but there was a part of me that worried now. He *had* been drinking since middle school since everything started to go to shit for him. Maybe Marshals's drinking isn't normal maybe he does need help. I had seen Marsh get really wasted before on more than one occasion, I was one of the few people who didn't regularly get hammered at Cade Danile's parties, but nothing about Marsh separated him from the people who did get hammered all the time. Sometimes it happened a lot quicker, usually when he was upset but he still... I tried to push the thought out of my mind.

"Kia, we heard yelling. Is everything okay?" my mom called from the top of the stairs.

"Yeah, and was that a girl's voice yelling?" my dad added.

Shit

"Yeah, Mom and Dad, everything is fine. It was just Winnie something about Marshal" *I really hate that girl.*

· VII ·

MARSHAL

I remembered everything from last night: what I did, what I said, and how I acted. I winched thinking about it. After I left Winnie's, I didn't go home; I didn't know where to go. I walked around town in the dark, smoking cigarettes and trying to sober up. I wasn't tired. The sun had come up, but I had no concept of time. I left my phone back at my house, surely dead. I doubted I had any dire messages from anyone. KJ and Craig were definitely still asleep. I wasn't talking to Kia after what he pulled yesterday at the lake, and even if, by some miracle, my parents noticed I was gone, they wouldn't waste the worry on me.

I realized it was inevitable that I would have to go home at some point. I kicked a rock along the sidewalk, now heading in the direction that was home. I really did hate my dad. He was so fucking stupid and always had been. It made me so angry to think how he had messed up so much of my life. My mom hated him, too, and my sister and I could see it. The constant fighting and screaming had only gotten worse when we moved out to the farm, but suddenly, over the winter, it stopped, and that's when I found the divorce papers one night. My parents have been sleeping in different rooms since my sister moved out, so I didn't think anything of it, but now it was like living in a house full of strangers, and I was a ghost to them.

When I got home, I was fully sober. I gave myself a quick breath check and smelled my clothes. I smelled like weed and cigarette smoke, so If anyone were home, they wouldn't bat an eye at it. My dad knew I smoked cigarettes, and it made him livid, so I did it even more. When I came home smelling like weed, he was almost relieved. Mom's car was gone, but his truck was still there. When I opened the door, my dad was sitting on the couch like he was waiting for me.

"She's gone, Marshal..." his voice shallow and small, trailing off.

"Yeah, I know. Her cars gone-"

"No. Marshal, she's *gone*.." he made sure to put empathies on gone.

"Wait, what?" my voice cracked a little. I knew it was coming, but still, my throat burned with the promise of hot tears.

"She packed up her stuff and said she needed to get out of West Richer for a while."

"Well, when's she coming back?!"

"She didn't say, just that she loved you." his voice was so small now he seemed like such a broken-down shell of himself.

"FUCK!" I screamed and ran upstairs, heavily thudding with each footstep. My bedroom door slammed behind me, and things fell off my walls, but I didn't care. I ransacked my bed and nightstand for my phone, somehow not dead, but very close. I punched in my mom's number.

Two rings, then her voice.

"Hi, honey!"

"Why did you leave me here, Mom!" I yelled into the phone, desperate.

"Oh, honey-"

"I hate it here! Why didn't you tell me?! Why didn't you take me with you?!"

"Marshal, honey, please, you need to understand I need some personal time. I'm on my way to visit your sister for a little bit and figure something out," I hated how calm she was, how casual she was about abounding her son. My sister had gone to college somewhere in California.

"Mom.." I was crying now, and the words I let out sounded more like whimpers, "Mom, when are you coming back?" my voice was quiet, and I wasn't angry, not anymore; instead, I was sad like a little boy missing his mom. I felt eight years old again, hugging my knees to my chest and sniffling. She was quiet for a long time before answering.

"I don't know yet-" I hung up before she could finish. My phone started to ring repeatedly with her photo on my phone screen, but I just let it ring. I couldn't handle it; it was too much. Everything was too much. In the same week, my girlfriend dumped me, and my mom abandoned me.

I wasn't angry now. I was a different kind of heartbroken, and I let out long, hard sobs that came from the bottom of my chest. It felt like I was slipping into some kind of age regression as I rocked on the floor crying. I missed my mom for the first time in years. I wanted to tell her how I felt, and I wanted her to hug me and tell me everything would be okay. I wanted to tell her how fucking sad I was about Winnie, about all my sleepless nights. She knew I was angry and wouldn't talk to her, but now that she was gone, I wanted to tell her everything I'd been keeping from her.

I hiccuped before started to cough. My cough turned into a wheeze followed by a series of gasping breaths and I crawled over to my bedside table, fumbling around feeling for my inhaler. Panic flooded me only adding to the already intent stir of emotions and I grasped my lips, pulling the trigger, letting the clean taste of medicine flood my mouth, and my breathing began to stabilize.

Now that I calmed down enough to breathe properly again, I looked around my room. I walked over to the heart-shaped picture wall and started tearing them all down, screaming and crumbling them up before they dropped onto the floor. I went into my closet and picked out all the things Winnie had bought me to match her, I shoved them all into my trash can. I collected anything she had gotten me, stuffed animals, books, and video games. I shoved them all into the trash bag I removed from my trashcan in the corner of my room. I collected the few things of hers she had left behind here and tied off the trash bag. I wasn't sad anymore now I was angry again. I returned from a scared and sad eight-year-old to a raging sixteen-year-old.

My dad slowly opened the door, "Hey buddy, having some uh... big feelings I can hear,"

"I hate you, Dad," I seethed out between gritted teeth.

"Okay, I can tell you're upset, so, uh, I'll talk to you later," he shut the door softly and I could hear his footsteps retreating.

· VIII ·

KIA

We all received the same message in the group chat from Marsh;
bonfire. my place 2night @ 8

So around 7:30, KJ was outside with Benji and Addie but to my surprise, Craig and Theo stood among them. Anywhere Craig went, Theo was soon to follow they had been together since grade school and were irreparable from each other like Marshal and Winnie were at first. Unlike Marshal and Winnie, Theo and Craig were going strong. I didn't understand how they fit together so well but I didn't question it either because somehow they were perfect. They were opposites in every way down to appearances even.

Maybe it was because Craig was freakishly tall or Theo was freakishly short, but when standing together, Theo only came up to about Craig's shoulders. Theo was already extremely pale but standing next to Craig who was a golden tan, Theo looked paper white, almost ghostly. Theo normally looked like he was on the verge of dying from how pale and skinny he was but that he had in common with Craig, who was also awkwardly skinny.

Some days I'd look at them and get hit with a pang of jealousy as I watched them holding hands or laughing with each other and wish I could have that too.

Craig and KJ had started getting a lot closer, the three of them almost always showed up together. I shouldn't have been as surprised to see them all there, but still, Marshal's message went to our group chat and that didn't include Theo and Craig.

"Come on kosher boy, just gonna stand there, or are we leaving?" Addie remarked.

"Yeah, yeah. Fuck you, Thatcher," I half-heartedly replied as I slipped out and shut the door behind me. The six of us all headed out to Marshal's place. He'd moved out of the neighborhood we had all lived in for the majority of our lives a couple of years ago because of one of his dad's random outbursts. Everyone had lived in the same development just a couple of houses down or across the street so his new place was slightly out of the way but not far enough we needed to drive. None of us drove yet except Craig anyway. KJ was the next closest to being able to drive legally, he had learned how to drive, and although he couldn't do it legally that didn't stop him. I smiled to myself, thinking about all the stupid things KJ did. He was an idiot and it wouldn't surprise me if he didn't live to see thirty but I loved him anyway.

I pushed my hands into my pocket to keep myself from picking at the skin on my fingers, I already wore three band-aids around both index fingers and my ring finger. For some reason tonight I was nervous about going over to Marsh's place.

"Why do you think Marshal wants to hang out all of the sudden after he ditched us huh?" Addie said breaking our comfortable silence.

"He didn't mean to ditch us so shut up Thatcher," KJ said back rolling his eyes in annoyance.

"Do ya think he's gonna have stuff for s'mores fellas?" Benji piped up. It was funny how almost childlike he sounded asking the question. Benji still had a very childlike look to him, a round face still with generous amounts of baby fat. His eyes constantly seemed to be wide and shiny, kind of doe-like, tonight I squinted noticing the small bit of sparkle on his eyelids making him somehow look more majestic in childlike wonder. Maybe I was just imagining it. The only thing that kept him from being mistaken for a child was his stupid tall height meeting me at almost six feet flat.

Craig snorted followed by a sharp jab to the ribs by Theo and a look that could kill immediately sclinincing him and whatever snide remake he was brewing up. I really didn't get how Marsh and KJ hung out with that asshole. I was too embarrassed to say anything but I had never eaten a s'more before. I knew what it was and the basic idea but I still thought the idea was odd.

"I sure do love marshmallows!" Benji said after no one said anything to his last remark.

"Well, I am expecting some kind of refreshments after all this walking I'm going to be starving." Addie pouted.

"Yeah and what's new Big Fun!" Craig spat out and laughed, "You could use the walking Thatcher you are a fucking marshmallow!" He continued. Addie's face turned a bright red.

"OI! Don't call me fat your fag!"

Craig stopped laughing. His face went completely blank and showed nothing but from how sudden his change was we could all tell he was pissed.

"Oh shit! Craig," Theo grabbed at him. Craig removed his arm from over at Theo's shoulders and got close to Addie.

"*¡Escucha, gordo bastardo!*" Craig yelled lunging at Addie and grabbing handfuls of his shirt collar, "You ever call me a fag again Thatcher, and I will break both your legs, *entiendes cerdo*?" Craig spat out in a hushed voice filled with anger.

"Fuck! Guys!" Theo's voice was filled with panic. He reached for Craig's hand and started trying to pull him back from Thatcher before anything else could happen. "Please don't- don't do anything, Craig, please?" Theo pleaded.

"Sorry *Amar*, you just know how I feel about that word," Craig shrugged solemnly laying a sweet kiss into Theo's blonde hair.

"So anyway fellas! Let's keep moving so we can get there by eight" Benji gave a weak smile trying to break up the tension. We all continued walking on and Craig huffed and stepped away from Thater. The tension was still high even as Benji tried to soften the mood back up. He was nervously snapping the band of a little beaded bracelet on his wrist while he tried to get us all talking again. Theo tried as well still holding on the Craig who was clearly still pissed.

Coming up the driveway to Marshal's place from behind the house we could see a cloud of thick white smoke rising through the air. We picked up the pace and headed into his backyard. Not living in the development anymore meant that Marsh had a plentiful yard and could do things like this. Marshal sat in a lawn chair with a can in his hand a bulky trash bag on one side of his chair and a cooler on the other. There was music coming from somewhere, loud rock some of his favorite.

"Hey, Marshal!" Benji waved excitedly calling out to him. We all said our hellos except Craig who just sort of grunted. Marshal's head whipped up looking back at us all.

"Common over guys let's get this party started," he smiled at us. I looked eyes with Marshal, his smile didn't seem genuine. It stopped short of his droopy-looking eyes that looked dull and empty. Slight red but the red you get from crying. As everyone made their way to grab a lawn chair around Marshal, I studied him a minute longer, my eyes went from his face to his hand back to his face. Bingo. *Beer can, that's why he's all smiles.* He must have noticed my staring as his face went red and he quickly looked away.

"What kind of party are we starting?" I shyly asked.

"Tonight," he was interrupted by a hiccup, tonight we're celebrating our freedom and we're celebrating being guys!" He threw his arms up in the air above his head and hooted.

"What's in the bag?" I asked

"Our kindling gentleman," he giggled, "and Craig." He tried to keep a straight face but every time he looked at Craig, he'd start again with stifled giggles.

God, when was the last time he giggled? *He's so...* I shook my head and cut myself off. The fire already had a decent start to it but when Marshal started pulling items out of the bag and passing them around we all understood.

"Fuck her!" he hollered throwing his hands up.

"Hell yeah!" Thatcher cheered, "Burning stuff!"

The rest of the boys cheered with him. I watched as Marshal clumsily raised himself from his chair taking a few uneasy steps to steady himself before starting to sway to the music. I watched him as started to spin a little and twirl some while waving his arms everywhere as he did. I smiled as I watched him carrying on like an idiot, a stupid smile plastered on his face while he acted in a way I hadn't seen him do in a while; carefree and having fun. I watched him some more feeling a blush creep across my face before I joined in adding things to the fire.

Marshal came over to me, red in the face breathing heavy, and his overgrown bangs sticking to his forehead and he took his hand in mine pulling me along with him. My stomach fluttered a small bit when he interlocked our fingers together smiling and laughing while we danced and jumped around together. Holding his hand, I spun him and he in return did a little dip with me. Each of us breathing hard and smiling so hard my cheeks were starting to ache. Marshal started to cough and wheeze letting go of my hand to fish his inhaler out of his pocket and catching his breath.

We threw things into the fire and watched them burn for a little, Marshal's smile never stopped it only seemed to get bigger as everyone laughed and danced around with him. The music was loud and we were all yelling, laughing carrying on like kids again. I felt a bit nostalgic for how everything was before we started growing up.

He's happy, and laughing it's been so long since I'd seen him like this.

I knew he was definitely buzzed the collection of cans around his chair showed he'd been drinking since before we all got there but he wasn't quite drunk. Even if he was this wasn't his usual type of drunk. Marsh was a sleepy and emotional drunk usually curled up crying himself to sleep or he got unreasonably angry but tonight he seemed so lively and full of life. Everyone including myself was at least one if not three beers deep. Even Benji who normally wouldn't, always our dependable DD. Everyone had kind of died down a little as it was dark and getting a bit cooler.

I took it upon myself to throw out the rest of the things in the trash bag that we couldn't burn. Before I left I gave one last tantalizing stare to Marshal, he was holding his stomach and laughing his face was bright red. I relaxed seeing him like this and went to go throw out the remainder of Winnie.

MARSHAL

The fire had started to die down a while ago. At some point, the music changed from rock to something softer. I looked around. Addie had gone home, and Theo was asleep on Craig's lap, who was sleeping in a lawn chair himself. Benji and KJ were out, too; the two had sort of cuddled up together. Benji curled into the fetal position, and KJ spooned him with his arm draped over Benji along with his tattered zip-up as a makeshift blanket. I laughed a little bit. My mind was hazy with a comfortable fog.

We finished most of the beers in the cooler between the seven of us, but I still had a couple left. I rummaged around in the melted ice of the cooler, fishing out a cold can. I cracked the can open with my teeth and took a sip, leaning my head back to look up at the stars. Craig was always the stars and light pollution; he was right. At my house, the stars were a lot clearer.

Kia's head snapped towards me when he hurt me open the can. He had been sitting by the dying fire, lighting sticks on fire and putting them out. He hadn't seemed to be as in the mood as everyone else was. He was laughing and dancing with us, but I'd catch him looking at me with a sad look.

"Are you sure you should be drinking that?" I gave him a puzzled look. *Since when did he care how much I drank?*

"Well, it's just- I talked to Winnie today," he swallowed, slowly speaking in response to my look of confusion. I got up out of my chair, taking a few shaking steps forward before taking a seat next to him in the grass. I shuffled closer and reached my arm out to him, pulling him close to me. At first, he resisted but caved in and rested his head against

34

my shoulder. His soft, bouncy curls overtook my peripheral vision. He was warm on my shoulder, the heat of his pale cheeks seeping in through my sleeve, and my insides felt static.

"Why'd you do that?" I asked, still enchanted by his hair. I always loved his hair. It was so unmistakably him. He pulled out of my arm, now going back to sitting straight up, continuing with lighting twigs on fire.

"She came to my house," he wasn't looking at me, but I was staring at him. The orange glow of the fire lit his silhouette, and the red of his hair almost matched the glow of the fire. In the dark, I could still sort of make out his features. A deep concern was etched into his face, his lips turned downward into a frown and his nose scrunched up the way it did when he was thinking really hard about something difficult. Right now, he could almost be beautiful. I shook the thought out of my head immediately. I finally processed what he had said.

"She came to your house?! Why?" He didn't say anything for a minute until he finally turned to look at me. I couldn't help but think how pretty his eyes were in the very little light I had to see him in. They were the perfect shade of jade green, and if you got really close, you could see the small ring of copper around his iris, only amplifying their beauty.

"She's worried about you and this," he gestured around him and finally to me.

"Yeah, what about it?" I asked, unsure what he was getting at exactly, my mind working slowly and still lagging behind.

"She thinks you need like rehab or something," he said in a small voice but scoffed and gave a forced laugh, "Kind of ridiculous, but she's worried, dude. I told her she was wrong because it's not like you're drunk, you're- you aren't.. like, doing anything bad," he stuttered a little unable to hold eye contact. "But Marsh, this tonight was the happiest I've seen you in a while, and it made me think, are you only this happy because you're drunk? I mean, yeah, I had a drink, and so did all the other guys, but you drank like half that cooler signal hardly," he continued. He was getting more anxious, fidgeting with his fingers and rubbing at the skin around his nails. He put his finger up to his mouth and bit at the skin.

"I'm not an alcoholic, Kia, if that's what you're saying!" I spat out. The idea was laughable, and I couldn't help the deep chuckle that bubbled up through my chest. "I'm fine! So what if I drank more than you? It's not any kind of problem, man," I was getting upset now. I looked away, staring deeply into the shining embers, a shade similar to Kia's hair.

"I know that's what I said, but maybe it's not normal for any of us to drink the way we do," he paused for a second, "or smoke, and I mean smoking anything." I watched him continue to bite at his fingertips.

"Unbelievable," I huffed; we both looked straight ahead as he turned away.

"Look, I just wanted to say something about it. Winnie was all freaked out. It was all so weird. She like yelled at me, then I thought she was going to slap me, but instead, she kissed me and was acting all weird!"

I grabbed him by his shirt, turning his shoulders to force him to face me, "You kissed Winnie?"

I asked again, bitterness in my voice. There was a building rage crawling out of my chest up my throat, and I could see him start to panic. " She just broke up with me, Kia! And you fucking what?! You fucking kissed Winnie!" I yelled, releasing his balled-up shirt in my hands and shoving him backward.

Kia's silence was the only answer I needed. I started to get up when he reached out for me. I was beginning to feel hot, and I needed to get away. My face was burning, and I started sweating. I needed to leave. My breathing picked up now.

"Wait! Marshal," he called after me, clumsily getting back to his feet, "She kissed me! I didn't want it!"

I whipped my body around to Kia, "But it still happened, and you didn't stop her!" I needed to escape.

"You're my best friend, Marshal! I wouldn't!" We were yelling, and I knew people were no longer asleep, but I didn't care.

I was so unbelievably angry, the rage that was building in my chest was starting to boil over now, making its way up my throat and soaking each venomous word I spat out at Kia. It wasn't his place to say anything about my drinking habits. He didn't have the right especially since there was no problem. It made me feel even worse that Winnie had put him up to this. I thought then about him kissing her. His lips and hers together. His lips.. on someone else. *His lips.* Kia was talking. I could see his lips moving, but I couldn't hear any sounds. I didn't want to hear anything else he was saying. My vision started to tunnel, and my ears rang.

Before I knew what I was doing, my fist connected to Kias's nose. I flung myself at him, and fist after fist hit him. I was on top of him now, hitting his face, chest, and the arms he'd raised to try and defend himself. He only held his forearms in front of his face and made no attempts to fight back. With each blow, I thought about how he wore KJ's clothes and how his lips had been on Winnie's. Those thoughts fueled my rage. I was flying off the handle, and I couldn't stop; it was like I was trapped inside my own body, watching as someone else controlled my movements.

I heard yelling behind us but couldn't focus on any of the words. I could hear my voice, but I didn't know what words were coming out.

A couple of different arms wrapped around my waist and pulled at me. I struggled against them and flailed my arms and legs backward, occasionally hitting something.

"Calm down, Marshal! What the fuck!" KJ and Craig were holding me down. KJ had pinned my arms down with my head on his lap while Craig held my legs down. I tried to fight free of their hold but couldn't. I realized I was screaming.

"I HATE YOU!" Over and over again. Kia was being sat upright by Benji and Theo, I watched as they walked away with him. My hands were wet and sticky with Kias's blood all over my knuckles and some of my own. I stopped struggling as much, and my screaming turned into a pleading type of cry to be let go. I was tired now and didn't have the energy to fight anymore. I watched the three boys walk off until I couldn't see them in the dark anymore, and I felt the grip on me loosen.

I lay on the ground; KJ held my head softly, telling me to count and breathe to calm me down. Craig gave me a concerned look trying to help KJ calm me down but was waved off by KJ. He had disappeared, and now it was just KJ and me alone in the yard. I started to cry again, hard sobs that I usually wouldn't let out with anyone around, but I couldn't stop. I was struggling to breathe, heaving all the air out of my lungs in cries that turned into screams of pain and heartbreak.

• X •

KIA

I tried my best to be quiet as I snuck into the house, hoping I didn't wake up my parents or Peter. My lip was split, and the blood from my nose was mixed with the blood from my lip. I wouldn't let Theo or Benji help clean me up, I had just pushed them both away. I just wanted to leave, and I just kept going despite their protesting. I lay on my couch and started to cry. Sobs escaped my throat muffled by the back of my hand as I tried not to make too much noise. I used my other hand to remove my glasses and folded them up, laying them on my thigh. I could feel my left eye starting to swell, along with all the busies beginning to form. My shirt had gotten blood on it so I just took it off and used it to try and clean up my face the best I could.

The stairs creaked, "Kia?" A small tired voice called down. *Shit.*

"Oh, Peter! I'm sorry I didn't mean to wake you up," I tried to sound as level as possible and balled up my bloody shirt shoving it behind my back and the back of the couch. "Go back to bed buddy," I called back to him. But rather than retreating he made his way down the stairs and gasped when he saw me.

"Kia! What happened!" He looked scared. I tried to cover my face and make it look like I hadn't been crying.

"Peter, it's okay just go back upstairs. I'm fine," I mumbled, "fuck moms gonna have a field day with this," I sighed. Peter grabbed my hand, wrapping his fingers around mine.

"Kia?"

"I got into a fight with Marshal," I choked on a sob. Saying it out loud was what made it real for me. I had gotten into a fistfight with my long-time best friend. Sure we had fought before but never like

38

this. Peter hugged me tight wrapping his small arms around my bony shoulders and squeezing tight and hugged him back while continuing to let tears far. Peter was the best brother I could ever ask for, I didn't know what Marshal was complaining about with his sister Shelby.

"Did you beat Marshal's ass?" He asked. I laughed a little bit and relaxed a little bit.

"Yeah," I lied, "I got him pretty good," Peter was my little brother, and I know he looked up to me. I didn't want him to know for some reason, I didn't even fight back; I didn't want Peter to see how hurt I really was right now.

"Good," was all he said before he turned away, I assumed to go back upstairs and back to sleep. Instead, he walked into the kitchen, and I heard the faucet turn on and off again. Peter came back and put a warm washcloth under my nose.

"No, Peter," I took the washcloth from him, "you're not supposed to be doing that- ugh! I'm your big brother; you aren't supposed to be cleaning me up," I laughed a little strained and obviously fake.

"Yeah, Kia, you're my big brother; it's our job to take care of each other."

I wiped my face grinning stupidly because this kid was wise beyond his ten years. I managed to wipe away the dried blood much better with the warm washcloth than I had my shirt, as Peter sat beside me watching.

"Hey, Peter?"

"Huh?" he yawned and rubbed at his eyes. I wasn't sure how late it was. I stood up and grabbed him by under the arms tossing him around to my back.

"Dude, Kia what the hell?" he laughed in surprise.

"Don't say that," I rolled my eyes and he smacked me upside the head. I gave him a piggyback ride up to his room. He was getting too heavy to easily pick up but I still tried my best.

"Good night Peter, and uh don't tell Mom about this?" He made the motion for zipping his lips and locking them, I smiled at him with a tired smile. *I love that kid more than anything* I thought walking into my room. I'd do anything for my brother and he'd do anything for me.

My room wasn't completely dark so by the light of some string lights I managed to make my way to my bed and collapsed into it. I hurt all over but now that I was able to fully process the fact that Marshal beat the shit out of me I was angry. I was ready to go to bed but couldn't, I was too upset so instead, I got back up and, using the mirror on the back of my door and I inspected my injuries. A nasty gash on my lip, another above my forehead, *one of his rings probably got me there,* bruises forming over my eye and the opposite cheek.

I looked rough and there wasn't going to be any way to hide it. I cycled through possible stories, *blame it on Craig? Then my mom would call his mom and then he'd actually beat me up, baseball? No, they know we all hate it so why would we even be playing? Another fight with Thatcher? Yeah, that could work I got into a fight with Thatcher that's not totally out of character. We fight all the time.*

Since it was the only thing I could think of I decided to go with it. I sunk into my bed and let my thoughts go. I was so mad at Marshal, and I was angry at Winnie, maybe she had a point but if I never said anything then maybe I wouldn't have a black eye.

Lately, there was been something weird between Marsh and me. There was a tension I couldn't place, the way he was always looking at me and how I felt when he looked at me. I started feeling this way a little while ago trying my best to keep it down and ignore the foreign feeling. When he'd look at me I'd stare sometimes in awe until one of our faces turned red. I'd catch myself staring frequently and Marsh was usually somewhere in my mind.

I started getting jealous when he hung out with KJ more even though that was beyond stupid but I wished it was me. When I was with Marsh, it was like the whole world stopped, my heartbeat would be in my ears and my face would get flushed. *Everyone feels like that about their best friend though. All guys hate their best friend's girlfriend and wish she'd go away, everyone looks at their best friend and gets embarrassed when they notice it's all totally normal. We all get a bit flustered being stared at.*

MARSHAL

KJ had taken me to bed and stayed the night with me. He put an arm around me leading me to my room whispering comforting things to me as my crying had started to slow down. I was still sniffling as he laid down in bed with me like we did when we were kids. He stretched his arms upward revealing a sliver of the pale skin of his abdomen, I saw a spot that looked red and purple. I thought back to when I was throwing fits and elbows and kicking when he tried to get me off Kia. *Shit, I didn't mean to hurt KJ.*

I went from KJ to Kia. My knuckles still had blood from hitting Kia, some mine most of it his I examined my hands. While I flexed them open and closed, I closely looked at the small parts of my skin that were split open. I knew Winnie was gone but still, I couldn't control how angry I was when he told me they kissed. I wondered what would have happened if KJ and Craig weren't there. I felt a wave of guilt but quickly shoved the feeling aside. Kia was my best friend and he betrayed me by kissing it was easier to be angry.

KJ had stretched out against the wall under my blankets and was softly snoring. It was nothing new sharing a bed with KJ or anyone really we always did when we slept over unless it was a lot of us then we'd sleep together on the floor, so I didn't mind that he had passed out wrapping himself in most of my blankets. I laid down beside him and tried to drift off finding rhythm in KJ's breathing.

When I woke up KJ was still passed out beside me, but he had kicked all the blankets off and somehow his shirt was half off. My door slowly creaking open woke me up and my dad stood in my doorway, the light from the hallway spilled in and I glared at him.

"Hey, Marshal-" he poked his head in the door and gave me a confused expression before continuing, "Who's in your bed?"

"Just KJ."

"Oh well, tell him I said hi,"

"What did you want, Dad?"

"Yeah just wanted to check on you Marshal, you were upset yesterday and I heard yelling last night-"

I cut him off, " I'm fine." I rolled over to face KJ. I pulled the covers back over him.

"Well if you want to talk Marshal I'm here for you buddy"

"I don't want to talk, especially not to you." I snapped.

"Okay buddy I'll be here when you do want to talk," he said ignoring my last comment. KJ sat up.

"Mornin' Mr. Langdon," he tiredly waved.

"Hey, KJ," he nodded at him. "Want any breakfast boys?" I sat upright abruptly from where I was lying next to KJ.

"Jesus Christ, Dad, stop acting like you give a shit!" I snapped, "Since when did you start caring? Huh? Wanting to talk and shit about my *feelings??*" I inhaled sharply before continuing, "You've never cared about my feelings! If you did we wouldn't fucking be here! Just because KJ's here doesn't mean you can try to play the perfect dad to look good! You've never offered to make me breakfast unless someone's over!" My face felt hot, and I had to catch my breath from my sudden rant. My dad looked hurt and turned away heading back downstairs.

KJ placed his hand on my shoulder, "Don't say anything, dude," I said under my breath. I sighed heavily and groaned before flopping backward into my pillows. I ran my fingers through my hair and gripped two handfuls. KJ patted my shoulder before getting out of bed. He looked at his phone and quickly got his few things together.

"I gotta dip, man, Katie texted me."

"Oh yeah, see you later KJ," I gave a half-hearted wave as he slipped out of my door, still sliding his shoes on. He left without saying anything else, just giving a slight nod in response to my wave. It was so weird to me that his home life was so fucked up but he would do anything for his family, mainly his sister but if his parents asked him to empty his bank account to bail them out he wouldn't complain. Maybe it was some kind of guilt. KJ's dad hated him, and KJ still tried so hard bending over backward and stretching himself in impossible ways for his family almost as if it was a way to prove himself and try to gain an ounce of respect from his father. KJ's mom wasn't much better, she definitely held some resentment for him but not to the degree his dad did.

Anyone could tell KJ hated his home life, his brother had graduated and left to join the military and originally KJ said he was going to do the same. None of us, especially his brother Jason could stand the idea of KJ in the army. He wasn't built for it and we all managed to talk him into trying to go to college. Now it was just his parents and sister at home. Katie was the only one left who actually loved KJ at home.

Their mom, Carrie, blamed Jason for everything wrong in her life being the reason she was 'stuck' in her shitty disappointment of a marriage, in a shitty run-down trailer, in an even shittier trailer park, stuck at the bottom of the living pay check to pay with the help of Danny's disabilities checks. Carried had gotten married to her husband, Danny Conwell when she was fourteen and found out that he, a man almost twice her age at the age of twenty-six, had gotten her pregnant. Being Catholic, Danny did what everyone said was the right thing and married her. From the day Jason was born, Carrie hated him, blaming him for running her life but it got really bad when KJ was born.

KJ was not Danny Conwell's son. He didn't actually know who his biological father was but he was made painfully aware that he was a result of his mother's sins, as so eloquently put by the rest of the family who hated him almost as much as his parents. Since the church doesn't allow divorce or abortion KJ was born as a 'consequence and punishment' his dad said for his mother. He took all of his resentment for both his wife and son out on KJ shamelessly, some times it was just verbal, and other times it was physical.

Still, somehow KJ was the guy he was, happy-go-lucky KJ, the golden retriever sunshine boy with a chronic smile that was contagious.

KJ was his sister's best friend and she was basically his whole world. His parents were prone to disappear going on benders showing up days or weeks later, some times he'd get a call to bail them out from the drunk tank and the whole cycle would start again. I didn't understand how his life could be so fucked up but he could be so compassionate and still love his family the way he did. Compared to KJ, my home life was paradise.

Even though my parents fought nonstop they didn't beat each other. My dad may smoke too much weed but at least he wasn't doing meth or going on benders, I still couldn't remotely say I cared as much about my family as KJ did his. My sister and I were never close like KJ and Katie or Kia and Micheal, our relationship had gotten better as we bonded over our mutual hate for our dad and started relying more on each other as a distraction as our parents screamed at each other.

Kia...

I looked down at my hands at the dry cracked blood I never washed off and the cuts on my hands. I flexed my hands mesmerized by the dry blood cracking and flaking away some. Some of the minor cuts on my knuckles reopened, fresh droplets of red pulling around the split skin, and I thought about what caused those cuts and cringed at the memory of my hands hitting his face repeatedly; the sound echoed throughout my head, and I shook my head violently as if shaking my head would stop the sound effect of my fist connecting to Kia's face, the loud thud and crunch as I hit his nose. For a moment I sat in disbelief, I was still mad at him but it wasn't as much for kissing Winnie as it was just me being angry. I went to wash my hands and shower. I needed to stop thinking about Kia.

I sat in my bathtub with the shower running letting the warm water run over my body, I wanted to disappear in the curtain of steam created in the bathroom, I wanted to be evaporated with the water, and I wished I could just float down the drain be anywhere but here, be anyone but me right now. My showers, when I took them, had started becoming less about cleaning myself and more of a safe place for me. I hated showers and avoided them as long as possible hating the effort to get up, get undressed, and get into the shower, only to be left feeling wet and cold. The only times I enjoyed showering were times like now, when something was eating ay my mind. It was warm and I felt safe in the blanket of steam I had created. I finally stood up and started to wash.

Kia was still in my mind. I scrubbed desperately at my skin as if that would somehow force the sharp face of my best friend from my mind, his eyes looking sad and afraid under me as I drew back yet another punch. I screamed and crouched down hugging my knees barely balancing on the balls of my feet in the tub. I moved my hands up to my hair gripping handfuls and squeezing hard enough my nails dug into my scalp.

"Stop it, stop it, stop it, stopstopstopstop STOP!" I started to smack myself in the forehead, crying now unable to get rid of the image of Kia's fucked up face.

The guilt had started to build up once I woke up but now it was over pouring. I heaved taking in uneven and sharp shallow breaths, becoming light-headed. I started coughing until I fell over on my side curled into the fetal position shaking.

"Stop stop stop stop stop stop it," I mumbled to myself almost as if it was a chant to ward off the guilt and despair in my chest making my throat close and restrsitcing my chest. Stop was all I could think. The sour feeling of bile rose up into my throat along with my panic and I scrambled to get upward off my side and now sat on my knees just in time for the sick bile of last night to slip out my lips.

I wretched at the taste, throwing up again, the guilt manifesting into a physical form as I continued to cry, heave, throw up, and choke in the thick, steamy air around me. Eventually, the water started to run cold, an indicator I'd been in the shower more than an hour. The cold water helped to calm my panic, my body still shivering either from the cool temperature or the shock still but I managed to get calm enough to get out of the shower and reiterate back to my room.

I didn't know how to apologize I didn't know what to say or how to fix this. He was my best friend and it wasn't his fault why did I let my stupid fucking anger explode and take it out on him. I shivered as I thought back to it I was blind with rage, by the mere mention of his lips on another person, and when I started hitting him he didn't even try to hit back. It bothered me like he knew I just needed to get out all the things I couldn't say and punching was the only thing I could do, I hated him for that.

His lips on hers... Why does that bother me so much? why the fuck do I feel like this? He's my best friend my favorite person at that I would do anything for him I love him but everyone loves their best friends like this so why does it feel so fucking weird?

Fuck what do I do? It wasn't even his fault. I probably just lost my best friend because I hated that he kissed a girl I don't even care about right now.

· XII ·

KIA

"Oh, mother of Moses! Kia!" My mom shrieked and grabbed my face, still tender from last night. *"Mayn kleyn beibi eyngl!* Your *shyen* face!"

She squeezed my cheeks frantically turning my head and looking at all the damage Marshal's fists had caused. It never seemed to be a possibility to my mom that I wasn't a little kid anymore, she still talked to me like I was nine years old. She thumbed over my split lip causing me to wince and she only cooed at me more.

"Mama, please," I sighed, knowing nothing I said was going to make a difference.

"Ezra!" She squealed, "Come quick, it's Kia!"

"What happened hun?" my dad called back from down the hall hurriedly thudding up the stairs with a tinge of worry in his response. After a moment, my dad was now in my doorway.

My mom turned my face so he could see, my cheeks still squeezed between her hand, "Look what happened to our *beibi*!" She was frantic now. His face dropped a little bit.

"Kia, what happened?" he asked with a deep frown his eyebrows raised and concern etched into his face. He approached much calmer than my mother had. I didn't know how to tell them I didn't have the words and I didn't want them to know, but the state of my face made that impossible.

"Nothing, it's fine, guys!" I protested, pulling away from my mother's grasp and finally moving my lower jaw from side to side.

"It's not fine, Kia! Your face is all bruised, and oh my! Just look at you! Your little lip is split and your nose is all swollen! This isn't nothing!" My mom whaled, grabbing at my face again to empathize.

"Ruthie, *sviti*, let me talk to him," my dad said managing to get my mom to let me go. I rubbed the tender spots on my face where she had been squeezing.

"I know your mother can be a bit... over dramatic, but she really cares about you, what happened?"

"I got into a stupid fight," I said dully

"Kia you should know that's not how we raised you violence isn't the answer," he paused leaving time for my rebuttal.

"Okay, a fight isn't the right way to describe what happened... more like.." I thought carefully about how to explain to my dad what had happened while causing the least amount of concern. "It's more like I'm bad at defending myself, I didn't fight back and I'm not really that great at blocking I guess," those probably weren't the right words. My dad looked like he was about to start going on about something, "can we just drop it?"

"Your mother won't like that," he sighed, shaking his head.

"I know, but I really don't want to talk about it. Can you talk to her?" I pleaded.

"I can try, but I'm not going to promise anything," he said, leaving my room. I sat listening to his footsteps go down the hallway and the stairs, muffled voices, and my mom's high-pitched whaling.

This is really not how I wanted my morning to start... goddamn it.

My mom had come into my room to leave me a basket of clean clothes, and then she saw my face. I woke up to her crying and violently shaking me awake. I was too tired to deal with anything happening since I wasn't able to sleep last night. I stared at my ceiling half hoping that it would collapse on top of me. Everything hurt my body and my soul.

It hit me last night, and it was still hitting me that my best friend beat the shit out of me. If it weren't for the guys, I don't think he would have stopped either. I had never seen him so angry and full of hate before. His eyes were deranged. I sighed *fucking, Winnie.* Things were so fucked up right now and it seemed to be all at once, nothing could be normal for us.

I rolled back over to face my wall, I just wanted to go back to sleep. I wished I could sleep for the next three months my face hurt and I thought about how I lost my best friend probably, *all over some stupid girl. God fucking damn it- I hate her!* I felt my eyes get watery and hot. Putting my face into a pillow, I began to cry.

I missed Marsh in so many ways. I missed how he was last night, smiling and goofing around, I missed how we used to be, and mostly, I missed the idea of him thinking he'd never want to talk to me again. I didn't want to kiss Winnie and it's not like I kissed her back, I tried to think about what possibly gave her the idea to kiss me. Marsh was so mad about it so it didn't matter, he seemed angry about so much more though. *I should have told her to fuck off, I was an idiot for even letting her in.*

I had never really been fond of Winnie. For so long, she was the only thing Marshal talked about. They were always together. I always watched them from a distance and got weirdly jealous of her. I never made it a point to get to know her all that well, and neither did she. We had a mutual dislike for each other but tolerated each other because of Marsh. Each of the thoughts of times they'd broken up for whatever stupid reason, I was always there to pick up Marshal, and each time I hated her more.

I was angry and crying, and it was exhausting. I shut my eyes and prayed I could just sleep for a little bit. Everything was fucked. I yawned. *Fucked* was the only thought I had before my eyelids were too heavy to keep open anymore.

I felt a little bit better when I woke up the second time, my house was quiet and the sun was getting lower, *shit I slept all day,* but I needed it. I was so mentally exhausted from everything that had happened still. I hadn't slept the night before and spent most of the night crying. After my mom woke me up, it just all seemed like too much. I checked my phone with a message from my mom saying that my parents and brother had left to go out to dinner. My dad didn't want to wake me up, she loved me, and they would bring me leftovers. There was another message from Benji checking up on me after yesterday. The message was sent four hours ago, I didn't bother answering. I scrolled through Instagram and got another message from Addie; this time: *Hey ass wipe! I see ur online so ur bitch ass better start answering*

I didn't have the energy to deal with him now, but he didn't stop ding after ding flooded my phone.

I typed back a short and sweet *kys*. I closed my phone and stared at my wall. I missed Marsh. There was a loud banging on my door and yelling.

"I'M COMING IN!"

God fucking damn it.

My front door opened, and heavy footsteps clumped up my stairs. Thatcher barged into my room, and there was a second set of footsteps behind him, probably Benji. I sighed heavily, I felt so alone.

"Thatcher, why are you here?"

"Benny was worried about you, and oh my god!" he burst out laughing, "I had to see it to believe it!"

"Addie!" Benji hissed.

"Did you just call him Benny? Dude, he hates that. It's what his grandma calls him," I asked, ignoring his stifling laughter and choosing to be the bigger person here.

"Oh, it's fine, Kia, you know it doesn't bother me any," Benji replied sheepishly.

"I can't believe I miss Marshal beating the shit out of you!"

"Thatcher, if you're just going to make fun of me, you can leave," I sighed. Benji sat down on my bed and put his hand on my back.

"I was worried about you, Kia," his voice said softly.

"Thanks, Benji, but I just want to be alone," I shrugged away from his touch but Benji was relentless. He gave a therapeutic smile before continuing.

"No way!" he exclaimed, "We need to get you out of here! Come swimming with Addie and me! We were going to meet up with Cade and Beth, and I don't actually know who else! It'll be tons of fun, I bet!" He forcefully rolled me over so I would face him and smiled wide. I couldn't say no to Benji. He wouldn't let me be and just wanted to help.

"Okay, okay, give me a minute, and I'll get my swim shorts on, and we can go," I said, smiling back at Benji.

"God, everyone around here is so depressing, I'm getting sick and tired of this!" Addie remarked before leaving my room with Benji. I stuck up a middle finger to his back, not like he'd see it, but I still felt some kind of relief from the jester. I kicked off the sheet that I had swaddled myself in and began the search for my swim shorts.

· XIII ·

MARSHAL

It had been almost a week since Winnie left me, my mom left me, and I punched out Kia. I was still mad at Winnie for everything, I hated her. She had broken my heart over and over again, but this time, it was a gut-wrenching, soul-crushing pain the likes of which I had never truly felt before. She left me and left me when I needed her most. All the reminders of her were gone, but still, the heartache remained. I hadn't talked to my mom since she left; my sister made her attempts to comfort me, which was just texting me saying it was kind of annoying having mom there with her. I didn't answer any of her messages or any of the messages from anyone else.

I hadn't wanted to see or talk to anyone, despite the efforts made by KJ. He tried to come check on me, but I wouldn't let him in, and I wouldn't answer his texts or calls. I had completely cut myself off and wanted nothing to do with anyone. The guilt I felt for what I had done made it so I couldn't face anyone. I missed Kia. I missed him so fucking much.

What the fuck did I do? I ruined the best thing in my life.

I stood in the bathroom, gripping the cool porcelain of the skin, staring at my reflection in the mirror on the back of our medicine cabinet above the sink. I pulled off my hat and shook my head a little bit. *Goddamn, my hair's long I look like I have a mullet.* My bangs now hung in my eyes, and the hair on my neck was well below my ears.

I took off my shirt, continuing to stare myself down. I picked myself apart, taking in every detail of my body. My shoulders and chest were broad but bony. My stomach made up for it with a decent-sized pocket of putty, like all the fat of my upper body had accumulated to this one spot. At least it didn't stick out as much as it used to. I had started needing to wear a belt in the last year or two when it had never been a problem before. I flexed my arms and gave myself a stupid grin. Somehow despite how much time I spent inside, I had a slight farmer tan, my chest my regular painfully pale shade, while my arms had gotten darker. I didn't exactly have anything to flex. My arms had a slight bit of muscle but were still thin and lanky. Scrutinizing eyes picked apart every detail of my bare upper body. I looked at every scar along my arm and grimaced; the tanned skin of my arms was permanently ruined by small circular scars that came from my inability to leave bug bites alone, picking at them until they were gaping wounds. I had too awkward of a build, I was too thin but not thin enough all at the same time. My arms were covered in minor imperfections of light and dark scars, nowhere as bad as the severe acne scaring on Craig's face, but I still hated it.

I hated who I was looking at, and something needed to change, *I* needed to change. I put my shirt back on and headed back to my room. *Phone. wallet. earbuds. Check, check, and check.* I made my mental list of what I needed to leave the house. I hadn't left the house in the last week after what happened.

"Marshal?" my dad called out as I reached for the door handle.

"What?" I groaned.

"Just long time no see, huh?" he nervously laughed.

"Yeah, you're not exactly my favorite person right now,"

"I know, Marshal, I've been a really shitty dad. I was a really shitty husband, too. Now that your mom's gone, I miss her... a lot." I turned back to face him now. His face showed a genuine kind of regret, and his voice was sad. I narrowed my eyes, not wanting to give into his pity party and then I noticed the red of his eyes and the lingering smell of skunk.

"Yeah, you have been shitty," he looked hurt, but I didn't feel bad.

"I want to do better."

"I think you missed your chance, Jerry," I said, glaring, "You and Mom have been at each other's throats my entire life. Never once did you or Mom take the time to think about me or Shelby! We are both suffering, but she got out! I'm still here, and you both keep treating me like I'm not. It feels like since we moved here, it's only gotten worse!" I started to get angry at him.

"For the last five years, my life's been a shit show, Dad. You guys are my parents; you're supposed to make it better, not fuck it all up! And now that mom is actually gone, that's when you realize," I continued pausing to take a deep breath. "You should have realized years ago, Dad that everyone here was miserable except you, " I stopped; my face was red, and I could tell my dad felt the hurt I had intended to give him.

"I'm sorry, Marshal," he said, looking down. It caught me by surprise to hear him say sorry and genuinely mean it. "You're right I should have realized earlier, and I should have seen what your mom and I were doing to you." he sounded defeated. I turned back to the door and was halfway out when he said something else.

"We did notice, Marshal, we did see the change in you. We just didn't want to admit to ourselves that we were the problem. " I let the door shut behind me, and for a moment, I stood on my front porch, letting what my dad said fully sink in.

As I started walking, I started thinking about everything that had been happening with my family. Throughout most of my childhood, my parents fought a lot, usually after my dad did something stupid or drastic, but they always made it up by the end of it. There was a time before when my parents separated, but it didn't last very long. That was the start of how bad it would get between them.

The fighting got frequent and more aggressive so to speak, and it took them longer to make up. Sometimes my dad would be on the couch, or my mom sometimes one of them would be in a motel. They never got physically violent with each other, just late-night screaming matches that would keep me from sleeping. It was always over the stupidest shit.

Once Shelby moved out, I noticed my mom and dad were sleeping in separate bedrooms, my mom had moved into Shelby's old bedroom. It was like living with two strangers. They avoided each other the best they could, and when they had to be near one another, it was always passive-aggressive, with high tension between them all. I felt like I was starting to fade away. The fighting started to get bad again. They'd scream at each other and then come to me and keep yelling about what happened.

After five years, I found the divorce papers on the kitchen counter; they didn't need to tell me. There just became an understanding that I knew. Now we were here, my girlfriend of four years or something like that broke up with me because I had too much shit going on, I guess, and my mom was quote "ruining summer break" for Shelby.

I stood outside the general store, hoping they had what I needed. I braced myself for entering, hoping I wouldn't run into anyone I knew. I wasn't sure if it was because I was thinking about what happened the last time the guys were all together and I didn't want to face that or if it was because of what I was about to buy. For some reason, it was embarrassing to go in and buy what I wanted, but I left the store content with my purchase.

◆ XIV ◆

KIA

Benji's mission was to make me feel better again. I told him a lot on our walk home from the lake. My curls were a wet mop on top of my head, dripping onto my neck and damping the neckline and shoulder of my t-shirt. The feeling of the wet fabric clinging to my skin made my skin itch, so I rolled my shoulders every few seconds, trying to keep the shirt from clinging too much to me.

"You okay, Kia?" Benji asked curiously.

"Yeah, just hate wet clothes, and I know my hair's going to be a mess when it drys," I groaned, thinking about the awaiting process of taking care of my hair, but right now, that didn't matter that was a future Kia problem.

Right now, Kia was living in the moment, walking home from the lake with Benji, the sun setting, painting the sky a beautiful ombre of pinks, yellows, and oranges. I took a deep breath in through my mouth slowly letting it out my nose and trying to focus my thoughts on the fun I had swimming and keep myself grounded. Despite the uncomfortable sensation of wet fabric clinging to me, it was cooling off now, the sun setting and it was enough to eclectic small shivers from Benji and myself.

I hadn't wanted to go at first, not really in the mood to swim, but once Addie threw me into the lake, any hesitation I had was gone. There were a couple of other guys there, a couple of girls I wasn't really friends with but knew nonetheless, Donovan Lambert, Cade Daniels, Beth Rook, Annie Maddigion, and so on. Donovan had set up a speaker playing a good mix of 2000s pop while we swam and ran around the man-made beach of the lake.

I was exhausted but smiled to myself because it was a good kind of exhaustion, the kind that comes from an afternoon well spent.

"I know this stuff with Marshal really has you messed up, so are you sure you're okay?" Benji reiterated his question to get the answer I had been avoiding, but he had been looking for. Still tender from the fight, I ran a hand down my face and sighed.

"What the hell even was that? Like, what happened? I just-" I groaned again, unable to put together coherent thoughts, but Benji looked at me expectantly, ready to listen.

I let all my pent-up feelings out and I felt isolated like I was losing everyone, they each had someone and I had nothing. My fight with Marshal had just been the thing to set it all in motion seemingly. If I lost him, the guy I'd been friends with my entire life, the other half of me, it felt like I'd be reduced to nothing. Without Marsh, it'd be like trying to live without water. My chest started to heave, and my breath quickened; Benji just hugged me tight and told me I wasn't going to lose anyone.

This was now the fourth time in the last week Benji had stayed over at my house. He had stayed up with me and carefully listened as I told him everything I was feeling. Quietly he'd nod along, waiting for me to be done speaking before giving me a reassuring smile. At one point he told me how much nicer it was sleeping over at my house. I wasn't the only one who felt alone, he told me, and now it was my turn to quietly sit and listen to him.

"I hope you don't mind me coming over so much, Kia," he started out.

"No, dude, it's fine. I need company. Without you here, I'd probably be wallowing in self-pity," I answered not looking up the mobile game on my phone I was playing. Benji just hummed in a satisfied way. "Maybe you know next time we could go to you're house, I bet you're tired of holing up in my room, and I bet you miss your own bed and whatever," I suggested, and out of the corner of my eye, I saw Benji go rigid.

"No!" he blurted out a bit too fast, "I mean, I just like it a lot better over here, is all." I looked over at Benji, sitting unnaturally straight on my floor, no longer focused on our game.

"It was just an idea Benj…"

"It's just I don't like being at home all that much; it's weird there," he mumbled quietly.

"Weird?"

"Uh- I don't know how to explain it..." he started looking flustered.

"Oh, dude, we don't have to talk about it if you don't want to. I didn't mean to pry," I felt terrible, but Benji started to relax.

"No, no, you ain't prying, but I'm sure you don't want to listen to me rattle on about my silly stuff I'd like that," Benji didn't face me, eyes burning into the carpart of my floor.

"It's not silly, Benj," I said softly, much like the way he would speak when it was me ranting, giving him that same expecting look he had given me so many times recently.

At home, he felt trapped and like he had no one to turn to, he told me he felt just as alone as me. Benji told me that he always felt some kind of tension at home like he couldn't correctly breathe or relax. He explained it was like he was an actor in a play with a role he wasn't entirely comfortable with.

"Benji, can I ask you something?" I asked him, sitting cross-legged on my bed as we watched Netflix.

"Sure?"

"How are you so happy all the time? There's all this pressure on you, but.. it doesn't seem to affect you."

"It's called a positive attitude, Kia," he laughed a little and playfully punched my arm.

"But dude, you straight up told me it doesn't feel like you can ever actually be one hundred percent yourself at home? You mean to tell me all that's bearable with a positive attitude?"

"You should really try it," I laughed with him now. The movie Benji wanted to watch was the sequel to some cheesy teen romance movie that I had never seen, agast he promptly hit play on The Kissing Booth and told me that I had to watch it and we would, in fact, whether I liked it or not be watching the second movie. So far, it wasn't terrible; it's just not something I'd ever watch on my own or want to watch again.

"Benji, how the hell do you like this movie so much?" I chuckled.

"Come on, Kia! We're not even halfway through," he said, resting his head on my shoulder. I put my arm around him.

"I'm never watching this again," as we both laughed. My phone buzzed with a message from Thatcher:

*Dude why is Benji at your house AGAIN? *

I decided not to answer until another notification: *Are you having some kind of jew orgy?*

I didn't even want to dignify that with a response, but soon yet another message came through; *Stop ignoring me you rat whys the other jew boy at your house??*

I typed back: *Why are you stalking him or something lol wanna join*

My phone pinged again: *No I'm just bored you homos! I'm coming over to break up whatever gay shit ur probably doing!!*

"Thatcher invited himself over," I sighed.

"Oh, that's cool," he didn't seem too enthused.

"I can tell him no if you don't want him here."

"Nah, it's okay, Kia! I haven't really seen him much lately, so he's probably losing his mind out of boredom," Benji giggled. We sat again in some content and comfortable science before it was rudely interrupted, and I sighed.

"Gay wads!" he yelled, entering my room and closing the door behind him. Benji quickly sat up, getting off my shoulder.

"Now, Addison, I thought I told you to stop calling me gay!" Benji Stammered out.

"Fine, how about Khosher homo?" Addie snickered, thinking he was the funniest person alive at that moment.

"Why do you always have to call Kia and me names?" Benji asked, sounding defeated with slight annoyance infecting his ordinarily sweet and almost angelic voice.

"Yeah, shut up, Big Fun," I remarked.

"Don't call me fat!"

"I didn't call you fat, I called you Big Fun," I shot back.

"That's a fat reference!" he argued, the color in his face reddening, I smiled shamelessly, indulging in pissing off Addie.

"Don't call Benji gay then," Benji and I laughed at how flustered Addie was. Addie set down a small drawstring bag and walked over to see what we were watching.

"Oh my god- seriously, The Kissing Booth, Benji, if you don't want me to call you gay, don't do gay shit like watch the fucking Kissing Booth." he huffed

"How'd you know it was The Kissing Booth?" I asked, grinning. He looked dumbfounded and started stemming while Benji laughed at Thatcher's embarrassment.

"I think he got you there, Thatcher," he wheezed out.

"Fine! I watched the Kissing Booth!" He yelled.

"So you're gay?" I said, smiling, I loved watching Thatcher getting all pissy and embarrassed.

"Shut your stupid bullshit-spewing mouth!" Addie shouted. "I can tell when I'm not wanted and it's not here!" Addie recollected his bag, flinging my door open and dramatically stopping down the stairs. Benji and I waited until we heard the heavy front door slam shut before we started laughing. That was the fastest an 'Addison Thatcher' tantrum had ever gotten him out of my house before.

"Do you think he's gonna come back?" Benji asked when we caught our breath from laughing.

"Definitely not he was *really* pissed" Benji and I readjusted ourselves so that I was leaning back on my pillow and Benji was between my legs leaning back on my thigh as we watched the movie. I squirmed a little bit and Benji sat up quickly.

"Oh, uh, sorry Kia if I made you uncomfortable! I didn't me to, oh jeez.." he trailed off, embarrassed.

"Oh, no, Benji, you're fine! sorry my leg just kind of fell asleep, you didn't make me uncomfortable at all," I reassured him, "Marshal and I did that-" I stopped quickly, "Marshal and I did that sort of thing all the time when we used to sleep over and stuff."

"Kia, can I ask you something really personal?"

"Sure, dude."

"And you won't get upset?" Benji looked at me, deadly serious.

"Yeah, Benj?" I was confused, Benji's demeanor scared me a little bit.

"Did you or do you maybe still have feelings for Marshal?"

"What?" my face heated up, so I quickly brushed a hand over my face.

"You said you wouldn't get upset, Kia."

"I'm not upset, Benji... Just why are you asking me that?"

"The way you are with him, Kia, it's just like there's something else there, and and.. what you just said You guys used to lay like that all the time" I could tell Benji was getting embarrassed asking me this. I pulled my hat back up and looked at him, both our faces red.

"We're best friends, doesn't everyone do that kind of stuff?"

"Addie and I don't"

"Well Yeah, because it's *Thatcher.*" Benji gave me a look that said he didn't believe me when I told him we were only good friends. "When you're friends with someone like that for so long you get really close, and it's nothing more than a solid broship."

"I see how you look at Marshal and normal best friends, even super best friends don't look at each other the way you look at Marshal."

"How do I look at him?"

"You look at him like he's the most beautiful boy in the world, you get so tense when you're around him we all started to notice the staring and how you'd get all red. You look at Marshal like he's everything in life."

"Marshal is everything to me, he's the person I trust the most I want to tell him everything and be with him like all the time, I don't know why I get so awkward around him and the staring, I just admire him I guess, his eyes are so pretty such a nice blue..." I paused to think, "WAIT! What do you mean you all notice??"

"Kia, when your face gets red, it basically the same shade as a stop light." he giggled I relaxed a little bit now that Benji had lighted up.

"Benji," it was hard for me to say what I was about to say, "maybe I did have feelings for Marshal, and maybe I still do, I'm so confused. I've been jealous of Winnie for years! Anytime she was around, I'd get so mad and had to leave, it felt like she ruined everything and was taking Marshal away from me. I see Marshal, and I get all warm, and my face gets red, and I- and I- I don't know, there's something wrong with me! why can't I like girls like everyone else? I've tried to like girls my whole life like everyone else!" my eyes started to fill with tears. Benji wrapped me in a tight hug.

"Kia, you are normal," he told me in a soothing voice, "You don't get to choose who you love, and it's worse to try to force yourself to try and like something you don't"

"Fuck" I cried, "I'm in love with my best friend, I just never wanted to say it, I didn't want to admit it!" I was sobbing now. I was so scared. I had been scared for so long. For so long, I had kept it buried down and told myself that everyone loved their best friend the way I loved mine. I kept lying to myself, thinking no one liked girls the way they said they did.

I've been in denial so long it wasn't going to go away, not saying it wouldn't make it any less true.

"I'm gay," I said out loud as Benji hugged me.

· XV ·

MARSHAL

I had been mindlessly scrolling through various forms of social media for I didn't even know how long.

"Okay, I've fucking had it with you, Marshal!" KJ barged into my room, and I jumped a little bit. I hadn't even heard him come in or come up the stairs. *Isn't the front door locked?* He looked at me and got wide-eyed he opened his mouth, but before anything could come out, I stopped him.

"Don't," I glared. He put his hands up as a sign of surrender.

"Wasn't gonna say anything," he laughed, his hands thrown upward in a defensive manner giving an over dramatic eye roll.

"So can I help you, or did you just wanna stare?" I asked, annoyed.

"Oh yeah, like I was saying, I've fucking had it with you, Marshal! This is pathetic! I haven't seen or heard from you in a week, dude I wanted to give you some space, but then I had to make sure you weren't, like, hanging from your ceiling fan."

"Still here," giving him eye daggers.

"Get your shit we're going,"

"Where?"

"Just get your shit, dude, you need to get out."

"Dude, I really don't feel like it," I sighed

"Not an option! It smells like B.O., dispairs, and stale beer; you can't hole yourself up anymore, dude," KJ grabbed me by the arm and dragged me to my feet. He gave me a little twirl and danced, and he was in an oddly good mood. Closely looking at his face, I saw how red his eyes were and knew he was high. KJ continued to hum and dance around, waltzing out of my room as he waited for me.

"Marshal, do you still play guitar?" The question seemed so random. "Uh yeah, why?"

"Good, I still play bass," he said singsongy, "Oh yeah, and I told Cade we could play at his dumb party, something about bAbEs LiKe gUyS wHo cAn PlAy," he said mockingly

"Goddamn it, you drug me out of my house to go to fucking one of Cade's parties? And why did you tell him that? We haven't like playing together in like..." I had to think about it for a long while.

"Irrilivent," he waved his hand at me as if to wave me away before he stopped and flashed a smile putting his finger to his chin like he was thinking really hard. "You know, I think we both played enough Guitar Hero to remember what to do. Plus, if Cade is right, maybe I can get your miserable ass laid," he raised his eyebrows at me, winking and laughing at himself.

When KJ was high, it was honestly entertaining to me; like Craig, he became a different type of person. He became looser, even more carefree than before. He danced, hummed, and sang; all his movements became amazingly flowy. He would start acting like life was a Disney movie and could take on the world. He could do anything, and it didn't matter what it was or how dumb it was.

I laughed at the guitar hero comment until the pang in my chest hit *Kia*. *We* had been really good at that game when we were younger, and it was our thing. I remember saving up weeks worth of allowances to be able to pull together with him to buy it and we played continuously for months. *At least there's going to be alcohol.*

We stood outside Cade's house, I could hear music from outside, and it already seemed like one of those raging house parties from every teen movie ever—*weak dude.* KJ grabbed me by my wrist and took me inside. It was hot in the house and crowded we had to scream at each other just to be heard. KJ went on a search for Cade, and I thought about what he said, maybe I could get laid tonight, I could use a distraction. I looked over and saw KJ pushing through the crowd with a guitar case in one hand and a red cup in the other.

"Here you are," he happily shoved the guitar at me, "oh, and loosen the fuck up!" He handed me the cup. Without thinking, I quickly drank the liquid. We made our way to the living room, where Cade was waiting. He gave me a drunken smile and threw his arms around me.

"Oh my god Marshal! I'm so glad you're here I haven't seen you in forever!" KJ laughed as Cade peeled himself off me. You guys should have everything you need, right?

Two amps, a tangle of cords, and a microphone, probably a shitty one. I saw KJ's bass guitar leaning against the wall. He must have brought it ahead of time. It was beaten up and covered in stickers. I remembered buying it at the thrift store with all my allowance money and an advance from my mom. KJ had been so happy when I gave it to him and taught himself quickly using YouTube tutorials to help him. He was already looking for an aux cord to get set up.

"Ken, what are we even going to play?" I shouted over the music.

"How the fuck should I know," he was preoccupied with his cords.

"Because you fucking got us into this,"

"Okay, well," he trailed off and threw a cord at me the guitar in the case must have been electric. "I have a lot of Nirvana and Queen tabs rattling around up here," he knocked on his head to punctuate his point excitedly speaking. I set down the guitar on the floor and opened the case; it was an electric guitar. It was thin and red and looked pretty new, unlike mine at home, which was acoustic. I ran my finger over the strings before getting set up.

"Well, I don't, dude," I rolled my eyes in annoyance. *This fucker*

"Yeah, you probably have a bunch of sad emo shit memorized, huh?" he grinned.

"I don't have anything memorized, Kenneth James!" I said between gritted teeth. KJ might have been one of my best friends, but sometimes his fuckery was unbearable if he didn't have someone else to entertain himself with.

"Ultimate Guitar.com dude, you have a phone use it," KJ supplied a solution. I was running out of reasons not to do this, and KJ knew that, smirking at me as if he'd just won some kind of prize.

"Fuck you, KJ, fuck you."

"Hey, are you guys almost ready?" Cade whined at us, "I told a bunch of chicks I was gonna have live music chicks love that!"

"Yes, cry baby, we almost got it all set up!" KJ yelled back as I messed with the cords and began to adjust the amps.

"Don't call me crybaby!" Cade whined.

"Then don't act like one!" KJ snipped back. They started going back and forth for a little bit more I sighed but still couldn't help but smile a little bit. After getting primarily set up, KJ and I agreed on some easy enough songs for me to just sight read, some crowd pleasers, and stuff everyone would know.

"Get me another drink, and we'll be set, you know, for confidence," I said, interrupting. Cade huffed at KJ and left when he came back; he turned off the music and handed me a cup. Everyone turned to look at the sudden change of volume. KJ leaned into the microphone while I emptied the cup in three big gulps.

"We are Sex-a-bob, and we're here to make you make you think about getting sad and stuff!" KJ yelled, quoting one of his favorite movies.

"You better fucking not be!" Cade cried out. I shoved KJ out of the way.

"He's an idiot ignore him," I said, monotone into the mic. KJ gave us a silent count, and he started the first song. My fingers moved clumsily over the strings changing the positions. I was beginning to feel more relaxed as KJ and I took turns singing, both yelling our favorite part of the songs each of us had picked.

No one seemed to care about how bad KJ and I sounded.

When we ended our third song of the set, I scanned the crowd, and Cade threw us a thumbs-up as he was now in a group of four different girls. I laughed and tapped KJ on the shoulder, directing his look to Cade.

"Ha! Guess he was right," I laughed. We picked another few songs, and I took another couple of drinks for confidence, as I had told KJ and Cade. We kept playing, and my playing kept getting sloppier KJ gave me a funny look occasionally as I'd hiccup through the song, but I'd smile, and we'd move on. No one seemed to notice anyway we would finish a song, and they would cheer for us.

"KJ, man, I need a break," I said out of breath. He nodded and announced our break into the microphone. I walked through the house, slightly stumbling, and that's when I saw him; Kia *fuck, he's beautiful.* *I* felt my mouth open slightly in an awe-struck sort of way. I watched him, and he danced around with *Donovan fucking Lambert?!?* Donovan held up Kia's hand above his head as Kia spun around.

His face was red with laughter as he twirled from Donovan's arm. They broke apart and swayed some more together. *What the fuck is happening?* As I watched them together, I felt this weird pang of jealousy in my stomach. *I need a drink*

"Hey, Marshal!" KJ yelled grabbing my shoulder slightly startling me, "Ready to get back to it?" We had to yell again since Cade had turned the music back on. *I need a drink.*

"I think I'm going to be sick," I mumbled, holding my stomach. KJ looked where I was looking and looked back at me his face was soft and empathetic. My stomach turned, gaze flicking between the scene of Donovan and Kia back to KJ's face; I felt sick, dizzy, and hot. *I need a drink.*

"Talk to him," he nudged me; my stomach tightened at the thought. Suddenly the room was too full, there were too many people, too many sweaty bodies in too small of a room, and everything was closing in on me. I looked at KJ, who raised his eyebrows, giving me a look that said, 'Go on, dude,' and I looked back at Kia. Instead, I ran away to throw up.

⬧ XVI ⬧

KIA

When Addie came to my house, he was more resilient against our gay jokes after he had stormed out yesterday. He pouted at us, telling Benji and me that we just *had* to go to Cade's party with him. I thought about it and raised my thumb to my mouth, biting off my skin. I could use a distraction, I hadn't left my room since last week, and I hadn't seen or talked to anyone much besides Benji, not including Addie's appearances at my house.

"Will it make you shut up if we agree to go?" Benji asked the two of us standing in the doorway of my front door while Addie stood on the porch making his case.

"Yeah then, Thatcher, we'll go with you!" Benji beamed, happy to make Addie happy. Benji opened the door wider, and we stepped aside, letting Addie in. Both Benji and I's parents had gone to some kind of conference with the synagogue in California. Neither of our parents had a second thought about leaving us home alone, especially with the amount of time Benji spent; my mother was thrilled. My mother didn't like most of my friends tolerating them, but she loved Benji. He was my only Jewish friend, as well as his father, was our Rabbi, which immediately boosted his likability with both my parents. Peter was staying with a friend, so I was home alone. Curfew wasn't going to be an issue, at least.

"*Benji!*" I hissed under my breath. He smiled at me and gave me a pleading look.

"Oh my god- just make out or something I want to leave!" Addie huffed, stomping a little. I shrugged and motioned for Benji to come upstairs with me to get ready.

"Guys! Where the fuck are you going!"

"We'll be right back, Thatcher. Don't get your panties in a bunch," I responded, and Benji laughed when we heard him grumble. We had been wearing the same shirts and basketball shorts for almost two days. I pulled out some clean clothes, and Benji revealed a neatly folded shirt and pair of shorts from a backpack he had been living out of for the last week. He also pulled out a small pouch.

"Kia, would you make fun of me if I wore makeup?" He asked.

"No?" I was confused as to why he asked.

"Okay, great! Now I just have to worry about Thatcher," he sang, unzipping his little pouch and pulling out various types of makeup. He walked over to my mirror, happily sitting on the floor in front of my door, and began to apply different products. I watched carefully; *where did he learn to do that, and when?* I knew how his parents were; his dad especially would never allow this, so this was a skill he had learned and practiced in secret. Something I'd picked up on was how not only strict his parents were in general but also how his dad would scrutinize him based on what was and was not appropriate for the Rabbi's son to be doing and how it would make the family look.

"How do I look?" He smiled, looking quite pleased. I examined his face. He had a light pink color on his eye eyelids making the deep brown of his eyes look brighter. Silver glitter was also spread over his eyelids but also down onto his cheeks, highlighting his cheekbones. The silver was suitable enough that you could tell it was there, but it still almost melted into his dark bronzed cheeks. There was some black stuff around his eyes I think it's called eyeliner I remember when Marshal wore it when he had his token middle school emo phase. *Ugh, Marshal.* I frowned.

"Does it look bad!" Benji got all red and embarrassed.

"No, no! Benji, it looks awesome," I said, panicked but smiled awkwardly. I let out a heavy breath through my nose and screwed my eyes shut, pinching the bridge of my nose, "Sorry, I was just thinking about… you know what? Never mind, just when do you even learn to do this?" I said, panicked. Benji's eyeliner looked much different than Marshal'a when he was goth. Instead of being heavy and dark around his eyes, Benji had a thin line from the corner of his eye out and back connecting to the middle of his eye.

"Oh, I thought you were gonna make fun of me," he smiled.

"I already said I wouldn't do that," I smiled at him, and he beamed back, basically engulfing his entire face. "But uh... well, actually, I was wondering... Benji, could you actually- uh, can you put some of that on me?"

"Sure Kia! What do you want me to do?" I examined his assortment of makeup carefully; all the colors he had were pretty bright or too glittery for my liking. I picked up the eyeliner and handed it to him.

"Can you do some of this on my eyes like yours?" I picked up a black pencil, "I like yours," I added. He nodded and uncapped the pencil, grabbing my face to bring it down to eye level as he put the pencil near my eye. I cringed. "Sorry!" I blurted out, trying to keep still.

"It's okay, Kia! I mean, I am coming at your eyes with a pencil after all," he giggled. The pencil swiftly moved around my eyes, and I looked in the mirror. My eyes didn't quite look like his, but I was still happy with it.

"OH, MY GOD, GUYS, IM DYING OF OLD AGE YOU FUCKS! I. WANT. TO. GO!" Addie shirked from downstairs. I rolled my eyes, and Benji and I left my room so we could finally leave before Addie died, even though I didn't think it would be all that bad if he did. At the bottom of the stairs, Addie took one look at Benji and me before laughing hysterically.

"Oh my god, guys! you look so totally gay!"

"Shut up, you fat fuck; he looks nice!" I snapped.

"What are you guys homo for each other?" Thatcher teased.

"Thatcher!" Benji snapped in a scolding way. "Can you just stop it? You're the one who wanted to go so badly, so let's go," Benji said, ushering us to the door. We walked silently to Cade's house; he didn't live that far. Before we had even made it the entire way to the party, we could hear the music. Standing outside, we could see all the people going into and out of the house, solo cups littered through the yard, and girls vomiting in the bushes out front.

"Nice," Thatcher murmured before walking up to the house and making his way into the party. I nervously picked at my fingers.

"We should get in there. Looks fun!" Benji said, slightly yelling so I could hear him clearly.

"Uh, you go ahead I'll catch up I just kind of need to prepare mentally," I said, trying to take deep breaths. Crowds always made me a bit anxious.

"Well, okay then! See ya inside, Kia!" he chirped and ran up to head inside. My fingers started to bleed a little now from biting at the skin; *good thing I always have band-aids*, I thought, diving into my never-ending pocket supply of band-aids and carefully wrapping one around my finger. I inhaled deeply. *Come on, Kia, you can do this.* Exhaling, I stormed to the door and started walking through the crowd. I didn't see Benji or Addie anywhere; the music was thunderous and I began to panic a little bit. I jumped when my hand landed on my shoulder.

"Jesus, man, you almost killed me!" I laughed, clutching my chest dramatically.

"Dude, you look like you could use a drink," Donovan Lambert, a sort of friend, responded with a warm smile. My pledge to sobriety after my hangover from the last party of Cade's I went to was now meaningless. My nerves had me too tense.

"I could probably use a few; these many people are making me anxious dude. I don't really see anyone I know, so thank god for you," I laughed as we navigated through the tight spaces to the kitchen. On the counter were red plastic cups pre-filled with beer, I assumed from the two kegs on the ground; *how does Cade even get his hands on this much alcohol?* I wondered taking a drink, followed by another, emptying the cups quickly in a desperate attempt to ease the tension. Donovan looked at me with a raised eyebrow as I whipped my chin with the back of my hand.

"Like I said, man crowds freak me out."

"Fair enough," he shrugged, offering to replace my again empty cup. I shook my head at him I was going to need something stronger than beer for how shitty I'd been feeling. Donovan watched in shock as I grabbed a bottle of rum, pouring what I guessed was the equivalent of a shot. My throat was on fire, but I didn't care. I closed my eyes tight grimacing, heavily breathing through my nose. I poured another, throwing it back just as fast as the last one. I shook my head and opened my eyes, trying to get rid of the grimace my face had definitely twisted into.

"Okay, let's go," I said, smiling.

"Dude-" I laughed at Donovan's shocked expression. While I was in the kitchen, the music had stopped briefly and was now replaced by what sounded like two guys with guitars, I couldn't exactly tell what room the music was coming from, but as Donovan and I found a less congested area I started to dance around a little, awkwardly saying to the beat picking up and moving in a less awkward way. As I danced, I had to grab onto Donovan a couple of times for support. My body swayed to the music, and I felt my head getting lighted, and the surroundings seemed to fade. I felt better and looser now. My need for Donovan's support became more necessary as we danced together. We were laughing both, and I could tell Donovan was pretty buzzed.

The boys' music stopped; *they stopped. They sounded so pretty.* I pouted internally, but soon the music had been replaced again by some shitty pop music. I didn't care, and it didn't matter. Donovan and I kept dancing, leaning on each other more. He took my hand and spun me around, twirling me around.

"Dude, I bet we look so stupid," Donovan laughed.

"Yeah, definitely! I don't know about you, but it's true Jews don't have rhythm I can't dance for shit!" My face was red and I couldn't breathe from laughing so hard it was the most fun I've had in a long time. From the corner of my eye, I saw the unmistakable form of KJ.

"I'll be right back, Donovan! I gotta go do something," I said, wobbling and stumbling over to KJ. I clumsily pushed my way over to him. "Oh my god, hi, Kenneth James!" I threw myself into a hug over KJ, almost taking him down as I leaned my entire body weight into my hug.

"Jesus Kia? What happened to never drinking again?" He said, making air quotes with his fingers.

"I haven't seen you in so long, KJ! Hey, man, I love you!"

"Kia, how much did you drink?"

"I like- really love you, KJ," I nuzzled my face into his neck, he smelled like sweat and cheap beer. "KJ, I'm so happy to see you an' I miss Marsh!" I yelled into his neck, "Wheere is heee?".

"WHO WANTS TO PLAY SEVEN MINUTES IN HEAVEN?" someone yelled in the background, a voice I couldn't identify, but I could at least tell where it was coming from. I pushed myself off KJ.

"Oooo we should play Ken!" seven minutes in Heaven was such a childish game but I wanted to have some fun. I started walking to where a group was gathering around the closest.

"Hey Kia, I'm gonna go get a new drink I'll see you over there, buddy," he said. I stumbled over, Donovan offered me his arm and I took it, leaning into his side tucked into the crock of his arm. I looked around at the group of kids. Some I recognized; Cade, Beth, Craig, Theo, Thatcher, Donovan, but then the rest, I wasn't sure of their names.

"Cade and Beth should go first!" Craig suggested and he winked at Cade, who looked back with droopy eyes, a red face, and a dopey grin that took up his entire face. He bit on his knuckles, entering the closest after Beth. We all laughed at what we heard in the closet and seven minutes later Beth and Cade came out with disheveled-looking clothes and hair, our attempts to keep from laughing weren't successful as Beth's face turned into a deep tomato-like red.

"I don't know what they were expecting to come out to," Donovan snickered and I let out a snorting laugh.

"Hey put Kia in there next!" someone yelled.

"With who? I don't want to spend seven minutes with him I don't think anyone else does either," another unidentifiable voice answered.

"Aye," I grumbled.

"Yeah, seven minutes with the right girl, and maybe she'll be able to pull the stick out of his ass!"

"Dude I'm right here," I snapped at the speaker able to pinpoint the unmistakable voice of Thatcher.

"No wait! Guys, shut up!" Donovan announced hushing the small group. "We *should* put Kia in there and I know just who to send in!" Donovan suggested.

"Who?" I asked pushing away from him as he turned away. He either didn't hear me or was ignoring me.

"Just get in the closet and I'll send him in," Donovan said practically shoving me in the closet and giggling to myself *I'm in the closet in a closet ha I'm hilarious!* I stopped and thought in horror, *Shit! Donovan asked 'him' does he know I'm gay? Did Benji tell him? Oh shit, man!* I started to panic slightly biting at my thumb harshly.

⋆ XVII ⋆

MARSHAL

I ran into the backyard, making a couple of uneasy steps off the back deck before emptying my stomach and throwing up, the image of Kia dancing replaying in my mind. I felt my face flush. I thought about how he looked dancing. He was stupid and goofy but his face was lit up, smiling so hard it made my cheeks hurt for him. He was laughing, and he looked so.... *adorable, almost beautiful.* The acidic burn raced up my throat, and I there up again. My stomach turned, and with shaking hands, I pulled out a cigarette from the pack I had in my back pocket. I placed the cigarette between my lips and before I lit it, I looked around at Cade's backyard. It was almost deserted except for a few couples aggressively making out.

I flicked my lighter a couple of times, trying not to bite down on the cigarette between my lips out of annoyance before finally a flame was produced. I eased up a little and took a deep inhale, letting the smoke fill my throat and lungs before exhaling deeply.

"Dude! Marshy!" KJ was running up behind me, I hated how he called me 'Marshy' but after years of it, the name had grown on me. "I know you saw Kia in there are you okay?"

"Yeah, just drank too much, and it was too hot in there," *lie.*

"Well, dude, you should like to go see him and talk to him,"

"And say what?"

"Kias kinda fucked up, man I think anyone could smell the liquor on his breath from across the room, and he was acting all weird. He like threw himself on me and kept telling me he loved me and shit, and I mean.. really go talk to him; he even asked for you," my heart jumped in my chest at that last part, but the feeling was quickly left when I fully

73

processed what KJ just told me. It was rare for Kia to drink and even more rare for him to get really drunk.

"Uh huh," I nodded lazily, still thinking about how Kia had asked for me i figured he would never want to see me again after what happened, all those things I said. KJ was saying some other stuff but I just handed him my cigarette, giving a quick pat on his shoulder before I headed back inside.

I looked for the boy, hoping to spot the halo of red.

"Marshal!" a voice yelled from across the room, I whipped around, hoping it was Kia, but subconsciously, I knew it wasn't his.

"Hey Donovan-"

"I was just looking for you, dude, so this is perfect!"

"Oh, uh have you seen Kia I really need to talk to him," I asked, trying to look past him.

"Yeah, he's in the closet, come on," he grabbed my worst, and we started walking through the crowded bunch of people.

"The closet?"

"Yeah, seven minutes in heaven i told him I'd send him in someone," Donovan laughed.

"Wait! Seven minutes in heaven, and you were intentionally looking for me to put in the closet with Kia! Dude, why?!" For some reason that freaked me out, the implications of the game and me and Kia together. Why the hell would Donovan throw us in there together?

"You guys need to make up to make out whatever!" *Make out?? what the hell is wrong with this dude?* The idea of kissing Kia seemed wrong and weird since we'd known each other since preschool and were super best friends but it also seemed oddly enticing.

"Donovan! What are you talking about!"

"Theo told me what happened at your little bonfire, and KJ talked to Benji about how he was worried about you, so Benji told him about how miserable Kia was; KJ told Craig about it, who obviously told Theo, who told me," That was a lot of information he dropped on me, but I had managed to follow what he was saying. When Donovan got back to the closet with me in tow, everyone looked at me weirdly as I opened the door shutting it behind me. there wasn't much light but here I stood face to face with Kia. In the dim light, I saw his face light up.

"Marshal!" He yelled, "Oh my god, your hair!" he ripped the beanie I had worn despite the summer temperatures, off my head, and all of a sudden, I was super flustered by this action. He ran his fingers through my hair.

"It looks so different!" I was suddenly worried about what he meant by different, and my stomach turned. " I like you, blonde," He smiled at me, and I felt a wave of relief. He leaned into me, face on the crock of my neck while his fingers reached the back of my head now, "You cut your hair?" he said muffled into my neck. I could hear the frown in his voice and I felt the panic start to build again. *Why is his response making me so nervous I've never cared this much!*

"Is it bad?" I asked. Kia's back still gripping my shoulders hard, like if he let go, I'd be gone.

"It's choppy," he looked puzzled, and my face deepened in redness as he leaned closer, "It suits you I liked your long floppy hair, but this seems more like," he put his finger onto his chin, "it's more you, everything is more you."

He threw himself into a hug wrapping his arms around my neck and shoulder while leaning his total body weight into me. I lost my balance and we fell. He was laughing hard. Maybe it was the stuffiness of the closest or the heat or Kia's body heat radiating onto me. Still, I felt my face get even hotter, my forehead dampening with sweat as Kia moved closer, basically sitting on my lap with his head over my pounding heart my stomach threatened to empty whatever was still remaining, *Fuck why am I like this I hope he doesn't notice, ugh I feel so weird what the fuck is wrong with me??*

"I miss you, Marshal, I love you, dude," he said into my chest. I felt my chest tighten and took a sharp inhale as he fidgeted with the charm on my necklace, *fuck he's adorable.* My palms started to sweat and all of a sudden the closest was becoming too hot.

"I miss you too, Kia, and I love you too dude your my super best friend, and- and- I was so horrible to you Kia. You're so sweet, Kia, and kind, you've always been there for me and always were there when I needed someone to pick up my pieces!" I could feel tears start to form in my eyes, I instinctively wrapped my arms around him. Now I was the one holding on for dear life, it felt like this could be the last time I got to hold him and if I let go, he'd be gone.

"I don't deserver you. I fucked up so bad and there's never going to be enough words to tell you how sorry I am- and K- I just," I was now crying a little, unable to keep the water from overflowing. "I can make up all the excuses I want but it won't take back the fact I hit you, I can't even tell you why and I don't deserve your forgiveness!"

"Don't be sorry, I love you, Marshal, and I don't know what I would do without you; just please never leave me again." He sounded so tired, and KJ was right. He reeked of alcohol I could smell it all over him. I cried as I silently hoped and prayed it wasn't just the alcohol talking.

"Come on, Kia, it's time to get up you need to go home," I hoisted him up with one arm supporting him he was pretty much passed out now, mumbling. I walked out of the closet

"Hey! it's only been five minutes, guys! It's against the rules," a girl yelled.

"I don't give a shit about your rules," I said in a flat voice, mainly focussing on getting Kia out of the party.

"HAHA YOU PUT MARSH IN THERE WITH KIA THAT'S TOTALLY GAY GUYS!" Thatcher shouted but I didn't even bother to respond I was now trying to think where I could take him as we exited the party, it was like I dragging a corpse as he struggled to keep up with my steps. *Shit, I can't take him home his parents would lose their shit, KJ and I both live too far away for me to drag him I could ask Craig, maybe? No, I don't want to leave Craig to deal with this FUCK!* I groaned.

"Kia? Buddy? Come on I need to ask you something really important," I shook him a little bit and he groggily answered with a groan. "Are your parents home?" I prayed to god the answer was no, so I could take him to his house, which was the closest, and then no one else would have to deal with him.

"No, my p-parents went on a trip and Peter, no Peter." Maybe there was a god.

I drug his limp body down the street a couple of blocks, struggling to keep him upright. When we finally got to his house, I was out of breath. I managed to dig out my spare key to the house I kept in my wallet, Kia had made me an extra copy years ago and especially now, I was extremely thankful. Kai was right and no one was home, thank god, so I wasn't worried about all the noise I made getting I'm to his room.

I managed by some miracle to get Kia upstairs and onto his bed *I wonder how many times he's done this for me it's weird being on the other side of it.* I carefully removed his shoes and covered him up, making my way out the door.

"Marshal," a small and exasperated voice called out, a warm feeling running through my body at the sound of his sleepy voice. "Don't go," I turned around and looked at him, snuggled in the blankets. I came back over to the bed and took a seat on the edge.

"I'll stay with you until you fall asleep okay?" I whispered.

"Don't go, Marshal," he pleaded. I noticed now the dark makeup around his eyes *is he wearing eyeliner it's cute. shit, he's really kind of beautiful, and his sleepy voice, why is that so cute all of a sudden?*

"I won't go anywhere yet, okay? go to sleep Kia," I reassured him.

"Will you sleep over Marshal, please? I don't want you to leave" he lightly gripped at my arm.

"Sure, Kia," I said without hesitation. He scooted over in bed and patted the space next to him he made. Sharing a bed during a sleepover was nothing new but for some reason, as I got into bed next to him, this felt more intimate. I watched as his breaths became more rhythmic, and he began to snore softly. Everything about this felt so right, so perfect. I felt weird.

· XVIII ·

KIA

My head hurt.

My head hurt.

My head really fucking hurt.

My head really really fucking hurt. I didn't want to open my eyes I knew it would be too bright in my room when I did. *I fucking hate myself right now; what is wrong with me last time I got wasted, it wasn't nearly as bad as this!* I was comfortable snuggled into my blankets and sunk into my bed. It was warm, but not too warm. All I wanted to do was stay forever in this blissful comfort and warmth even in the middle of summer.

I heard my door open end and quickly opened my eyes, flinging back my blankets away from my face, my vision blurry but still clear enough to see the clear figure of Marshal standing in my doorway like he had been caught doing something wrong. He looked flushed with a glass of water in one hand and an in the other hand. It was starting to get warm as we held uncomfortable eye contact, and suddenly, the comfort I felt from under my blankets became too warm. I quickly kicked them all off and sat up.

"Uh, I was going to leave this for you, then I was just heading out," he said quietly, "Your pills and some Tylenol are on the plate,"

The light in my room hurt my eyes and I squinted, my head pulsing from how fast I sat up and still groggily trying to catch my brain up. He handed me the glass of water and set down the plate on my bedside table.

"Thanks, man," I said with a crack in my voice before embarrassingly clearing my throat, and I slowly drank the water holding my hand against my temple, as Marsh sat on the edge of my bed, putting his shoes back on.

"Wait," I said as he got up. Grabbing at him hard enough to leave small crescent moon indents in his bare arm of my fingernails, "You don't have to go, Marsh... please," he stopped and looked at me slightly red.

"Oh, okay sure,"

"Thanks for staying with me, and thanks for taking me home," I rubbed the back of my neck, embarrassed. I had a vague memory of the night so vague I brushed it off as a dream until I saw Marshal standing in front of me.

"Yeah, you really didn't want me to leave and I mean- you've probably done this kinda thing for me a thousand times," he shrugged, seemingly ashamed, and shifted uncomfortably on the edge of my bed.

"Could you get me another glass of water?" he looked relieved for an excuse to level my room as I gave him the empty glass. My face was burning when I thought about how I pleaded with him to stay last night; *shit I told him I loved him. This is so fucking awkward.* I let my thoughts spiral deeper.

"Kia? Dude?" Marshal had reappeared, a fresh glass of water in hand. He set it down next to the untouched plate on my bedside table and took the hand that I had brought up to my mouth without realizing it. "You were chewing on your finger, I think it's bleeding" he looked concerned as he gripped my hand in his own. I quickly brought my hand out of his seeing the almost hurt feeling that flashed in his eyes.

"Oh, yeah," I said quietly to myself. I reached into the drawer of my bedside table unwrapping a new bandaid. Marshal took the bandaid away from me, to my surprise, and carefully wrapped it around my fingertip. I blushed furiously. "Thanks," I mumbled, refusing to meet his eyes. Something about the gesture felt far too intimate. I quickly drank the water he had brought me.

"So, how are you feeling?" he asked.

"Well my head is fucking killing me, I don't want to ever do anything again, Jesus," I sighed.

"What do you remember?" he asked, eyes wide and he had a hopeful look i was almost sad kind of hopeful like he was looking for a specific answer and begging me to give it to him but he also was looking slightly doubtful.

"Most of it, actually, I went with Benji and Thatcher but lost them before I even got in the door but I found Donovan. We danced, and uh, oh, there were these guys I guess Cade got some kind of shitty garage band, they seemed out of practice, but man, their voices were so pretty," I smiled, thinking about the voices of the boys. Marshal's face turned a deep red and he snapped his gaze downward.

"Yeah that's was, KJ and I."

My cheeks were hot, my entire body felt flushed and I slightly panicked but tried to act like nothing was wrong. "Oh, you guys sounded pretty good," I said nervously. "What I meant by shitty was just out of practice and I'm... I-" I trailed off, embarrassed.

"Yeah, we were; it's fine, dude. No offense taken anyway." he brushed it off, and we sat a couple of beats without saying anything before Marshal spoke again, "I don't know what KJ was thinking," he laughed, "we were actually shitty," he smiled slightly. We sat yet again in a semi-uncomfortable silence, this time longer, before Marshal cleared his throat. "What else do you remember?"

"W-well the closest..." I sputtered out, embarrassed to think about it.

"Did you mean all those things?" his eyes wide, a brilliant shade of grey, almost electrifying to look into.

"Did you?" my voice came out barely above a whisper; at some point, we had started leaning into each other, getting closer, our faces inches apart.

"Yes, everything I said, I meant it, I still mean it," his voice the same low volume as mine. That was all I needed before I hugged him, closing the distance between up and gripping onto him tightly, trying to bring him impossibly closer, and his body tensed before relaxing and hugging me back. "So you meant it all, too?" he asked quietly. I didn't give a verbal reason just making a noise of agreement out of my throat, muffled by his shoulder that I had buried myself into. "So we're back to normal and super best friends again?"

"The super-ist of super best friends," I said into his chest before he let me go.

"I love you, dude," and when he said that, my heart beat a bit faster, we told each other we loved each other so many times why was this any different? *Because I wasn't in love with him before.*

· XIX ·

MARSHAL

"So where are your parents?" I ask Kia from his floor. We had been switching around in different positions on either his floor or bed for the past couple of hours being hungover. I was used to the feeling, the headache, and the nausea just a minor annoyance, but Kia was the embodiment of misery. The house was quiet and we had just been either watching movies or scrolling on our phones together with no interruptions in his empty silent house.

"Oh yeah, my parents went to some kind of conference or a convention thing with our synagogue in California so they're out of state,"he explained. Kia lay on his bed sprawled out on his stomach with his head hanging off the end of his bed. He looked angelic. I knew Kia hated his hair but I thought his curls were brilliantly beautiful the color of his auburn hair was breathtakingly bright. Kia was one of the most beautiful people I knew.

"What about Peter?" I continued.

"He's been at a friend's house and I hate to admit this- but I don't actually know where *exactly* he is," Kia rubbed the back of his neck in an anxious manner.

"Oh, okay." I continued to just look at him a flutter in my stomach starting as I soaked in all of his feathers, committing every small detail to memory.

"Isn't your sister in some dumb art school in Calli?" he asked interrupting my staring.

"Oh yeah... mom's out with her too," I tacked on quietly.

"Oh cool! How is Shelby?"

"She's happy to be out of West Richer, she really hated it here man"

"How long is your mom going to be visiting her for?" I sharply inhaled and hesitated before responding.

"Yeah well, she's not really visiting," Kia turned to me and I could see his face drop, "I think she was just using that as an excuse to get out of West Richer, 'visiting' but she left Kia, like- like it's not just her that's gone it's her stuff too. Like all her clothes and- and-," I could feel a lump forming in my throat my body feeling like it was on fire burning from the sudden and overwhelming emotion. I hadn't talked about this to anyone, I hadn't even said it out loud because saying it made it more real. I felt so pathetic wiping at my nose sniffling trying to keep myself together.

"I don't know when she's coming back, I don't think she is." I continued, my head hanging trying to protect what little dignity I had left at this point and not let Kia see me get all fucked up but instead, Kia got up from his bed and came over to sit with me on the floor. We were both cross-legged facing each other and I looked up to meet bright eyes, *I can't find the right words to describe that green of your eyes,* I thought deeply looking into them. He had light freckles across his nose and I smiled a little at him. I looked back down shamefully no longer able to hold eye contact seeing the slight discoloration around his eye, remnants of a fading green and yellow bruise.

"Shit Marshal! I'm so sorry dude, when did she leave? Like I know that your parents weren't together but I didn't know she like left," he slipped my hand into his, gently rubbing his thumbs across the backs of my hand.

"Last week," I said quietly now trying to avoid looking at him. I felt sick.

"Oh my god Marshal I'm so sorry," he said in a hushed voice, one that would be used to console a small child.

"It's okay I guess, I mean it was going to happen anyway," I shrugged and leaned back so I was laying back on the floor and staring at Kia's ceiling. He laid back on the floor with me slightly resting his head on my chest. *This is nice, him, here, with me just like this. Right here, just like this.*

"Dude it's not 'okay' it fucking sucks," he said close to a whisper.

"Yeah it really fucking sucks Kia, everything just went to shit so fast," before I realized it, I started ranting about everything. Kia listened quietly and all the internal rage that was built up slowly came out. It felt like it was hours' worth of ranting and it could have been I wasn't sure. At some point, I had wrapped my arm around Kia while he listened carefully while he leaned into me and I cradled him in my arm. He was warm, a nice warm.

"Oh sorry," I pulled my arm as back as much as I didn't want to but he gave me a confused look, "You just kinda looked uncomfortable,"

"No, I wasn't it's fine. I was kinda comfy actually," he smiled at me, I slightly missed holding Kia in my arm, it felt so right but also weird because that was the way I'd hold Winnie while she listened to my bullshit. I must have done it subconsciously out of habit and to not be rude Kia just went with it like it did.

"Dude you're way too nice," I said.

"What?" he laughed, "What do you want me to do act like Thatcher?" We both laughed at this.

"I didn't mean to like ruin the mood with all my meaningless bullshit, and you just let me go on."

"It's not meaningless Marshal I really care about you dude, your life is important to me and even if it's a 'mood killer' I'm always going to listen to what you have to say. I know I yelled at you the other day about moping around and I'm really sorry about that-"

"Dude you ARE too nice I was being a massive dick and now you're apologizing even though I was wrong," I Cut him off. "And jeez maybe you should spend a little more time with Thatcher, your habits can rub off on each other maybe," we laughed a little bit then the air between us went flat.

"You had a lot of shit going on, even though I was right I shouldn't have been such an asshole to you,"

"Kia, dude, I love you but shut the fuck up before I punch you again, for being too nice," I laughed but Kia didn't. I looked at him and the look on his face was sullen. "Shit too soon huh?" *Fucking idiot yeah it's too soon his eye is still black.* It was awkward between us, Kia and I had fought before but it was never like this. He sighed and sat up now looking down at me.

"It's not that like, I'm really all that upset that you hit me and shit but that you didn't tell me anything before, you didn't call me or text me or even try to come to see me after you fucking beat the shit out of me Marshal," he sighed and I could here the uneven tone in his voice.

"Kia you should be mad I hit you!"

"No I'm mad because let's face it we're not super best friends anymore," I broke at those words, "Were just more like best friends, I watched as we got further apart and you kinda replaced me with KJ," I sat up to face call and cupped his face in my hands, his cheeks were warm and his face flushed.

"I know Kia but it's not my fault! I just- we aren't like we used to be I know but there's no replacing you dude! You just always seemed distant and I missed you so I kinda started hanging out with KJ to fill the void not replace you, dude. I miss you now Kia, I can't replace you but you're the one that you pulled away from everyone." I said a bit annoyed, how could he blame me for us growing apart when he was the one falling back?

"I'm sorry," he whispered pulling away from my hands, "Marshal I feel so weird, everything feels so fucking wrong," his voice quivered unevenly and I realized he was crying.

"I'm always here Kia don't think this is one way, your life is important to me too. Everything everywhere all the time is so fucked up," we leaned close to one another, our foreheads almost touching, " I want it to go back to normal." We were close enough I could feel the warmth of Kia's breath on my lips when he spoke. His perfect lips were close to mine. *he looks like he would taste like vanilla his lips are so perfectly plump, I bet they're so soft.* I realized in horror, both our faces were horribly red. I quickly let him go and backed away.

"Yeah I want it to go back to normal too," he said between what seemed like gritted teeth slurring the words as he spoke. His face had gone to a lighter red now. *What the fuck is happening to me?*

"Dude," he laughed. "That was really super gay," we both started laughing, it seemed forced and artificial from both of us, and to some degree, I think it was. I didn't know why I felt like this with Kia. For our entire lives, we'd been best friends but recently I felt different about him it was like the way I felt with Winnie but he was a boy.

· XX ·

KIA

Marshal had spent almost the entire day with me. It was amazing like I hadn't seen him in a thousand years. I missed him, every little thing about him. Earlier played through my head on repeat. The way his face was so close to mine, our lips almost touched and I thought about what would happen if they did touch. I found myself wondering if Marshal would taste like the lemon scent that clung to his skin and suddenly I'd be overtaken by a wave of shame and guilt for letting my mind go there and thinking that way about one of my best friends. The day went on and my headache was starting to fade away.

We sat down in the living room lazily playing rounds of Super Smash Bros, I was losing terribly and usually that would bother me immensely but today I didn't care because I was playing with Marsh, and he was here, so that was all that mattered.

"Dude last time I got hungover I was at KJ's house and like, he gave me the grossest thing known to man to drink it was like super disgusting,"

"Oh my god he gave you the Con-get-well hangover cure too?" Marshal laughed.

"The what?"

"That's what I named his hangover cure," he announced proudly "and it might be gross but he's on to something it works dude."

"Marshal you're crazy," I rolled my eyes but couldn't help but grin. "You couldn't pay me to drink that again!" and I stuck out my tongue in disgust.

"What's worse? Being hungover or drinking the elixir of the gods made by KJ?" We both laughed at his question.

"Are you implying that KJ is a god?" I said trying to keep a straight face but unable to shake the grin plastered on my face.

"Maybe I am," Marshal smirked back and we both burst out laughing. Marshal started wheezing a let out a sputteruing cough which had me slightly concerned but he let out a steady breath and we calmed down before he spoke again. "Admitt Kia it made you feel better than you do right now?"

"Okay yes I felt better," Marshal smiled and gave me a teasing shove, "But only a little bit!" I snapped back at his teasing. As our laughing died down I heard the front door open.

"Kia! You didn't come and pick me up are you here?!" Peter called out.

"Shit dude I was supposed to get Peter from his friend's house!" I face palmed, "Yeah Peter I'm here! I'm in the living room with Marshal!" I called back. Peter ran in and tackled Marshal with a hug.

He fell backward on the floor and I laughed at his surprise at my brothers' sudden appearance. "Jesus Peter hey there," Marsh wheezed out after having the wind knocked out of him.

"Shit Marsh your losing your touch, getting taken out by a sixth grader," I said with a huge grin. Peter rolled over on my floor laughing.

"Wanna bet Shwartz?" Marshal grinned back giving me a playful look. Before I could think about what he was implying Marshal pinned on my floor laughing, "Quick Peter get him!"

"No Peter save me!" I yelled out giggling, he looked between Marshal and me before jumping on Marshal again causing them both to collapse on top of me. We wrestled around on the floor laughing hysterically until we all couldn't breathe.

"Can Marshal stay the night?!" Peter asked excitedly, Peter had always been fond of Marshal, he was like another brother in Peter's eyes. If you asked him who was in his family he'd tell you his mom his dad, and his big brothers Marshal and Kia. I jokingly gave Marshal a pleading puppy dog look.

"Oh please Marshy," giving him a fake whine. He gave me a general punch on the shoulder.

"Yeah if it gets you to stop calling me Marshy," he retorted.

"We should build a pillow fort!" Peter his excitement compared to a puppy. Marshal and I exchanged looks before silently agreeing. We moved around the house collecting the necessary materials and when we reconvened Peter and Marshal started to work constructing the fort.

"We should call KJ too!" I exclaimed, " It could be just like when we were kids," I laughed excitedly.

"What are we going to make popcorn and watch scary movies too?" Marshal joked.

"No, I'm serious! It would be fun we haven't had a sleepover in forever, what about it Peter? That okay with you?" Peter nodded still hard at work perfecting his pillow fort masterpiece.

"This is so stupid," Marshal sighed shaking his head and smiling, and called KJ who agreed adding that it wasn't a stupid idea it was a good idea.

"Ha, I was right!" I teased. A little bit later KJ knocked on my door. When I opened it he gave me a grin and held up two shopping bags full of chips, candy, and diet soda.

"Hi KJ!" Peter waved poking his head out of his almost-finished pillow fort.

"Hey, little buddy what's up? I haven't seen you around much Katie is starting to miss you," he asked Peter who now suddenly looked embarrassed.

"Wait what? Peter are you not telling me something?"

"Ooooo Peters' been caught!" Marshal teased giving him a playful punch who responded by giving Marshal a slap to his arm. KJ stepped into the house leaving his bags of snacks by the door and removing his shoes.

"Yeah," he started to explain, "Peter's been hanging around with Kate a whole lot getting pretty close," he said in a token dramatic tone of his.

"Peter and Katie sitting in a tree K-I-S-S-I-N-G," Marshal started and I joined in teasing my horrified-looking little brother.

"Shut up you assholes!" Peter yelled in protest his face a deep red, while we all made fake kissing noises. "What are you guys? Twelve?" he scoffed. We stopped and laughed at his embarrassment.

"Don't worry Peter we're just teasing," I reassured him.

"Hey Thatcher's on his way," KJ added back into the conversation.

"Wait Thatcher why?" I asked annoyed.

"He's tired of being left out apparently you 'hogged' Benji last week and now both me n' Marsh," KJ smiled a little at Addie's stupidity.

"Guess it really will be like when we were kids with you guys at each other's throats," Marshal chuckled. *I could listen to this laugh forever it's so rare anymore I love him, I love how light his laugh is, how his chest shakes, and his head falls back, his eyes sparkle.* KJ smacked the back of my head.

"Dude what's wrong with you, you're smiling like an idiot over here and totally spaced out," he remarked.

"Nothing wrong I was just thinking," I smiled at Marsh.

"Gaywad!" KJ snapped his fingers at me, "I'm talking to you, not your boyfriend," KJ said annoyed

"He's not my boyfriend!" I quickly protested embraced and my stomach turned. Hearing Marshal being called my boyfriend made my heart skip a beat, even though Thatcher had called Marshal and my super best-boyfriends since middle school now I realized how much I wished it was true.

We got into the pillow fort starting to dig into some of the snack supplies KJ had brought with him and we searched for scary movies we could watch with Peter. My front door opened for what felt like the millionth time now adding Thatcher to our sleepover.

"Hey big bonded!" We all welcomed him.

"Really?" he whined, "This is so totally gay guys," Thatcher remarked.

"You can leave like you did last time," I responded without giving him a glance.

"I'm not going to leave I'm not letting you dick holes leave me out any longer!" He snapped in protest.

"Okay we'll get in the pillow fort and help us pick a movie," KJ yelled back to him holding the remote and taking his turn to search through Netflix.

"Fine I will," he made his way into the space making it slightly tighter than it was before. It was a tight fit between the five of us. I was wedged between KJ and Marshal while Peter was on my back. I missed the feeling of Marshal's warmth on my skin and was glad to have a reason to feel it again.

"Let's watch this one! It's not that scary don't worry Peter," KJ suggested we all agreed, and as he hit play. I leaned against Marshal as the movie started. *This is so perfect right now I wish this wouldn't end.*

MARSHAL

We all sat in the dark living beneath our pillow fort basking in the glow of the TV playing whatever movie KJ had picked. There was something nostalgic about the moment and again I felt like I was back to being a ten-year-old boy where life was simpler. We hadn't had a time like this since middle school it was like we had all changed and would never change back but right now we had changed back. I ladies on the edge of our pillow fort next to Kia who had wedged himself between me and KJ. Thatcher was on the other far side while Peter sat between Kia and me on our backs intently watching the movie captivated by the story.

A monster made a sudden jump on the screen and we all laughed as Peter yelped jumping back. I looked at my childhood friend group with the same intensity Peter watched the TV with. Thatcher had grown up he was less fat but still on the larger side. His face had become less round and slightly more grown up. KJ's face still had dimples when he smiled, a smile that had a gap from when one of his adult teeth had been knocked out. He sported a silver ring that went through his lip and a couple of studs in his ears. His hair was shaggy and chopping cut much like mine and his hair looked close to a mullet. He had a long thin white scar that ran across his crooked nose to the outer corner of his eye.

I had watched Peter grow up, he was eleven now and rather tall for his age. There was no mistaking his relation to Kia. His face was still round with plenty of check pudge. He had yet to lose the innocent sparkle in his eyes yet and the light in his face was still bright. Although he and Kia weren't blood relatives you could see the similarities in the way they smiled and their laughs. Kia was breathtaking. I hadn't ever truly noticed the ways we had both changed until recently as I started looking much closer at his features. His eyes were a shade of green I couldn't ever figure out what color to call them to truly depict their beauty. His pale skin made them truly pop from his face perfectly framed by his auburn eyebrows. His face was thin and his cheekbones stuck out from his face that no longer held any trace of the childish chub. His jaw was sharp and strong I admired his beauty.

As the movie ended Thatcher snatched the remote and quickly selected the next movie not caring whether we all agreed or not. Peter shifted now more between Kia and KJ while the four of us lay on our stomachs, Peter lying on his side across the backs of KJ and Kia. The poor kid was tired but wouldn't admit it even if we could all tell. he didn't want to go to bed because he liked the movie too much to miss it and was having too much fun at his 'grown-up sleepover' we all smiled glad to indulge him. It was around midnight though when small snores started coming from Peter.

"Kia-" KJ harshly whispered, "Peter's asleep what do I do?" KJ whisper shouted more urgently not wanting to wake Peter up.

"Dude Peter could sleep through an earthquake," I said at a normal volume. Peter didn't stir.

"Yeah I'll take care of him," Kia said shimming out from under Peter's legs. His limp body was unresponsive to the sudden change of support his breathing was still steady. Kia scooped up his little brother slightly struggling to maneuver while putting him on the floor next to KJ.

"See kid sleeps through anything," Kia agreed.

"Jeez, you make the smallest noise and Katies up and at you're throat," KJ smiled fondly.

"Now that the kids out you guys wanna watch a real scary movie?" Thatcher asked.

"What did you have in mind?" I asked.

"Hopefully something graphic," KJ said, still whispered.

"Yeah bring out the slasher movies and the gore," I happily added.

"Got it," and Thatcher yet again picked another novice hitting play. We all watched carefully monitoring Peter in case he woke up as some slasher clown committed horrifcly sick twisted acts of violence. I watched uncomfortably and noticed that Thatcher was also snoring now.

"Dude how the fuck did he fall asleep during that!" I said shocked.

"I think I'm gonna be sick I doubt I'm sleeping," Kia joked

"Could've been worse," KJ added causally, causing both Kia and I to give him horrified looks.

"How!" We both explained together. KJ laughed hard.

"You guys don't wanna know then, come one dude we should probably clean all this shit up Kias gonna go into a diabetic coma just looking at it," KJ joked.

Kia gave KJ a smack as we closed open chip bags and collected the candy wrappers and empty soda cans to throw them out while Thatcher and Peter slept. In our absence, Peter had sprawled out into the middle of our fort. For someone so small he took up a large amount of room. Thatcher too had spread out but not to the same degree.

"I'm gonna take him upstairs guys," Kia said gently nudging Peter, but the gentle nudges quickly turned into a violent shaking to wake him up. He whispered to his brother that he needed to sleep upstairs who tried to protest but ended up agreeing anyway. I loved the way Kia acted with his brother. They were so close to each other, they had a strong bond that I didn't think could ever be broken and it just added to Kia's beauty his love for his family, and how well he took care of his baby brother.

"Marsh? You good? You look like you're about to cry," KJ said breaking our silence.

"No, I think there's something really fucked up with me,"

"What's fucked up Marsh?" Kia asked I was unaware of his return.

"Oh I don't want to dump any more of my problems on you guys let's just go to bed we can talk about it later," both Kia and KJ threw me a sideward glaze of concern.

"We can talk about this later," KJ whispered in my ear. He seemed to be able to tell I didn't want Kia to hear what I had to say.

"Yeah I guess it is pretty late," Kia said lying down he frowned at me, "but it's not too late to talk Marsh," he added on.

"It's really okay, good night K," he turned away from me and I turned to face KJ, "night KJ," he gave me a sleepy groan in return.

"I love you Marsh and I'll always be here," Kia's voice hung in the air and was the last thing I heard before falling asleep.

• XXII •

KIA

It felt weird to tell Marshal I loved him. We had exchanged those words hundreds if not thousands of times to each other, and of course, we meant it, but now there was something different. Something had changed between us now, and I hoped if I said it enough, maybe he would understand that I meant it more than in a platonic way. I hoped he'd understand that I was in love with him.

I lay awake listening to everyone's breathing out of rhythm from one another, Thatcher not so softly snoring. I was on the edge of a tangle of legs and arms now. Thatcher and KJ kept their movie-watching positions, but Marshal and I had some reason to switch. Thatcher lay on his back now with his legs spread out inside down from the rest of us, his head next to one of KJ's feet. KJ was lying diagonally, with one food next to Thatcher's head and the other across his chest. KJ was slightly twisted, and he rested his head on Marsh. Marshal lay on his side, curled almost into a fetal position, with KJ's head nuzzled into his side. Marshal had wrapped his leg around mine, and I couldn't help but smile as we all lay together in a massive tangle.

Everyone one of them looked younger in their sleep, more innocent, and not like we were all constantly hanging to life with a death grip. I continued to stare into the darkness, trying to sleep while I got the occasional kick or elbow or someone groaned in their sleep murmuring something. I envied them all for being able to sleep so soundly while I couldn't. I had a heavy weight in my chest, like someone was holding down my chest. In so many ways, we'd all grown up, but we were all still the same boys who met in elementary school and became the type of friends that never really changed or grew apart. I knew inside that everyone in this room would grow up together, and we'd always be there for each other. The thought made me happy but sad all at the same time.

Marshal frowned in his sleep and groaned. He extended his arm to reach over me and pulled me closer to him I could tell even in the dark he had a slight smile on his lips. I suddenly felt the sleep coming on as I yawned, settling into Marsh's warmth. I closed my eyes, wishing we could sleep like this all the time I miss him even when he was right here I wish he knew how much I loved him and how much he meant to me.

I was awoken by a flash and a click from a phone camera followed by a laugh I could only place as Thatcher's. I angrily opened my eyes.

"Oh my god, guys, you look so totally gay!" He shouted as Marsh started to wake up. KJ was still asleep wrapped up like a burrito in all our blankets. Marsh still had his arms around me and pulled me close to his chest, and he let out an unhappy groan before opening his eyes as well now finally realizing the gravity of the situation. I breathed in the scent of cigarette smoke embedded in his t-shirt along with the lemmon scent on his soap that clung to his skin. The comforting scent was quickly pulled away from me as Marshal quickly unwrapped his arms from me. I was slightly disappointed.

"Thatcher, what the fuck are you doing?!" Marshal yelled.

"Fuck, Marshal, my man, why are you yelling this early?" KJ mumbled, half asleep.

"Because beefcake over here is being a dick. He was taking pictures of Marsh and me sleeping!" I yelled.

"Thatcher leave them alone, dude; it's too early for your antics," KJ grumbled audibly, annoyed.

"But they were so totally being gay for each other! Super best boyfriends!" Thatcher teased.

"Sorry, Kia, I didn't mean to be all cuddly and shit," Marshal said embarrassed. *Don't apologize I don't ever want you to let me go.*

"No, dude don't worry about it I usually wake up holding a pillow. It's nice to hold something in your sleep," I reassured.

"Yeah, you probably imagine it's your super boyfriend!" Thatcher snorted and revived a swift kick to the head from KJ, who was by no means a morning person.

"OI! KJ, what the fuck!" He yelled in response, rubbing the spot KJ had kicked him in.

"I said shut up I'm tired," KJ pulled the blankets further over his head. I felt my face getting red and hot from anger. I was sick and tired of all of Thatcher's teasing I hated him calling Marshal my super-best boyfriend. No matter how much I wanted that to be true coming from him it meant to be an insult and demeaning.

"K? Your face is all red. Are you okay?" Marsh asked in a sweet soft voice. "I think I can even see the vein pulsing in your forehead," he said with the same softness but with some teasing in his tone as he flicked my forehead. I grunted annoyed and recoiled from his touch. I wasn't in the mood for his joking around.

"No Marshal! I'm not okay! I'm tired of Thatcher's shit!" My feelings started to boil out. "I'm tired of him calling everyone gay even though he's the one who watched the Kissing Booth, not me! I'm tired of him always ripping on me, and I'm sick of hearing it towards everyone else!" I snapped

"The Kissing Booth?" KJ asked voice rough and still full of sleep. He now was sitting and looked around slowly blinking at us.

"Yes, the fucking Kissing booth!" I yelled at KJ.

"Kia, calm down," Marshal grabbed me empathically.

"No! I'm not standing for this shit in my own house when I didn't even invite him because I knew this shit would happen! Fucking delete the pictures of Marshal and I, you retarded fat fuck!" I demanded, not releasing how loud I had gotten.

"It's not a big deal Kia," Marsh tried to calm me down.

"It is to me!" I protested, "And if anyone's going to have pictures of us sleeping together I want it to be me," I said quietly but not quietly enough.

"Dude, what's that supposed to mean?" Marshal laughed awkwardly. My face flushed.

"It's the principle! I don't want Addie to take pictures of me and you sleeping unless I want the fucking pictures that's what I meant!" Marshal nodded his head, letting me know I had successfully covered up the true meaning behind my statement.

"Jeezus Kia you sound like your mom," Thatcher rolled his eyes.

"I do not!" My voice cracked a little.

"If it will make your vagina stop bleeding then I'll delete the picture," he sighed.

"You're. Not. Fucking. Funny." I said between gritted teeth.

"Look, Kia, it's all gone," he showed me his photo gallery with no sign of me or Marshal anywhere.

"You guys suck! I'm going upstairs to go back to bed fuck you all!" KJ yelled, making his way out of the blanket fort, still wrapped up in blankets. We all took a moment and then burst out laughing at KJ's childish outbursts.

"The dude's 's not a morning person," I laughed.

"What is it so funny when he gets all bitchy like that?" Thatcher giggled.

"I don't know, but it's always funny when KJ gets tired like that," Marsh remarked. Our laughter died down and we sat together now catching our breaths.

"Well, I think I'm gonna go, guys I haven't changed and brushed my teeth in like two days I feel gross," Marshal said, gathering his things and ready to leave.

"And if Princess KJ is going to continue to be sleeping beauty, there's no reason for me to stay either," Thatcher said, gathering his few things. Both of them left, and I started to disassemble our fort, putting away the blankets KJ hadn't taken and putting the pillows away. My phone rang, and I saw an incoming call from my mom, I slid across the screen to answer the call.

"Hi, *beibi*!" She excitedly squealed.

"Hey, mama, how's California?"

"It's very nice, Kia lots of sun, and your father and I are having a wonderful time! How about you boys I called Peter but didn't get an answer,"

"Yeah he's still asleep-"

"What at almost noon?" She cut me off.

"Yeah, we had a long night he asked if Marshal could come over so we built a blanket fort in the living room and invited KJ and Thatcher over too. We watched movies really late, and he didn't want to go to bed because he was having too much fun," I explained

"Aw, Kia, I'm so glad you let your little brother hang out with your friends like that! It's so sweet!" She went on to ask about all the boys and Benji as well. She continued to complain, things such as, about a restaurant she went to and the hotel pool but still told me what a great time she was having. My mom told me my dad was busy but he missed both Peter and me, and she said before hanging up she missed us both and to have Peter call her when he woke up. Twenty minutes later, I hung up, telling her I loved her and missed her too, and almost on cue, Peter came downstairs, wiping the sleep from his eyes.

"Where is everyone?" He asked.

"Marsh and Thatcher went home, and KJ moved upstairs. I started taking down the blanket fort. Sorry buddy."

"Oh yeah, KJ's asleep in the hallway I think he's mad because I tripped over him," I laughed at the thought.

"Mama wants you to call her by the way," I told him.

"Jeez, Kia let me wake up first!" He squeaked at me and I laughed.

· XXIII ·

MARSHAL

I was so confused, I had so many feelings, and I couldn't place any of them. The way I felt when I was with Kia was similar to how Winnie made me feel, only better, but he was a boy. Thatcher calling us super boyfriends made him so mad, but I kind of liked the idea. It hurt knowing how upset Kia had gotten because of it. When he told me he loved me, it felt different than I had before I couldn't tell why, and this morning I woke up with him in my arms, his sweet vanilla smell, it all felt so right. My head was swimming now. It was like my nerves were on fire anytime Kia was around. I had so many different emotions and it all felt so wrong and right at the time. It was all good and all bad I was so fucking confused.

I started walking to the only place where I could find the help I needed. I held my breath while I waited for an answer after knocking on the door. When Theo opened the door I felt slightly relieved.

"Okay, great! This is perfect, you're both here I need your help," I pushed past Theo, grabbing his hand before grabbing Craig in my other hand and dragging them both upstairs to Craig's room. I shut the door and locked it.

"Hey Marsh, we like you and all, but not like that; keep it in your pants," Craig laughed.

"Suck my dick Craig, this is important, and I don't want anyone to know," I retorted back

"Again Marshal I'm flattered but the only dick I'll be sucking is my boyfriend's."

"GAK! CRAIG DON'T SAY THINGS LIKE THAT TO PEOPLE!" Theo yelled. Craig kissed Theo on the forehead while he tugged at his hair.

"So what's so important that you had to barge into my house, drag us upstairs, and lock us in my room? " Craig asked while he took Theo's hand out of his hair and interlaced their fingers. "Usually I wouldn't mind being locked in my room with Theo-"

"CRAIG!" Theo screeched. "Dude, you're freaking me out," Theo explained, the anxiety clear in his voice.

"'How did you know you were gay?" I asked them in response, I got a dumbfounded look.

"Do you have brain damage?" Craig asked.

"I'm serious how did you know you were gay?" I asked again.

"How did you know you're straight?" Theo asked sarcastically.

"God Theo, when did you get so sarcastic? You've been spending too much time with Craig," I scoffed and rolled my eyes. I crossed my arms over my chest and huffed, "Come on guys, just," I paused, squeezing my eyes shut and pinching the bridge of my nose. "… Please?"

"Probably because I could only jerk off to gay porn," Craig said, looking bored and annoyed. Theo smacked him and I scowled.

"Gross dude, I don't need to know about your jerk-off habits!"

"I'm just saying- no straight dude watches gay porn without being gay."

"I just- Well, I mean- okay, but like-" I sputtered out before giving up, "Fcking gross, Craig," I spit out, finally abandoning any attempts of forming a coherent sentence.

"Don't try to deny it, Langdon," he smirked.

"Serious fucking answers, *please*!"

"I was honestly really confused as a kid, I never liked girls, I never wanted to like do anything of the stuff I was 'supposed' to do I guess. I honestly thought something was wrong with me, but then I started hanging out with Craig, and it was like my entire worldview changed."

"Aw thanks, *Amar*," Craig responded kissing Theo."Kinda long-winded way of saying I'm special," Craig grinned, and Theo laughed.

"That's it? Just because you guys make each other feel special?" I asked, dumbfounded.

"It's more than that, Marsh," Craig said as he rested his head on Theo's shoulder. "It's like when that person is always on your mind, all you do is think about them day and night, you lay away awake thinking about them and wish you could be talking to them all the time." I watched the admiration grow in Craig's eyes while he looked at Theo speaking.

"Suddenly your whole day is about this one person, you can't wait to see them next waiting for the next time you can see them and want to tell them everything you think. When you're not with this person you think about how much you miss them. You look at this person in a way you've never done before. You look at them and stop... and he's just, he completes you. You can't stop thinking about how beautiful they are, how lucky you are to be so close to them; this person is YOUR person," Craig stopped. Theo grabbed his face and kissed him deeply on the lips. Craig ran his fingers through Theo's hair as they pulled each other closer.

"Hey, can you guys like not fuck each other while I'm here?" I interrupted and they both looked very flustered. "But guys, isn't that just really good friendship?"

"Marsh, if you think that's friendship, first of all, go see a neurologist. You probably have a brain injury, and second your super fucking gay," Craig said, breaking away from peppering Theo's face with kisses in a deadpan way. Theo tugged his face back down, putting their lips together and my face curled in a slightly disgusted way ."Now get the fuck out of my house," he said, flipping me off. I quickly left Craig's room before I had to witness any more of him and Theo basically eating each other.

Not everyone feels that way about their friends?

I left Craig's house, not knowing where to go now. I didn't know what to do now with myself. I pulled out a cigarette, lighting the sweet stress relief, and took a drawn-out drag. I let the taste of the smoke fill my mouth. Every time I smoked a cigarette, I savored the moment. I made sure to take in everything about the moment and how exactly it felt between my lips the exact taste in my mouth and down my throat, and how I felt in that moment. It was like a sacred ritual for me. I slowly exhaled the smoke from my exhalation. I closed my eyes and tried my best to take in every part of this moment.

I needed a drink.

On my way home, I smoked another two cigarettes feeling better than I had at the start of my walk. My head felt clearer then, and I felt a calm sensation running over my nerves, but it wasn't enough. My dad's truck wasn't in the driveway, so I knew it was safe to be home. I looked at the empty house and flung myself back on my couch, just breathing, trying to steady myself.

I needed a drink more than anything I wanted a drink. I needed something to make me feel better, I needed to become numb again. I didn't want to feel confused anymore. I didn't want to feel anything anymore I wanted the thinking to stop. I got off the couch and opened the liquor cabinet taking out a bottle of scotch.

Fuck glasses, these are bottle-worth feelings.

I let the warm brown liquid slide down my throat, savoring the woody texture as it ran past my lips, across my tongue, and down my throat. I kept thinking about Kia, and the more I thought, the more I drank. The bottle was empty but my mind was not. I threw the now empty scotch bottle across the room and watched as it shattered. I thought between what Craig had said and Kia.

"Marshal, if you think that's friendship, you're super fucking gay" rang out in my mind. I thought about Kia and how he made me feel. The way I felt was a type of happiness only he could produce, he completed me. I pulled out my phone to call KJ I needed him right now, he was my best friend besides Kia and I needed him now when I couldn't have Kia.

"K-KJ..." I said once I heard him pick up, "I need y-y-ou," I stammered.

"Dude, it's like three o'clock are you drunk?" he sounded disappointed.

"Just come over, please it's important."

Before I knew it KJ was sitting next to me, looking concerned.

"There's something wrong with me, KJ!" I cried on his shoulder. "I don't know what it is but I feel all weird nothing's like it was, and I want it back. I want to stop feeling like this!" I ugly sobbed

"What happened?" he asked me softly.

"I think- I think I love him," I choked out into KJ's chest where he held me.

"Who Marsh?"

"Can you love both boys and girls?" I asked. He frowned at me and gave me a sad look.

"I just fuck to fuck, It doesn't really matter to me but I don't know this whole sexuality thing it's so confusing. It's just expected you like girls and only girls, and if you don't, then your fucked up! it's all so fucking stupid!" KJ let out a deep breath of frustration.

"I-I'm sorry KJ."

"No it's okay dude," he gripped my shoulder tightly, "you can figure this out." I was so confused and my head hurt I was angry and tired. I was exhausted from every feeling I was having all at once it was too much.

"I just need someone right now. I don't want to feel anything anymore." I told KJ quietly, "I don't want to feel anything anymore." I started crying again. "You're my best friend KJ and I- I love you so much I don't know what I'd- what'd I do without," I stammer out.

"I know buddy," he patted my shoulder.

"I think I love him, I miss him he's so pretty I think I love him," I nuzzled into his shoulder, thinking it was Kia. I smiled to myself, suddenly overcome with sleep from my emotional exhaustion. "Mhm, *Kia*," I murmured into his shoulder.

· XXIV ·

KIA

With our living room cleaned up, I watched as Peter played with legos. The TV was on and Peter had it playing some kids' show in the background.

"Peter never grow up," I didn't want him to lose the parts of him that made me my baby brother. Peter looked at me, confused and I just smiled at him. We both turned to the stairs when we heard movement from KJ, who now making his way down. Due to the day's rising heat, KJ ditched the pile of blankets he had taken upstairs and now wore his hoodie fully zipped up and a pair of red boxer briefs.

"I gotta go where are my pants," he asked, still half asleep. When cleaning up I carefully folded the clothes that were forgotten and put them in a pile with the other ideas not belong in our house. It seemed that we could never take home everything we brought to each other's house as this happened each and every time. I pointed KJ to the pile that held his black jeans.

"Anything else yours there?" I asked as KJ struggled to get into his jeans again.

"No, that's Marsh's phone charger, Thatcher's belt, and Marsh's rings," he said, zipping up his pants and putting his shoes back on. "Thanks, man for some reason I think we all needed this," KJ said before leaving, grabbing Marshal's things to take with him. In middle school, during one of Marshal and Winnie's stupid breakups, he was on this hard-core emo persona for a while. The only habits he took away from his time were still occasionally painting his nails, drinking black coffee which he now liked more as we got older than back then, but also wearing simple pieces of jewelry. He wore the same things every day, a black band ring around his thumb, a silver band with the moon phases on it that was one of those spinning rings on his index finger on the opposite hand, and of course, our necklace. I thought the simple pieces suited him, and I'd never say it but I liked when he would put dark polishes on his fingers.

KJ gave Peter and me both a goodbye that consisted of mumbling groans and slipped out the door.

"Man, Kia. KJ should have gone to bed with me," He giggled.

"Yeah, he really hates waking up," I smiled. I had always found it funny how late he stayed up and how he could never keep a sleep schedule, but then how horrible he was at waking up but never fixing the issues. I didn't know how Peter was so fresh I felt exhausted even if I slept quite contently under Marsh's arm I was still whipped out.

I felt warm inside thinking about waking up still cuddled with Marshal and how he had reached for me and smiled in his sleep once I was in his grasp. I hated the method I had woken up in but I'd do it a thousand more times if it meant that Marshal would cuddle me to sleep every night and wake up with me every morning. *God, I'm so down bad for this boy.*

Now that I faced how I felt about Marsh, my every waking thought was about him. I knew deep down I'd loved Marshal for such a long time. He was more than my best friend. He was my reason for getting up every day. Once I finally expected that I loved him, it was like I couldn't stop it. The years' worth of representation came out in daydreams about kissing him, thinking about how perfect everything about him was and how perfect he felt in my life.

I knew I was gay and I knew I was in love with him but my parents had never expressed to me that it was okay to feel that way. I was deep in denial, trying so hard to ignore what was so obvious. I cherished the moments when those feelings would be humored, like holding his hand on the bus or in the hallways, things it was normal for friends to do and only *friends.* it was like a switch flipped in my head, and everything felt so much more complicated.

"Peter, I need to tell you something."

"Yeah?"

"I think I'm gay," it felt good to say it to someone other than myself. It was like a band-aid got ripped off. I didn't worry about how he would react I felt safe in saying it to him because he was little and didn't really understand the gravity of what I was telling him.

"Is that why you've never had a girlfriend?" I was right he was too young to understand the gravity and gave me the exact reaction I needed and expected.

"Yeah Peter that's what that means," I smiled knowing that at least someone knew, of course Benji knew but he knew even before I did. I ever since I talked to Benji about it, I tried not to be alone so I wouldn't have to think about it, and for the first time in five days, I was alone, and that meant with no distractions, I had to face my reality. I was in love with Marshal, the boy I'd been friends with since I was 4 years old, and the boy who dated one girl off and on since forever. My reality was that even though I expected all these feelings, they would never be recuperated.

Peter and I lay around the house most of the day doing nothing while the hours passed us by. I needed to do something for dinner and we needed to eat something that wasn't chips candy and diet soda.

"How would you feel like going out for dinner?" I asked him, and Peter agreed. My mom had left us some money for this and once I found it in the kitchen we headed out. We walked around town browsing our options, we ended up settling for pizza. Sitting at the table waiting for our pizza, I started to realize how much my brother and I were alike in ways that weren't. We both had a lot of the same tendencies and habits and I laughed a little bit, earning a confused look from Peter. I reassured him it was nothing. I got a call from my mom while we ate.

"Kia, it's loud where you are, are you out with your friends? Where's Peter?"

"No, Ma I took Peter out to get pizza wanna talk to him?"

"In a minute, but Kia, did you know Marshal's mom left?"

"Is that why you called me?" I asked, trying to hide the borderline disgust in my voice.

"He's your best friend for crying out loud! Why didn't you tell me!"

"Mom! That's not important unlike *some* people I don't pry into other people's personal lives," I said getting snippy but paused. I took a deep breath, I needed to contain myself so I didn't accidentally unleash the motherly wrath of Ruthanne Schwartz upon me. "And anyway, I didn't know until like two days ago."

"Young man, you better tread carefully with that tone," she snipped back, but finally, what I said must have been processed because she was squealing in my ear again in an obnoxiously high-pitched voice.

"Two days?!? She's been gone for almost two weeks! How didn't you know?"

"Is this seriously the whole reason you called?" I was highly annoyed with her gossiping that she always had to share with me. Why she felt the need to share all the housewife gossip with her 16-year-old son, I'll never know.

"No, not exactly I wanted to let you know that both your father and I are leaving tomorrow afternoon, the trip got cut short, and there are certain things I'm expecting out of you boys for when we get home," my mom went on to list a couple of chores she wanted done like making sure the laundry and dishes were caught up and the trash taken out. She finished up her list by asking me to hand the phone to Peter. He didn't say much to Ma, which was hard to do anyway since she never allowed you the room to speak, so he just gave her a couple of vocal signals he was listening.

Once we said goodbye, Peter sighed. Talking to my mother was a chore in itself.

"We should probably get going and start those chores we haven't been keeping up with any housework," I said, sucking in air threw my cheeks as we gave each other the exact look that said, "Eek". I paid our bill, and we started the walk home. I looked into store windows and as we passed Ians Coffee Co., the place Theo's parents owned. I saw Craig carrying a bus tub full of dishes and Theo behind the counter, "you up for dessert, Peter?"

"Yeah! What are we getting?" He asked eagerly.

"We're gonna stop in and see my friends Theo and Craig," I smiled, opening the store doors for him.

"Hey, Kia. Welcome in," Theo said.

"I didn't know Craig worked with you," I said as he walked back from a store room.

"I don't," he replied before Theo said anything.

"Yeah, he just hangs out and won't let me pay him for the coffee he makes or the dishes he washes," Theo laughed.

"Okay, so I'm going to get a cold brew with sweet cold foam and Peter?"

"I want a brownie!" He pointed to the baked goods display case.

"Coming right up, guys!" And Theo disappeared off to work. Craig opened the pastry case handing Ike a brownie, and I paid him, knowing Theo wouldn't expect my money.

"How's Langdon?" He asked it seemed random out of the blue; Craig didn't usually care about what other people were up to and hadn't seen him since he pulled Marshal off me. It had been two weeks so he had plenty of time to check on us if he was still thinking about the fight to ask us how we were doing.

"He's fine," I said hastily

"Seen him recently?"

"Yeah, he just spent two days at my house," Craig's expression changed to an odd look that was his version of surprise. "Why?" I was confused and could feel my heartbeat starting to increase.

"Nothing," *okay fuck you too, Craig.* I stared at him intently, hoping maybe I'd be able to force out whatever information he was hiding.

"You guys okay?" Theo interrupted, bringing out my drink. He could pick up on the atmosphere of the room and was starting to look anxious himself as he twisted a strand of hair around in his fingers with his free hand.

"Yeah, hun, don't worry," Craig quickly moved to his boyfriend's side, placing a kiss on his forehead. I watched the effect this small action had on Theo and wondered if people ever saw things like that between Marshal and me.

"See ya guys! Thanks for the coffee and brownie," I waved as Peter and I left, continuing our way home. Peter and I hadn't exactly been home, so the dishes weren't a problem it was the laundry and trash that stood in front of us in massive mounds.

"Divide and conquer?" I asked

"Divide and conquer," Peter agreed, and we began cleaning up trash and doing loads of laundry.

XXV

MARSHAL

Kia's parents came home, and when his mom found out about what happened with my parents, she demanded I come over for dinner, correctly assuming that I wasn't getting any home-cooked meals anymore. It was unavoidable that she would find out, and I was honestly surprised it took this long, but still, I dreaded having to face Ruth now. Kia's mom was always on top of everyone's gossip and always had something to say about it, everyone. Kia's whole family basically saw me as one of their own, but I knew this dinner would hurt a little as Ruth would probably grill me with a million questions about things I didn't want to talk about. I took a deep breath before knocking on the door, *why do I even knock I used to basically live here and their expecting me.*

I was greeted by Kia's dad and let into the house. I sat on the couch next to Peter, who was watching TV. He smiled, happy to see me back again.

"I missed having you around all the time, Marsh. You basically lived here before, then you were just like…gone," Peter said.

I cringed, "Yeah…"

"Was that Marshal at the door?" Kia yelled from somewhere else in the house.

"Yeah, I'm watching TV with Peter!" I yell in response. Kia came bounding around the corner and rolled over the back of the couch to join his brother and me. He laid on his back, kicking his legs over the back of the sofa.

"You sure seem in a good mood."

"Yeah, I guess I am," now that I pointed it out Kia looked like he had to think about how he was feeling. "Yeah, I do feel good today," he said again like he was reassuring himself. Kia moved his head so it was now on my thigh I felt a little butterflies in my stomach. I raised my eyebrows at Kia, and we both started smiling and laughing.

"You guys are fucking weird," Peter said, annoyed we were interrupting his show, "always giggling at each other like girls, it's gross,"

"Peter, what happened in the last twelve hours that no longer makes us best friends?" I asked pinching his arms. He swatted my hand away annoyingly turned off the tv along out of the living room. "Dude what is his problem," I laughed. Kia flung his legs backward rolling onto the floor and sitting on his knees facing me.

"He's all pissed with my mom for not letting him play Minecraft all day," He said. From all of Kias rolling around, his hair was disheveled, and without thinking, I reached a hand out to brush a curl back into its rightful spot, I didn't stop. He was too close to stop now. I ran the back of my fingers along his cheekbone feeling his soft skin.

"What are you doing?"

"What do you mean? Just fixing your hair; it's a mess," I responded, confused.

"No shit, dumbass I'm talking about that stupid goofy smile you have plastered on your face and the way you just touched my face."

"Oh, I don't know," I couldn't think of anything to cover up my actions. I just wanted to feel his skin and I've always wanted to run my fingers along the strong bone structure of his face. I had the urge to trace over every part of him with my fingertips creating a mental map of all of him the way he felt and where he was sharp or soft.

"Marsh?"

"Yeah?"

"You okay? You're all like spaced out and your face is red,"

"Oh... yeah I'm fine by the way what for dinner?" I was desperate to try and get Kia away from asking questions centered around how I was feeling.

"I think salmon and cucumber couscous," he said thoughtfully.

"Oooh pulling out all the stops for me?" I teased. He hit my knee.

"Nope, you get dog food we bought it just for you," he joked back, giving me a wide grin.

"Okay I see how it is," I grinned. "Maybe if you're going to act like that I shouldn't have tried to fix your ugly ass jew fro," to which he responded by sticking his tongue out at me and I just laughed.

"This is why you get dog food."

"Well, it's gonna be a great dinner if it's with you," I laughed.

"Dude that's like super gay," he said blushing.

"Looking in the mirror, you're super fucking gay," I responded laughing a little. Kia laughed, too, but it seemed forced.

"Yep... that's me.. super gay," he said sarcastically.

"Yeah, Kia's gay that's cool! right?" Peter said walking back in.

"PETER ALAN!" Kia screamed red in the face, "Don't go saying that!"

"But you-" Peter started saying

"NO! Don't say anything else Peter!"

"Ma says dinner ready," he said looking just as confused as I was by Kia's outburst.

"Kia are you-" I started to ask.

"Just don't!" he snapped at me cutting me off, "Sorry I just said something to Peter and I guess... I don't know, kids weird," he threw in a nervous laugh while he picked at his fingers I grabbed his hand and put it in mine prevents him from further peeling away the skin on his fingers. I could feel my heartbeat in my ears while I held his hand, and we just stared at each other.

"We should probably go eat," Kia suggested, I nodded separating our hands. I wanted to keep holding his hand but I still let him go before any more gay jokes were made since that caused his outburst to upset him. Dinner was as I predicted, Ruth asking me all sorts of questions about my family and about my mom leaving. I tried my best to keep my answer short and simple but it still became overwhelming. My breathing started to pick up and I felt a panic start to set in.

Under the table, I felt Kia interlace his fingers with mine and give me a squeeze. He was staring straight ahead so he couldn't see my look of surprise. The warmth of his hand felt nice in mine and sent a tremendous wave of comfort over me. I returned his squeeze and continued to field Ruth's questions. After dinner Kia and I were put on dish duty.

"God that was exhausting," I said drying the dish Kia just handed me.

"I know, dude I'm sorry," he looked like he had to say more but instead turned away and went back to the task at hand.

"It's all good at least I got a decent meal out of it I swear I haven't eaten something that didn't come from a can or a package in like... forever," I laughed it was the first time since my mom left I had someone cook for me. My dad wasn't one to cook, even when he thought he could when encouraged by the cooking channel.

"Marsh?"

"Yeah?"

"That thing that Peter said?"

"Yeah, what about it?"

"I am gay," he focuses intently on the dish he had been scrubbing even though it was clean.

"You are?" I felt the little butterflies in my stomach again he didn't say anything and I could see he looked like he wanted to cry. The silence was killer. "Do your parents know?" I asked finally.

"No just you, Peter, and Benji," his uneven voice said.

"Benji?"

"Yeah, he helped me figure it out."

"Wait you guys didn't like..." I trailed off hoping he would pick up on what I was implying.

"Gross Marshal! Sick dude!" he made faces at me while handing me dishes. "No we just talked and asked me if I liked this boy, and I do like a boy it's just that I felt like I couldn't like him like that and we're only ever going to be friends. I think I'm in love with him and have been for so long I was just trying to keep it all down and not deal with it." he continued on. My heart sank a little bit when he mentioned liking someone.

"It's okay K," I hugged him tight, "I'll always be here with you forever, I want you to be happy with who you are and it means a lot that you told me this," I wanted to sounded as reassuring as possible now he needed me. "I'm always going to be here for you too. I love you dude you're my best friend."

"Want to stay over again tonight?" he asked me with a small smile.

"Yeah that would be great," I said letting him go. We got back to the task at hand which we had abandoned.

XXVI

KIA

Thanks to Peter, I felt like I was forced to tell Marshal I was gay. I was terrified to have it out there for him to know but also heavily relieved now that, somehow freer. I didn't know why but it was almost like I didn't want Marshal to know. I was so afraid to lose him. I felt like our friendship was so deep and unbreakable but also still so fragile, if I did the wrong thing now it could destroy everything. I loved Marshal but if I let any indication that it was more than platonic I thought I could lose him. I was terrified to lose him to anything, let alone my own doing. Marsh was my whole life. He had been there for everything. I watched as Marshal started to get ready for bed. I asked him to stay because I felt like if he left my secret was leaving too, so I wanted to keep it a little bit longer.

Since Marshal wasn't planning on staying I gave him a shirt of mine to sleep in and watched as he took off his shirt replacing it with mine making my heart jump to my throat. Marshal and I were similar in height but I still had a couple of inches on him. We were both decently skinny but I had more muscle and he had more belly fat. His hands felt weird in mine when I occasionally held them, I had long slender fingers which my mom called 'piano hands', while Marsh's were rouht and calloused. He had thick fingers and his palms were larger than mine. The shirt I gave him was old and clung a bit to his broad chest, it was a bit long and hung loosely over his stomach. I felt weird watching him change, it always had but now epically.

Marshal usually slept in a t-shirt and his underwear or just his underwear but since it wasn't quite time for bed I gave him some basketball shorts as well so that he didn't have to pull the drawstring tight to keep them up like I usually did. I like seeing Marshal wear my clothes.

"Want to play something on PS4 or something for a while?" he asked, joining me in the bed.

"Yeah, sure, what did you have in mind."

"I don't know let me look at what you have again?"

"Marshal we have basically the same games and have had the same games since elementary school, you always say you need to look but you always end up picking Apex so cut the crap," I teased.

"Yeah I guess you're right," he laughed, "I know every game you have but I like the idea of looking, you know just in case I'm in the mood for something different," he justified sarcastically.

"Shut up you're full of it" I punched him in the shoulder before getting ready to play. He smiled at me.

"Prepare to lose," he smirked. We played for a couple of hours until I looked at the time and realized we'd actually been playing close to 4 hours.

"Wow, time really flies where you're kicking your best friend's ass," Marsh smugly remarked.

"Shut up I literally only own this game because you like to play it with me," I said with a pout.

"Maybe you should play it more to keep up," he laughed and I laughed with him. His laugh was contagious and over the last couple of years, it had started to become rare. I savored the sound when I heard it, it seemed he only really was happy when we were together. I smacked him upside the head jokingly for being a smart ass.

"Yeah whatever, I'm going to go wash my face and brush my teeth, I suggest you do the same, we still have your toothbrush here," I said getting up.

"You still have my toothbrush?"

"Yeah, remember my mom bought you one last summer since you basically were living here and she was tired of dealing with your rank morning breath," I joked. I slightly hurt inside since over the last year Marshal and I were growing apart but now everything started to feel normal.

"Shut up," he grinned at me, "Because yes your morning breath is the most fresh amazing amazing-smelling thing ever," he said rolling his eyes. we left my room and walked across the hallway to the bathroom. I put on a headband to pull my hair back while I washed my face and Marshal gave me a funny look.

"What?"

"Washing your face is such a girly thing to do, and it's totally gay that you have a skincare routine, which I guess checks out since you are totally gay," he paused and smiled.

"You have oily enough skin. I could fry french fries with it," I shot back

"Ouch, okay," he rolled his eyes but still smiled. Marshal didn't say anything more as we brushed our teeth together.

"Hey, Ky?" Marshal asked, wiping white foam from around his mouth with a washcloth.

"Yeah?"

"I think I might like boys too," he said quietly, intently focusing on twisting his spinny ring, "I mean, I obviously like girls, but there's something weird happening with me," *Did Marshal think being gay was weird??*

"Something weird? Like, liking boys is weird?" I was hurt.

"No!" he said in a panic, "I mean weird as in I've only dated girls and I like girls but then I started to look at this boy. I started to think about him and the way he makes me feel, well it's like how I used to feel about Winnie but he's a boy," he went on. "I look at this boy and I think about how cute he is all the time, I think about how much I want to be him, just in the same room is enough. I feel all warm inside when he's around and happy, like truly happy. I haven't really felt like this in a while. I thought I loved Winnie, but the feels this one boy gives me are better than anything I ever felt with her," he finished. I felt like someone had grabbed my threat from my chest and was squeezing it as hard as they could. It wasn't only the mention of Winnie that made my chest feel too tight, it was the crushing reality that I would never be loved by Marshal the way I loved him.

I felt my throat close up, I couldn't think or speak my mind just swam in the reality that I would never be loved back. Marshal looked up and looked extremely concerned when he met my eyes presumably seeing the hurt in my face.

"Are you okay?" he asked, *no! I'm not okay! my whole fucking world is collapsing around me!*

"I'm really happy you told me that," I said, trying to sound happy while my voice shook. I threw myself into his chest, wrapping my arms tightly around him like if I didn't, he would be gone forever. He hesitantly hugged me back.

"Are you okay?"

"Yeah, Marsh, I'm thrilled!" I said in a high-pitched voice. I let go of Marshal and quickly walked back to my room, trying to hold everything together when It felt like my world was dying and my heart was in my stomach. Marshal followed after me.

"K? Please, what's wrong?" he said quietly.

"I'm scared, Marshal! I'm terrified of my own feelings. I've been in love with this boy since probably forever but I knew he'd never love me back! I just pushed it all down and tried to deny it, I've known for a while I was gay but I didn't want to accept it. I didn't want to deal with my own feelings because I'm in love with a boy, he will never love me back and I'm terrified to lose him but I'm hurting the more I'm around him," I felt like I was yelling but I wasn't. Everything in my head was so loud and my thoughts were screaming inside my head drowning my mind. I had my back to him so he wouldn't be able to see me crying.

I flinched at the feeling of two arms wrapping around my waist, then Marshal laying his head on my shoulder and standing on his toes.

"I said I liked this boy right?" *I don't need reminding,* "Well I'm scared too because this boy is my best friend and has been since kindergarten. I'm so confused because I don't know who or what I liked and I've known this boy so long but all of a sudden I'm starting to want to be more than friends. I want to do things with him that friends don't do and I'm scared that if I do any of these things I think about he'll never want to see me again." every word he said dug deeper ripping at my heart. I turned around with tears in my eyes to face him.

"I-is it KJ?" I choked out. His face quickly went from sad and thoughtful to alarmed.

"*KJ?* As in Kenneth James? Are you seroisu," he grimaced.

"Well yeah... I mean you guys spend so much time together I just kind of figured-" Marshal cut me off by placing his lips on mine grabbing my waist with one hand and placing the other on the back of my neck. His lips were soft and I kissed him back savoring every moment of what was happening. I held his face now while shocks of electricity ran through my entire body. I never wanted to stop as our kiss deepened and I could taste the minty toothpaste he had just used. My whole body melted into his while inside I rejoiced. A euphoric sensation sent waves through my body and Marshal pulled away. Our noses almost touched,

"Gingers are more my type," he said, lips only centimeters from mine. I quickly realized what he was saying and I could have sworn my heart was going to jump from my chest.

"I probably just ruined this all, but I needed to know what it would be like to kiss you," he said, explaining himself, "I had to know what it would be like if it was anything like I imagined and it was better. I need to know because not knowing was making me crazy, I haven't felt this way about anyone before, and now I'm kind of less confused," he finished.

"I like this boy, and he's my super best friend since kindergarten and his name is Marshal Langdon," I said, awestruck, looking into his eyes. I reconnected our lips, missing the feeling of them already. The tingling sensation they had left behind made me long for more of him. He pulled me closer again in response to my kiss, now asking for entry into my mouth and his tongue. His hands were on my waist, and he squeezed me a little as he explored the inside of my mouth with his tongue. We broke away again, gasping for air I didn't want to stop but Marshal was panting starting to wheeze.

"Jesus's...Christ," he between deep inhales, "get my inhaler from my pants," he asked still trying to regain his normal breathing rhythm.

"Fuck dude, I can't believe you're getting an asthma attack just from making out," I said, feeling through the pockets of his pants, eventually feeling a bulky object and tossing the inhaler to him. He took a deep breath and released the trigger, and his breathing started to return to normal.

"Sorry, I just didn't want to stop," he smiled red in the face. His facial expression changed quickly, and he covered his mouth, "Shit! I think I'm going to be sick!" and he ran out of my room to the bathroom. All I could do was laugh.

· XXVIII ·

MARSHAL

It felt good having Kia be my little spoon despite our height differences. I had him tucked under my arm, holding him close against my chest, this just felt right. I nuzzled my head into the crock of his neck, breathing in his sweet vanilla smell. I loved this boy, I knew that more than ever.

"I'm still confused," I whispered into this neck.

"Why?" Kia squirmed in my arms, and I loosened my grip, allowing him to turn to face me. I couldn't help but kiss his nose. I had thought about kissing him before putting my hands in places I shouldn't, holding him in ways more than platonic, and now that I had kissed him, I couldn't stop myself.

"I like girls," I sighed "But I also like boys," I said pressing my forehead against his. I slid my hand up the back of his shirt feeling his body tense before he relaxed again. I just wanted to touch him and feel the warmth against my hand.

"You can like both boys and girls," he said softly, "it's a thing called being bisexual," he explained.

"What's that mean?" I hadn't heard the term before.

"Well, there's not just two sexualities, more than just gay and straight. There are so many different sexualities and one of them is when you like both boys and girls, it's called bisexual."

I thought carefully about what he was saying, "Yeah. I guess that sounds right," I gave Kia a quick kiss and he smiled against my lips.

"You don't sound entirely convinced," he said putting his head on my shoulder.

116

"It's just... I feel like I need to have a label but I still don't understand how it all works, all I know is I liked Winnie but now I like you. I just don't understand why I feel this way and I don't know how to label it." I explained to him sweetly.

"I'm sure you'll figure it out, Marsh," he reassured me. Kia kissed my neck sending an electric wave through my body as he snuggled closer to me. I closed my eyes and smiled, feeling a new kind of warmth spread through my body as I held him close, drifting off to sleep.

I woke up laying on my back Kia sleeping soundly on my chest with his legs and arms wrapped around me. I reached for my phone, plugged it in on Kia's nightstand, and snapped a picture. I wanted to remember how beautiful he was right now on my chest. I changed the lock screen picture of my phone to the new one of Kia and smiled to myself. I watched as his back slowly rose and fell while he took steady breaths. I started a bit longer until Kia groaned and stretched out his arms and legs.

"Good morning," he said in an adorably sleepy voice.

"Moring," I said kissing his head. Kia looked up at me now and whipped the sleep out of his eyes before putting his lips against mine. I kissed him back, and our lips fought against each other in a new passion that we now shared. Our good morning kiss started to become a sloppy make-out, despite his morning breath, I couldn't get enough of him and wanted the taste of his lips to never go away.

I broke away for a moment to sit up in Kia's bed and he looked at me puzzled for stopping also sitting up. I went his lips, trying to deepen the kiss as I began to lean Kia back into his bed straddling his lap, which he allowed.

"M-Marsh," he said into my mouth.

"Don't talk," I kissed his jawline, "just kiss me, you loser," I returned my lips to his.

"No," he said all breathy, " can we just stop a minute?" I was a bit surprised but pulled away.

"What are we doing?"

"Isn't it obvious? Making out," I started to lean in again, eager to continue one of my new favorite activities, but Kia pushed me away with a firm hand to my chest.

"No Marshal, I mean like what are we doing here?"

"Kia, you're one of the only people I know who can overthink making out," I told him before starting to kiss the freckles light that ran along his face. They were barely noticeable and you had to be within kissing distance to really see them.

"Dude seriously stop screwing around I'm trying to have a real conversation with you," hearing the frustration in his voice I stopped and felt awkward sitting on his lap now. I slid off laying down alongside him.

"What does this make us?" his voice was quiet.

"I don't know..."

"I mean, we both like each other, so what are we? Does that make us boyfriends?" My heart skipped a beat as he said *boyfriends* and I felt my face start to warm a little bit.

"I would like it if you were my boyfriend," I said, admiring the perfection of his beauty.

"I would like to be your boyfriend," he said, red on the face, and kissed me more innocently than I had wanted. I tried on my best 'puppy dog' eyes and gave a fake pout.

"I want to taste my new boyfriend again," I said, giving him the best seductive smirk I could muster.

"Gross!" he grimaced but couldn't hide his smile. "I love you Marshal but let me brush my teeth first," I laughed and watched him get out of bed. I smiled to myself as I fixed my eye on his ass watching the way his hips swayed slightly while he walked. I felt somewhat guilty thinking about my best friend's ass, but I quickly pushed away this guilt because my super best friend was now my super best boyfriend.

"Hey, K!" I yelled, now giggling a little at what just came to mind. Kia mumbled something and walked back into the room with toothpaste foam around his mouth, still brushing.

"So you know how Thatcher always made fun of us and calls us super boyfriends," he rolled his eyes and nodded, "I guess he was kind of right," I said through laughter.

"Oh my god Marshal don't even," he walked, looking absolutely horrified but in a comical way. "Oh, and if you want to continue what we were doing, I suggest you follow me," he grinned. I sighed and followed him to the bathroom. I watched as he rinsed his mouth out, getting rid of the last of toothpaste remaining.

"What are you looking at?"

"The prettiest boy in the world," I said grinning. I began to brush my teeth, and Kia stood behind me, wrapping his arms around my waist and pressing his face into my back while I finished brushing my teeth.

"You're getting clingy," I laughed.

"Shut up, Marshal; you have no idea how long I've waited for this," he mumbled into my back.

"I never said I didn't like it," I said back interlocking our fingers in one of his hands. I walked back to his room. Once he closed the door, I pinned him against the wall and kissed him.

"Marshal!" he gasped in surprise at my sudden action. I felt him smile against my lips while we continued the make-out session we started what felt like forever ago. I couldn't get enough of him. The taste was addicting. I had to stop needing to breathe again to prevent another asthma attack and pulled away breathless. I looked at him, lust clouding my judgment, wanting more of him the taste of his lips wasn't enough. I kissed along his jawline down to his neck, and Kia let out a breathy hum of pleasure as I started to suck on his neck slightly

"Marsh?"

"Hmm?" I bit down, sucking on the skin between my teeth, now a bit more aggressive

"Marsh, can you- Marshal! Stop!" I jumped back at the urgency in his voice

"What did I bite too hard?"

"No it's just kind of a lot," he l looked scared.

"Oh my god Kia I'm so sorry I just kind of got a little carried away and wasn't thinking I'm so so fucking sorry," I said quickly feeling bad.

"No, it's okay I just kind of want to take things slow, you know while we figure them out," he said to me giving me a reassuring look.

"I'm still sorry I just really *really* like kissing you and because I'm an idiot... I just am kind of touch-deprived, and I want to kiss you a lot. I'm sorry."

"Marshal stop apologizing *now* you're being an idiot," he gave me a peck on the cheek.

· XXIX ·

KIA

I was on my couch while Marshal and my brother played Minecraft, mindlessly scrolling Instagram and tapping through everyone's stories. There was something that I saw that caught my attention, someone had reposed a flyer for the Fourth of July fair that sets up every year.

"Marsh! The Richer County Fair opens tonight! we should go!" I said excitedly.

"Why it's the same crappy fair every year, it sucks," Marshal said without looking back at me.

"But Marsh," I whined, "It's only here three days a year."

"You won't miss much Kia trust me, it's the same food vendors, the same rides, and the same games by the same old people with the same firework display," I extended my foot out and lightly kicked him in the back.

"But Marshal I whined again, "It won't be here long, and we only have to one of them." I gave him a pouty look trying my best to persuade him with my cute pleads.

"K, there's going to be all these people, and it's gonna be all stupid and lame," he spat out excuses.

"Please, pretty pretty please," I begged "Are you scared you'll have fun or something?" I teased.

"Fine if it will make you shut up," he said sarcastically, " it'll probably be less dumb anyway if I'm with you," I smiled at his sweet comment.

"Great I'll go ask my mom," and I happily jumped off the couch to go talk to my mom. I found her in my dad's office on the computer.

"Hey, Mamma?"

"Yes, *beibi*?"

"Can I stay over at Marshal's tonight? I want to go to the fair with him tonight and figured we'd be up late, so it would be easier if I just slept over at his house.

"I mean... I guess that could be okay," she said hesitantly, " You can sleep over at Marshal's house tonight if you take your little brother with you to the fair," she added.

"Thanks, Mom! You're the best!"

"I'm glad to see Marshal around so much again, it was weird that you boys weren't talking or hanging out as much," she said as I was halfway out the door.

"Yeah... It was weird but now everything is better," I smiled.

I was slightly disappointed to have to take Peter but didn't mind since it meant I got an extra night of Marsh. Since we had confessed to each other we hadn't really been apart. The most he had left was to go back to his house and grab some clothes so he could stop wearing mine. I was also slightly disappointed in no longer getting to see him in my clothes, *my* boyfriend in *my* clothes. I loved the idea of being able to call Marshal mine. It was a sickling feeling of pure joy. I rejoined Peter and Marshal in the living room, where they continued their game.

I stood back and watched as Marsh and Peter freaked out fighting Minecraft zombies. I couldn't help but think how adorable he was the way he played with my brother.

"My mom said I could stay over tonight, and we just have to take Peter with us." I beamed at Marshal.

"Yay! The fair!" Peter cheered.

"I'm going to back a bag for the night Marsh," I called back, heading to the staircase.

"Here, I'll come help you," he said, following close behind me. As we walked up the stairs, I got a slap to the ass.

"Marshal!" I hissed in embarrassment.

"You're cute when you're embarrassed," he grinned. I hoped Ike didn't see the ass slap.

"Why do you need to pack?" he asked me.

"Well, I figured I could stay over?"

"Yeah, sure, but still, you can just borrow some of my clothes and stuff, dude," he said as we walked into my room.

"Okay, but like, I need stuff for the fair and my meds, but what about, like a toothbrush and deodorant? We can't share everything, Stan."

"Yeah, we can; we could share that too."

"Ew, sick dude! that's disgusting!" I grimaced in disgust.

"What?" Marsha lasked alarmed.

"Sharing a toothbrush! Deordent isn't as bad, but still, that's fucking gross!"

"Okay, so hold on... let me get this straight," he rubbed his temples like he was deep in thought. You'll let me stick my tongue in your mouth, but sharing a toothbrush is too far?" he asked with a puzzled look.

"That different!" I stammered out, "It's just gross." Marshal leaned in and kissed me.

"You're so weird, dude," I kissed him back, "good thing I like weird," he said into my lips. Marsha pulled a backpack out from my closet and began to fill it carelessly with an assortment of clothes. I walked up to him and put my hands on his face making him look at me.

"Marshal, you know I love you, right?"

"You might have mentioned that before?" he said more like a question than an answer confused.

"Please, for the love of god, never pack for any kind of trip ever," I said seriously.

"What! Why! what's wrong with how I pack?"

"You can't just throw things into a backpack; there's a system!" I cried out, "And it's a very fragile one at that. There's a certain way to do things Marsh and packing is sacred."

"Kia, I love you too, even if you are fucking insane," he said lovingly.

"I'm not crazy I just don't live like an animal!" I protested.

"Okay, fine, you pack, and I'll just enjoy the show," he said, walking over to my bed and flopping down on his back.

"What show?"

"The world's cutest boy in his natural habitat." he flashed me a brilliant smile.

"Sometimes I hate you a little," I said in a voice laced heavily with sarcasm.

"Love you too K." I worked in comfortable silence seeing Marshal's eyes follow me back and forth as I worked to put together everything I would need.

"How long are you staying?" he asked curiously.

"Until you get tired of me or my ma wants me home," I laughed.

"Let's go with the first one," he grinned

"Oh, okay, well, I think I have everything ready to go."

"Cool, I guess we can just hang around here until the gates open for the fair. When do they open again?"

"Six o'clock, so that gives us a couple of hours," I said looking at the time on my phone, it was currently only 2:30.

"That's a lot of hours, actually what are we gonna do?"

"I don't know I was content just lying around doing nothing, " I said adding on, "Like doing nothing with you it's fun," my face grew a little bit red.

"I like doing nothing with you, too, we should watch a movie or something," he suggested.

"As long as it's not the fucking Kissing Booth." Marshal raised an eyebrow.

"The Kissing Booth?"

"Yeah, I had Benji over here like all last week before he got grounded. He made me watch it," I explained, and Marshal laughed.

"Want to rewatch The Walking Dead with me then?"

"Oh, my god Marshal that show sucks. How many times are you going to rewatch it?" I rolled my eyes.

"The show doesn't suck! Maybe like the later season but the first couple are still good!" he defended his favorite show.

"What's this going to be your twentieth time rewatching it?" I teased.

"No... just the eighth," he mumbled in a low voice.

"You are so stupid, dude," I sighed, pulling out my laptop to open Netflix. I could think of about twenty different plot holes and no matter how many times I explained to Marshal the show was poorly written and stupid, he refused to believe it. Marshal excitedly took the laptop and pushed play on the first episode. He snuggled his head into my chest, wrapping his arms around me, and I removed his iconic beanie to play with his hair which was now a light bleach blonde with his dark roots still showing. I missed his dark hair, but the shaggy choppy blonde hair he had now seemed to somehow suit him. I ran my fingers through the brittle texture.

· XXX ·

MARSHAL

Kia's mom dropped Peter, Kia, and me off at the entryway to the fairground, and we all thanked her for driving us and got out of the car.

"I'll be back at nine o'clock, boys to get Peter," he said before leaving, giving us three hours.

Peter was bouncing on his toes, bubbling with excitement as we made our way into the fair. The Fourth of July fair was the exact same thing every year since probably before my birth. There were the same food vendors run by the same old people and the same fair rides that ran about as well as they looked not to mention the same games each year occasionally updating the prizes they offered.

Peter and Kia both had huge smiles on their faces, excitedly looking back and forth, pointing to various things.

"I'm going to go us and get us some ride tickets!" Kia said, running off like a little kid. Peter ran after him, and I followed behind, less enthusiastic. When I caught up to them both I watched as Kia gave the woman in the ticket stand several twenty-dollar bills in exchange for three sheets of tickets.

"I got us each twenty tickets," he smiled, handing Peter and me our sheets.

"I can't believe you actually want to ride these things, I feel like if I look at them wrong it's going to fall apart."

"Marshal, you suck at having fun," he giggled back, "Come on, what should we ride first?" he grabbed both Peter and me by the hands running off to the assortment of rides.

"I want to go on that one first!" Peter exclaimed pointing to a marry mixer.

"Okay yeah, let's go get in line!" Kia said, basically skipping over to the line. He looked back smiling, "Come on, grumpy pants!" he saved me. I shook my head and laughed but still went through the crowd to stand with Kia and Peter. We stood talking and moved slowly up the line. When we finally reached the gate, Kia tore off nine tickets for all three of us. The ride operator led us to an empty cart and locked us all in.

"Kia, when we die, I will blame you," I said, wrapping his arm around him. Peter was seated between us, but my arms were long enough to read around to his shoulder. Kia looked at me, slightly uncomfortable, but still smiled at my comment.

"You're not going to die, Marshal, all these rides have to pass a safety inspection, and obviously this one did, so it's totally safe," he said, giving me a look of both sarcasm and seriousness. The ride jerked forward, and I quickly gripped the bar across our laps. The ride spun us around to a point where I lost all sorts of direction and was heavily nauseated. I watched Kia's face light up as he and Peter screamed with childish joy. After the ride stopped I sat in the cart trying to regain my sense of direction. The ride operator unlocked the lap bar letting us all out, and I stumbled, still not over how dizzy I had become.

"I hate you both," I said as they laughed at my inability to walk in a straight line.

"Stop being so dramatic Marsh!" Peter laughed, "Kia let's get lemonade! And then Marsh can sit down and stop being such a sissy," he pointed to a lemonade stand not too far off and was thankful there was an empty bench right next to it.

"I am not being dramatic I'm being realistic," I sighed as I was drug along.

"Kia, I might need you to carry me," I joked and grabbed his shoulder dramatically. If Peter was going to call me dramatic I figured I'd give him a reason.

"Marshal stop it," he laughed pushing me off, he still had that same uncomfortable look when I grabbed onto his arm that he had when we were on the ride. I looked at him oddly. I sat down on the bench next to Kia, and Peter brought us three large cups of lemonade. I took a long drawn-out sip trying to calm my stomach.

"Marshal we should go on the Salt and Peper shaker."

"Are you fucking insane?" I said deadpan, and he didn't say anything else. "No way dude! I choose life!"

"No, come on, dude it's my favorite ride, and Peter's not tall enough for it yet. Please Marshal," he begged, "I don't care that we're in public I will get down on my knees and beg you," I could tell he was completely serious which terrified me.

"You, sir Mr. Schwartz are a manipulating douchebag," I punched him in the shoulder and finished off the last of my lemonade which was the perfect mix between sweet and sour.

"You know you can't resist my charms," he smirked.

"Yeah yeah, whatever it takes you to not embarrass the shit out of all of us." We got up from our bench, tossed the styrofoam cups, and returned to the area with the ride. I watched in horror as Kia's favorite ride was currently running and swallowed hard. "Jesus Christ, I am going to die today, " I mumbled to myself.

"Peter, you stay right here while I scare Marshal to death," he ruffled Peter's hair, and they shared a good laugh at my expense. Kia and I stood in line and my heart started to beat faster I reached for his hand and Kia pulled his away.

"What's wrong?"

"Nothing, just my hands are really sweaty, and I don't want to hold your sweaty hands and get even more sweaty and gross," he explained with a noticeably uncomfortable look. Before I could press further it was our turn for the ride. Kia and I each handed the ride operator 4 tickets and were strapped into the cart.

"God, I know I'm not the most devout catholic, but please don't let me die," I said, looking up into the sky.

"For the last time, you're not going to die," He laughed. As the ride started to rock slowly beginning to move into action, I tensed and grabbed tightly onto the bar. While Kia screamed in joy, I screamed in pure terror. The ride stopped, and my heartbeat started to slow down. Ike was still standing where we left him, almost doubled over laughing.

"Marsh, man, come on, you scream like a little girl!" he wheezed out.

"That's it I'm not letting you terrorists pick any more rides! I'm picking the next one," I said, scanning the selection. "Come on, we're going on the Ferris wheel. We walked over and were lucky enough not to have a long line.

"Kia, I wanna go by myself. You can ride with the big sissy," he stuck his tongue out at me. We got the next cart after Peter, and the Ferris wheel moved smoothly through the air. I leaned over and kissed Kia.

"Why did you do that!" he responded with panic rather than returning my kiss.

"What?"

"Kiss me!"

"Because you're my boyfriend?" I gave him a confused look.

"But, like what if people saw!" I could tell by the shake in his voice he was nearing a panic attack.

"Kia, what's wrong?" I tried to stay calm, "Wait, is that why you wouldn't hold my hand earlier?" I tried to keep my frustration hidden.

"No, it's not like that!"

"Okay, then how is it?"

"Well.. uh, okay, it is like that," his voice was small.

"Are you embarrassed of me?"

"No! Marsh not fucking at all! I'm so happy it's just-"

"Just what? Do you have any idea of how shitty you sound right now?" I started to get upset and made sure to let him know it.

"Marsh please just listen," he pleaded with me his voice was shaking and sounded like he was on the verge of panic.

"I don't really think I want to right now your being an asshole," I turned away, putting my back to him the best I could in our current situation.

"Marsh, it's not like you can leave right now!"

"Fine!"

"It's just like our relationship is *ours* and no one else and I want to keep it like that, just something for us and no one else to see. I don't want to be all public and stuff. It just makes me really anxious about what people will say and do about it. I'm not out Stand and I'm scared ot be out. I'm not even out to my parents yet and I just need some more time before I can really tell them. I just need some time to really get used to everything, I'm gay and I have an amazing wonderful boyfriend, it's all so new. I'm not really ready to share that yet. I want to keep our moments just to us and not in front of everyone." The anger started to melt away as he quietly explained how he felt.

"Fuck man I feel like such a dick now, I didn't me to get upset but it just kind of felt like getting rejected and I'm sorry I'm fucking this relationship up already and it barely started," I barrier my face in my hands out of embarrassment.

"Marsh your not fucking up anything, we just need to figure ourselves out and figure out how to do us," I looked at him still red in the face feeling shitty. I planted a quick kiss on his forehead.

"Sorry couldn't help it," Kia smiled at me. The ride began to slow down and we watched as Peter got off before us and waited by the gate until we could join him.

"Now what?" I asked.

"I'm starving! How about you, Peter?" Kia said.

"Yeah, fair food!" Peter rejoiced. I watched as my two favorite members of the Schwarts family ran away to where the concession stand was located. I scanned through the crowds looking for my boyfriend's unmistakable brightly colored hair. I saw him in line for a funnel cake and followed him and leaned on his shoulder.

"Where's Peter?"

"He went to get snow cones and pizza, I'm on cotton candy and kettle corn duty after my funnel cake, of course," he gleamed.

"Dude, you guys are so gross," I laughed, "I can't understand how you guys can eat all this shit, cotton candy? That's just pure sugar you're going to send yourself into a comma," I smiled back at him. "And wait? You don't even like kettle corn?" I added on.

"Oh yeah, that's for you," he said and I blushed. Kia received his funnel cake and began to devour it, covering himself in powdered sugar. I watched as this spectacle unfolded and couldn't help but find him adorable even as he messily ate a greasy funnel cake. We waited in line for my kettle corn while he ate, and he paid for a large bag.

"Dude, you didn't have to get me the biggest bag!" I said excitedly. I was actually very excited that Kia remembered my love for kettle corn and thought of it to buy some for me I felt my face starting to heat up thinking about his small actions. It was the small things that Kia always remembered about me that made everything feel so special. I saw a dark-haired little boy run up with two snow cones and a piece of pizza.

"Hey! Marsh and Kia! I got you and Marsh a strawberry snow cone to share like you asked!" Peter handed me a red mount of shaved ice with two spoons. I looked at Kia and raised an eyebrow at his now-red face.

"You guys are crazy," I said, taking the snowcone Peter held out to me.

• XXXI •

KIA

Marshal and I quickly ate our snow cone I got us to share each with our own spoons. We walked around some more and headed down an aisle with all the games. I looked around from stand to stand, eyeing all the prizes they each offered.

"Hey Marsh," I tapped his shoulder, "Bet you can't beat me at the water race game," I grinned.

"Is that a challenge?"

"Yep!" I ran over to the game and paid for Marshal and I to play. He laughed at my childhood antics but as the game was getting ready to start he gave me a mischievous smile.

"You're going down Schwartz," he said. As the game progressed I ended up winning the race.

"Suck it, Marsh!" I laughed.

"What prize do you want, kid? You can pick from these two shelves," the man operating the game said, pointing to two shelves in the middle holding an assortment of stuffed animals.

"Can I have the cow?" I asked and he handed me a cheap cow stuffed animal.

"Really, a cow?" Marshal rolled his eyes.

"Yes, Marshal a cow," I said back in a snarky tone.

"You see that huge teddy bear over at the ring toss?" He asked and I nodded, "I'm going to win that for you," he smiled. He pulled out his wallet and handed the game operator enough money for a medium bucket of rings. Peter and I watched as Marshal missed every single bottle and tried not to laugh.

"Whatever that game's rigged," he grumbled walking away.

"Okay," I laughed, "my turn!" I bought a bucket of rings the same size and as I went through them missing most of the bottles I ended up getting two rings in the bottleneck.

"How!! How did you do that!" He yelled in both amazement and frustration.

"Luck I guess," I smiled and asked for the teddy bear Marshal wanted to win me. Once I received it I turned around and handed it to Marsh who blushed at this small act.

"Bet you can't beat me at anything else! You're on a losing streak," I laughed.

"Fine, you're on!" Marsh said. We ran around the games playing everyone we saw until our wallets were empty. I laughed as Marsh had lost almost every game we played. A couple of times Ike took us by surprise and won some himself.

"Better luck next year," I teased. I gave most of my prizes to Marsh but also a couple to Peter as well so between the two of us, we had a large bounty of small cheap stuffed animals.

"Next time Thatcher calls you some demeaning name or makes some comment about your religion or- or some other bullshit I'm not defending you because I don't think it's right that I lost just about every game to the two of you," he laughed. I punched him in the arm.

"Yes, because Peter and I used our magical Jewish powers to make you lose every game," I rolled my eyes and Peter laughed.

"Wow, it's 8:40 what should we do for the last twenty minutes?" I asked

"Well, we have no more money," Marshal started.

"We should call Ma early without money this is boring," Peter said.

"Okay, I'll call in our surrender," I pulled my phone out and called my mom's number, walking away a bit. I asked her to pick us up and also to take Marshal and me back to his house. We had done enough walking around for the day and didn't feel like walking the long exhausting way to his house.

"Okay, Ma said she'll be here in ten minutes and she said she'd give us a ride, Marsh," I said, rejoining my brother and Marshal. We made our way to the front entrance and waited until my mom's car pulled up.

"Did you boys have fun?" she asked as we all got into the car.

132

"Yeah, we ate a bunch of junk food, tortured Marshal, and lost all our money to games," Peter exclaimed.

"Kia! You boys should have been more responsible all this fair food is bad for your health!" My mom yelled back to us.

"Mama, please, I'm fine. I promise," I said, annoyed.

"But *beibi* I worry!"

"I know, Ma but I feel fine," I tried to reassure her.

"I still don't like you eating all that horrible food," she responded.

I sighed. We drove most of the way in silence as Peter beamed about what a great time he had I looked at Marshal, who was watching the world go by through the window. He was so beautiful without even trying to be. I reached out and brushed his fingers against his cheekbones, to which I got a surprised and questioning look back from Marshal.

"Did I have something on my face?" I shook my head. I just wanted to touch his face. I wanted to run my fingers along every part of his body, making a mental map of every curve and edge where his strong bone structure protruded. I wanted to feel his soft skin against my fingertips. We Pulled up to Marshal's house and I got my bag out from the back of the car.

"Thanks, Mama!"

"Have fun, boys, and be safe! I love you, *beibi*!" she said as Marshal and I waved goodbye from his front porch. We opened the door and we were hit with the overwhelming scent of weed as we walked into the living room, his dad sprawled out on the couch in his underwear, surrounded by a cloud of smoke.

"Jesus, Dad! Have some fucking decency!" Marshal's hand flew over my eyes.

"Oh, come on, Marshal we're all boys here!" Jerry protested.

"Goddamn it, Dad! why do you always have to get high in the living room in your underwear? Common K," Marshal pulled me upstairs and we shut ourselves in his room.

"I'm sorry, Kia my dads a fucking idiot," he said in a voice laced heavily with annoyance.

"Dude, it's okay," I tried to reassure him placing my hand gently on his shoulder. He shook away from me.

"No, it's not," he said angrily.

"Come on, it's not like I haven't seen your dad laying around high off his ass in his underwear."

"Yeah, and I don't want my boyfriend to have to see that, I don't even want to see that," he sighed heavily.

"Marshal it's not that big of a deal," I said softly, pulling his face into mine and giving him a sweet kiss. He was tense and I could still tell he was really pissed.

"Love you K," he said putting his forehead against mine, "Still just because you've seen my dad high off his ass almost naked doesn't mean it should be a reoccurring sight for you," he sounded so defeated.

"Yeah it's kind of weird that seeing your dad like that is kind of normal," I shuttered.

"Oh for Christ's sake it is, isn't it?" he grabbed his forehead.

"Yeah, it kind of is."

"I'm going to kill him," Marshal sighed and hugged me tightly. I melted into his embrace and hugged him back letting him absorb me. Marshal rubbed his hands on my back. He reached up running fingers threw my hair.

"You have the prettiest hair, it's so perfect."

"I'm tired can we go to bed?" I mumbled into his chest.

"Sure, I'll let you get changed and I'll go brush my teeth."

"Can I wear your clothes tonight?" in the darkness of the room, I could still see the red across his face.

"Yeah, of course, just- u, fuck!" he quickly ran out of the room and I heard from a distance as Marshal threw up in the bathroom.

"Marshal!" I called out concerned, "Are you okay?" I followed him to the bathroom.

"Don't come in, Kia!"

"Why, what's wrong?"

"I'm just really happy," he responded behind the closed door. Marshal had always had a bad habit of throwing up when he was too happy or excited so I giggled a little going back to Marshal's room. I opened a couple of dresser draws and pulled out a Richer High School athletics t-shirt from the short period where I convinced Marsh to join the basketball team, and a pair of boxers quickly changed as I heard Marshal's footsteps down the hallway.

"Okay, I cleaned myself up, used extra mouthwash and everything, I cleaned up the bathroom too, so you're good to use it now," he looked up and looked me up and down, blushing red, "Shit you look really good in my clothes."

"Please don't throw up again," I said and giggled a little. His shirt was a little big on me but was a similar enough fit to my own clothes. It had a comfortable smell of faint cigarette smoke, fabric softener, and a little bit of his signature lemon scent.

"I won't throw up again... well, probably not." I kissed him softly and he ran his finger through my hair as I left to go finish getting ready for bed. When I came back to Marshal's room, teeth freshly brushed and face cleaned, Marshal was already snuggled into his sheets. I couldn't help but admire how adorable he was.

"Are you just going to stand there, or are you going to join me?" he said from his bed. I smiled at him and jumped into his bed, snuggling into Marshal's arms.

• XXXII •

MARSHAL

I opened my eyes to the bright red curls of my boyfriend in my arms. I inhaled deeply breathing in the vanilla scent and a vague smell of cigarettes lingering from my clothes. I nuzzled my head into his neck and closed my eyes. Kia groaned in his sleep and trashed in his sleep. I looked outside, and it was still dark out. I let go of Kia and searched through my sheets to find my phone, it was 3 am. He tossed back and I watched as he slept but he didn't look peaceful. His face was scrunched tightly, and his brow furrowed. He groaned again and grimaced. I pulled my sweet boy closer to me, and he started to mumble things I couldn't make out. I held his head into my shoulder, twisting one of his soft curls around my fingers.

"I love you, Kia; I love you to the moon and back," I whispered in his ear, continuing to play with his unbelievably soft hair. I listened to the peaceful rhythm of his breathing and kissed his neck sweetly. I had so much love for this boy, and now more than ever, I wanted him to know it. He looked so perfect and amazingly beautiful in his sleep. I watched as his face turned to grimace, making him look distressed but still perfect in every way. I kissed him again, I didn't know if he could tell but I wanted to know I was there for him. The dim lighting from the moon outside outlined the features of his face, and there was a perfect cast of moonlight across his nose, highlighting his faint freckles.

"M-Marsh?" he mumbled in a groggy voice that made my heart skip a beat. *He's so cute when he's half awake.*

"What are you doing away hun?" I whispered.

"Hun? Hmm, I like that," his voice barely audible threw the sleep.

136

"Go back to sleep hun," he squeezed me tightened nodding into my chest.

"I love you too Marshal, please never leave, I can't do it without you," he yawned.

"I'm always going to be here," I responded sweetly, his grip on me loosened slightly and I listened as his breathing slipped back into a soft sleepy rhythm and his heartbeat returned to normal. I frowned as I thought about how scared he'd been. His dream must have been terrifying and I felt the need to protect him more than ever. I felt so helpless as I lay on his chest for how scared he had been and how I couldn't do anything for him. I couldn't get back to sleep instead I just watched now as Kia slept peacefully hypnotized but the shallow rise and fall of his chest. Closing my eyes I tried to get some more sleep and drifted off to the sound of Kia's heartbeat.

When I woke up the second time it was to an alarm Kia had set to take his pills. I groaned still tired from my restless night.

"Kia?" I whispered into his ear gaining a groan in response. I ran my fingers threw his hair.

"Morning Marsh," he said speaking threw a yawn. I closed my arms around his thin frame."Did you sleep okay?"

"I'm sorry I woke you up," I said as we started to get out of bed.

"Oh you didn't, I just kinda wake up sometimes for a minute or two and pass right back out," he explained.

"Oh okay," I smiled fondly, *god he's beautiful.*

"What were you doing awake?" he questioned

"I just kinda woke up and couldn't sleep so I was looking at how pretty you were while you slept, sorry if that sounds creepy."

"It kind of is creepy but in a sweet way," Kia said, blushing.

"Your hair is so pretty," I said quietly, Kia blushed profusely.

"What is your obsession?" he shook his head with a slight smile.

"It's pretty and like bright, just like you, it's like a sunshine halo," I said without trying to filter what I said to him, both tired and no longer caring.

"Come on let's get up," he said quickly.

"I mean it."

"Marshal, it's not your just saying that because I'm your boyfriend," he said annoyed.

"Kia, I've always thought it was beautiful, I just never said it because it sounds totally gay," I said smirking. My comment earned a snorting laugh from Kia.

"You're totally gay dude," he laughed.

"No your *totally* gay," I said kissing his soft lips.

I swung out of bed Kia followed me. We headed downstairs and my dad was nowhere to be seen, thank god, Kia was wearing my shirt he slept in and no pants just his boxers and there was a warmth that filled my stomach when I looked at him, watching as he tiredly wandered around my kitchen preparing to take his pills for the day and get breakfast. I searched through the cabinets searching for something for Kia and me to eat for breakfast.

"Are pop tarts okay?"

"Yeah I'm good with that," he responded as he took one from the box I held out. I watched in horror as Kia unwrapped and ate his pop tart un-toasted.

"What?" He said between mouthfuls with crumbs falling out of his mouth.

"You're a monster," I said dramatically pointing to the pop tart in his hands.

"What!"

"Pop tarts are only good if you toast them!" I responded, laughing.

"Nope, you're wrong there, cold is way better," he said, taking a bite out of his cold pop tart giving me a spiteful look.

"I can't watch this monstrosity any longer," I dramatically covered my eyes waiting for my pop tart in the toaster. When it popped out I wrapped it in a paper towel and glared as we stood on opposite sides of the kitchen eating out pop tarts. I stared at Kia and even if he was eating a cold pop-tart I loved him. I liked seeing him in my clothes. right now he was so unintentionally attractive. I watched him eat his pop tart seemly in his own world and I watched him awe-struck.

My shirt hung loosely on him. Kia might have been taller than me by a couple of inches but he was more slender than I was. There were hints of muscle on my arms but my skin still hung close to my ribs while Kia still had a small bit of belly fat. His arms and legs were long and he had a thin frail looking frame. My build was broader and more compact I hated my body and showing it off in any way. Kia looked so perfect the way he was built and the way he fit so well into it. I liked a loose baggy fit and since Kia and I were around the same size, my shirt still had that baggy fit to him. It came down to about his mid-thigh.

"What?" Kia said noticing my staring.

"I want to wake up with you in my arms wearing my shirt every day," I said almost like I was out of breath. His face turned a bright red and Kia walked across the kitchen, grabbed me, and without saying anything kissed me again. It was a hungry kiss rapid with desire and hungrily tased each other like we were each other's air. The kiss started to become more sloppy and passionate and we melted into each other's embraces. I began to let my hands wander, my fingertips grazing his lower back. I noticed Kia breathing heavily, figuring it was from the aggressiveness of our kiss neither party breaking apart. I gripped his thighs and realized how tense he was I pulled back and immediately stopped, he was hyperventilating.

"K?" I said concerned, he only looked at me with panic, "Kia? dude come on talk to me babe," I pleaded.

"I- Just-" his words catching in his throat, I encouraged him to breathe showing him what to do in a manner that would calm him down and I managed to get him calm enough to speak again. "I'm so sorry, I don't know why I freaked out, don't be mad."

"Kia, why would I be mad?"

"I didn't want to stop you, but- I- I can't do any of that yet dude, I just need some time to settle, and like you seemed really into it but then I started to panic."

"I'm not mad, I'm never going to be mad that you're uncomfortable," I said in a soft and sweet voice.

"I'm still sorry," he sighed heavily

"Don't be," I gave him a small innocent peck, "I need to shower, I'll be back," I said painfully, pulling away.

Last night, he made me promise to never leave but what if he left? What if I pushed him away? He had a panic attack because of me, I did that, I'm pushing him away, I'm going to lose him. Everyone always leaves, Winnie, and my mom, they always left me because I was always part of the problem.

They all left because of me I always fuck up good things and now I'm going to fuck up my lifelong super-best friendship because I'm too much. What was wrong with me? My chest felt tight and a familiar burn started to spread throughout my body.

No, please, don't. Stop. Just stop. Fuck. Fuckfuckfuck stop it.

I need a drink.

· XXXIII ·

KIA

I wrapped myself back into Marsh's sheets and waited for him to finish his shower. He'd been in there a while, and I was starting to get worried until I heard the water stop, soon followed by the shuffling sounds of him making his way back to his room. He stood in the doorway and looked at me before quickly looking away. There was something on his face I couldn't recognize, shame? Guilt?

"K can you leave real quick?" He said in a quiet, almost sad voice. I sat up on the bed, looking closely at him, his skin was bright red in some places, and he held the towel loosely around his waste. His wet shaggy hair hung messily in his face and I watched as water droplets fell and slowly ran down his upper body.

"Why it's not like I haven't seen you without clothes on before, and I might wanna 'enjoy the show,'" I added, quoting him with a giggle.

"Please." Voice flat and blunt, not hint of amusement.

"Are you okay?" I asked, the mood changing suddenly.

"Kia get out, this isn't a request it's me telling you now," sudden frustration in his voice. I looked down and quietly left his room. I rubbed my fingers and started picking at the skin, pulling a long strip away from around my nail bed. I made my way through Marshal's house feeling lost. I wrapped my mind around why he suddenly got so angry so fast. What did I do? Lost in my own mind, I sat down on Marshal's couch, watching the little bubbles of blood build around my fingertips before putting my finger in my mouth and sucking away the metallic taste.

I was wrapped deep in my mind fogging up with questions and sudden worry. I pulled more aggressively at my skin until I heard footsteps down the stairs and I snapped around to face the source of the sound.

"Marsh?" He walked past me to the kitchen, "Marsh?" I called out again.

"I heard you the first time K," he responded annoyed. I heard some shuffling and glass clinking.

"Marshal please talk to me," I debated following him careful of his sudden mood change. He reappeared now facing me with an emotionless expression holding a bottle that contained a brown semi-clear liquid. When I saw the label I recognized it, *Jack Daniels*. I cocked an eyebrow in confusion.

"Marsh?" He removed the cap from the bottle and took a long sip grimacing, "Please!" I said my voice shaking. He lowered the bottle and pitched the bridge of his nose.

"I'm fine Kia," he sighed.

"It's 10 a.m. and your drinking Jack," I retorted.

"Yeah?" I walked over to him and saw the sad look in his eyes. I reached for the bottle in his hand but he jerked away quickly. He brought it to his lips taking a long drawn-out sip before lowering it again.

"You were fine forty minutes ago, did I do something?"

"No Kia you didn't," he groaned. I stepped closer putting one hand on his face and pulling it closer to mine, our forehead's almost touching together. I looked into his dull and dark-looking eyes. His face was now soaked in emotion, some I didn't quite understand. He looked so hurt and ashamed. He looked so far away, deep somewhere else in pain he couldn't communicate.

"Marshal? Talk to me I'm right here," I cooed softly. I wanted too badly to understand. Marshal pulled away from my grasp and returned the bottle to his lips and I watched as he drank the liquid, hit Adam's apple bobbing as he quickly swallowed like he was trying to down in it like it was his life force and he would die if he didn't get it all down now.

"Marshal, what are you doing?" I asked concerned.

"Drinking, hun what's it look like?"

"Marsh I mean, why? What are you trying to cover up?" My voice slightly shook when I asked.

"Jesus Kia nothing is wrong stop fucking interrogating me!"

"It's not an interrogation just talk to me," I pleaded my voice cracking a little, " I don't understand," he groaned and started chugging the now less-than-halfway-full bottle, grimacing as it passed through his lips.

"Not everything is about you K I have my own shit to deal with, and you're not part of it, Jesus."

"Marshal please just stop! I don't understand," My voice cracked a little with this plea. He gave me an angry scornful look. I reached for the hand with the bottle in it to lower it away from his mouth he gasped for air now. "Why are you acting like this? What happened? You were so happy and lovey and now all of a sudden you flipped so fast, what's wrong, please tell me!"

"You don't understand?" He gave me a dangerous smile the look in his eyes was a mix of anger, guilt, and fear, "Honey, I don't understand!" he laughed wildly.

"What?"

"You weren't here! you don't know! nothing is wrong *Kia*" he hissed my name. His lips twisted upward into some kind of joker-looking smile.

"Why are you acting like this? I'm here now!" I yelled on the brink of tears. I was starting to get scared of the anger etched into his features and twisted around his sweet face into someone I couldn't quite recognize.

"This.." he waved his arms around motioning to himself, "is me. This is who I am, Kia!"

"Marshal, please-"

"This is who I am," he repeated more softly. He continued his drinking and I felt a new kind of fear creep in.

"Why are you shutting me out right now? I care about you, I love you and right now I'm here! So let me fucking in!" I cried out.

"This is what I am, Kia! This is what I do! You'd know that if you'd been there but you weren't!" He yelled in response.

"Marshal, that's not fucking fair-"

"What? How is that not fair," he hissed, "because it's the truth? And I'm calling you out? You left me K! And now all of a sudden you're back, flinging yourself on me, suddenly in love with me?!"

"Suddenly? Marshal, I've *always* been in love with you! I just didn't want to say it! I didn't want to admit it!"

"I loved you too! You pushed me away! And all I wanted was to forget I loved you!"

"Marshal don't do this-" I felt the lump building in my throat. Hot tears started to flow out. "Please," I choked out, "don't forget now." What he said stung, and his words cut through me. Marshal sat down on his sofa with a heavy sigh now nursing off the last of his Jack. I followed him back and sat next to him. He turned to face me and I reached out putting my hand along his jaw. I softly ran my thumb over his cheekbone back and forth and he looked at me with teary eyes.

"Kia don't!" He snapped, "I don't need this!"

"Marshal, PLEASE! I'm worried and I'm scared for you!"

"I don't need you right now!"

"Marshal please," I started sobbing. The way he so easily said it and the emotion behind what he said. I felt my heart break a little. *He didn't mean it.*

"Fine," I said more even-toned, "I'll go." I got off the couch and stormed upstairs slamming Marshal's bedroom door behind me. I leaped into his bed, inhaling the smell of him letting out loud, heartbroken sobs. Downstairs I heard a yell and the shattering of glass while I continued to sob into one of Marshal's pillows. I knew he didn't mean it, he couldn't have, and he wouldn't say that to me. I got up and swiftly worked to gather my things, I found a pair of shorts and put them on, slipped on my shoes, and started to make my way downstairs. I looked over my shoulder into the living room and saw Marshal on his knees chest heaving and a broken bottle across the room. I didn't look back as I left.

When I got home, my mom looked at me surprised, "*Bibei*? I didn't expect you home so early!"

"Yeah, I didn't expect to be home this early," I mumbled.

"Baby? what's wrong with my *klyen ingl*?" she asked, her voice less chipper than it usually was.

"It's nothing. Marshal and I had a stupid fight," I sighed.

"Oh no!" she said with that motherly concern in her voice.

"I just want to be alone right now Ma," I said simply dragging myself up the stairs. I dropped my bag by my door and fell face-first into my bed. I didn't understand. *What was that look?* the way he looked at me, the emotion on his face was foreign to me. Marshal and I could often so easily read each other but it felt like he was purposefully trying to keep me out. I didn't understand and I didn't understand why he was saying the things he said.

He was right about some of it, I had pulled away because I didn't want to feel the feelings he made me feel but I didn't know how bad it must have gotten for him. I wanted one person right now and only one person but the person I wanted didn't want me.

Why Marsh?

• XXXIV •

MARSHAL

I hated how I felt. I hated all the feelings I had pushed down and how now they all started to resurface. I didn't even understand myself, Kia kept pressing for an explanation, but I didn't even have one. All I could think was how guilty I felt for everything. I remember the bitter feelings and the anger. all I could think to do was drown it out. None of my thoughts were clear when I started yelling at Kia. My mind swam around in the Jack I so quickly downed. I wanted to feel nothing, and Kia was trying to make me feel something, so I lashed out at him. I saw the look on his face, and the guilt and shame I felt deepened.

Kia stormed upstairs after we yelled at each other, I didn't know why I was so angry or why I took it out on him, but I was feeling these things because of him. I yelled out and threw my empty bottle across the room at the opposite wall letting it shatter. I sunk down on my knees, wanting to cry, and as my chest heaved, nothing came out but raspy breaths. My front door slammed, and I slumped over on the floor, just lying there, not quite asleep, not quite alive, not quite dead, but not fully alive.

What did I do? Why am I fucking like this?

At some point, I had fallen asleep on the living room floor. My head throbbed, and my stomach violently turned as I woke up, feeling the intense need to throw up. I tried my best to stand up with my legs shaking, and I couldn't will myself move forward. My head hurt too much every time I moved, and I threw up directly in front of me before falling back onto the couch. I pulled out my phone, slowly dialing KJ's number, with my heartbeat thudding lowly in my ears, mixing with the pounding on my head. The phone went on ringing, and I felt so desperate to give up before KJ finally picked up, his sweet yet raspy voice giving me a new type of comfort.

"Marsh?"

"Dude, can you come over?"

"Yeah? Where've you been? I haven't like seen or talked to you in a couple of days, dude," he said with a concerned voice.

"Just come over," I groaned.

"You sound like shit dude, you good?"

"Thanks, princess," he wasn't here to wittiness my eye-roll that came out with my response, "Just get over here," I hung up the phone with a sigh.

I grabbed a couch pillow, using it to cover my ears as if it would help soften the pounding in my head. I pressed my face deep into the couch cousin still tightly holding the pillow over my head. I have not seen nor heard from my dad this entire time, and usually that would be perfect, but I wondered where he was now. My stomach turned again, sending a wave of sickness through my body, and I sat up only to throw up on the floor again. I still hadn't cleaned up the first puddle of vomit, and now, as it mixed with the new puddle, I didn't feel like dealing with it; *future Marshal problem*, I thought to myself. I snapped my head back to the sound of my front door clicking open.

"Kia?"

"Nope, sorry to be disappointed," KJ shrugged, walking in, "Are you too drunk to remember who you called?" he teased while he welcomed himself into the house.

"No- just- displeasurably sober," I groaned, gripping my head in my hands.

"So then, why did you think I was Kia?" he asked with a raised brow.

"He stayed over last night, we had this ugly fight, and he stormed out. I don't know, man," I had no idea why I thought he was coming back. Maybe it was because I subconsciously wanted it to be him walking through the door. KJ approached the couch, and he looked at me, the puddle of vomit and the broken glass; his expression drastically changed.

"Marshal, dude," he pinched the bridge of his nose between his fingers and leaned his head into his hand. "What happened?"

"I don't want to talk about it, dude I feel like shit. That's why I called you because you make me not feel like shit."

"Well, you look like shit, dude, and this is gross," he gestured to the sense before him, "Come on, let's get this fucking mess cleaned up," he said, annoyed. I lay back on the couch, pulling my knees into my chest and wrapping my arms tight around them, holding myself as if I would fall apart if I let go. KJ cleaned up the vomit and broken glass, ensuring I knew how annoyed he was the entire time. When he finished, he took a seat next to me.

"KJ?"

"What?"

"I love you, dude, you are my best friend, and I really appreciate everything you do."

"Shut up, that's so cheesy," he lightly punched my shoulder. "I love you too dickwad," he mumbled, and I let out a small laugh.

"Thanks for coming over. I really needed someone, I don't want to be alone right now. I don't know where my dad is, and K and I are fighting, I guess? I don't know anymore. I think I ruined everything," I said, feeling a knot build in my chest and throat.

"Oh dude, your dad's with my dad on a fishing trip with my uncle Ned."

"Oh, fucking wish he would have told me," I groaned.

"But what's up with you and Kia?" he inquired.

"I don't know," I sighed.

"Well, try to explain it," KJ said reassuringly. He put my hand on my shoulder, and I moved my head so that it was now on his thigh. I looked up at him. His eyes gave me a look that made me feel safe.

"I just feel so fucking guilty about everything. All of it. I don't know why but Kia came back around, and now I just feel... bad. He and I just drifted apart, we had that big fight the last time, but we made up, and we got better. Better than ever actually, we're not just best friends, we're..." I cut myself off, *boyfriends*.

"Super best friends," KJ finished for me, listening carefully.

"But now that he's here, I feel so bad about everything that happened, he pulled away from me- and- I just said the wrong things, and I don't understand how can I make him understand?"

"You guys are Marshal and Kia; you'll make up like always," KJ smiled and ruffled my hair, "So you never told me. What the fuck is with your hair?" he laughed, and I couldn't help but to smile at him.

"I didn't like who I was, and I needed a change."

"Okay, but bleaching your hair?"

"Shut up, KJ, it doesn't look that bad," I scowled at him.

"No, it doesn't. It's just different and, I guess, *a* change," he said, shrugging his shoulders.

"KJ, you're full of shit," I gave a shy grin pushing myself off his lap and into an upright sitting position, "Come on, you little shit head I need a smoke," I said, standing up on shaking legs. KJ stood up with me and held an arm out for me to grab onto for support. I gladly took his arm, and we made our way to the back porch. We sat on the rear steps, and I pulled up a plank that underneath held a metal tin where I stashed some extra cigarettes, hiding them from my dad. I opened the pack and frowned at the few remaining cigarettes, making a mental note to get more for this hiding spot.

I pulled one of them out, putting it between my lips and handing one to KJ, who did the same. With shaking hands, I held the lighter under his cigarette and tried to light it unsuccessfully.

"Fuck!" I mumbled, frustrated with my fingers' inability to work.

"Dude, I just let me–"

"No! I can do it, KJ, shut up!" I snapped back, and finally, after a few more attempts, I was able to light our cigarettes. I took a long drag, holding in the smoke before slowly relating it. KJ took a couple of short drags, and we sat in silence we surrounded ourselves with separate clouds of menthol smoke.

"KJ, I'm an idiot, and I think I'm in love with someone, like, for real, in love," I said, breaking the silence between us.

"Yeah, not shit," a long stream of smoke blew out between his lips, "You've loved Winnie since the third grade."

"What? No," I grimaced, "I don't give a shit about her, I'm in love with someone else."

"Who is she?"

"Well, that's the thing, it's not a she."

"Oh," I tensed up for his response as he took another drag. "Who is he then?"

"You're not surprised at all I like boys?" I asked, deflecting his question. KJ turned to me, giving me a dumb look.

"Dude, it doesn't matter who you fuck, I don't care. Personally, I think this whole sexuality and gender thing is blown way out of proportion; it's all so stupid. I mean, it's just expected you are this one thing, and if you aren't, then it's a big deal, but why? I mean, we don't act like that about anything else, but when it's about sexually, suddenly the world is going to end Sorry, I'm going off on a tangent," he paused, and I gave him a questioning look.

"Are you...?"

"Gay? No, I don't do the whole labels thing. I don't have a sexuality; I'm just sexual. I just fuck to fuck. I don't care what's there." He inhaled deeply and exhaled quickly.

"Kenneth James, I think that is probably one of the most intelligent and most insightful things you've ever said," I smirked at him.

"Shut up, Marshal, I gotta lotta good stuff up here," he knocked on his head.

"Yeah, whatever," I shoved him jokingly, and he dramatically toppled over, sending us both into a fit of giggling.

"Thanks for coming over, man," I said, feeling my smile fade into something sadder.

"Yeah, you seem less shitty now," he grinned at me.

"I feel less shitty with you here, dude." I tried to smile back.

"So, who are you in love with?"

"I don't want to talk about it, I guess I just wanted someone to know. I guess I'm something, and it's not straight," it felt good to say out loud, almost like a weight was lifted from my chest. I put my head on KJ's shoulder as we finished our cigarettes, and with shaking hands, I lit another. I basked in the calm glow the smoke that filled my lungs gave me, and a wave of calm surged through my nerves.

· XXXV ·

KIA

I lay in bed staring at my wall, the air conditioning in my room was turned up high making it so it was cold enough that I could wrap myself comfortably into several blankets.

"Kia?" Peter's voice said as he cracked open my door.

"Hey buddy," I said weakly, and I heard his little footsteps shuffled closer.

"Are you okay?" Peter crept closer sitting on the edge of my bed. I rolled over to face him, his small face twisted into deep concern.

"Yeah man, I'm fine," I lied trying to hide the upset in my voice.

"But you look sad," he frowned.

"Yeah, I'm a little upset, but I'll be better," I tried to smile at him but I knew my eyes would tell him I was lying. Ike wrapped his small arms around me in a loose hug. "I love you, Peter, and thanks."

"What's wrong?"

"Marshal and I had another fight," I sighed.

"Again?" he raised his eyebrows and frowned, "Did you beat him up this time?"

"No, it wasn't like that." I closed my eyes tight thinking about everything he said to me and how deep it cut. Ike let go of me and slid off my bed.

"It'll be okay Kia!" he smiled brightly before turning around and bounding back out of my room. I lay in my bed unmoving for I don't even know how long, just a while. I rubbed my fingertips with the thumb around the nail bed feeling for a good piece of skin to start peeling away. I found a hang nail on my ring finger and with my other hand pinched the small pieces of skin between my index and thumb, slowly pulling it back. I wanted to enjoy the slight stinging sensation it gave me for as long as I could. I felt a sense of calm when I peeled away small parts of myself like I was getting rid of the things that made me worry by getting rid of such a small part of myself. I continued to mindlessly pick at my fingertips wanting Marshal, who clearly did not want me.

I still didn't know what to think. I was scared, by the way his mood changed and how fast he became so angry, and it seemed for no reason either. I just wanted to know what was wrong but he shut me out. All I wanted was to help him, I felt so helpless seeing the hurt on his face and wanted to make it all go away but didn't know how. I felt so empty now and I stared at my phone which was an arm's reach away on my nightstand and debated calling him, I wanted to hear his voice again. I didn't have the mental energy to pick it up and call his number. I didn't know if he was sober or not and whether or not he would want he would even want to talk. I didn't know what this fight meant for us.

We've had plenty of fights before but this one was different. We weren't just friends now we were together now. Maybe. I wasn't sure anymore. I didn't think he meant what he said it was just the jack talking but also, he hadn't been drunk he'd just been drinking. *But he was upset no one means what they say when their upset AND drinking.*

I picked up my phone and opened my messages. There was nothing from Marshal or anyone actually, and I opened my messages to Marshal and started to type a new one out. I would start to write one but deleted it to rewrite it. I did this four times before finally hitting send.

I'm sorry about this morning, and I know you're hurting, but you hurt me too. We need to talk about what happened. *I put my phone down on my bed not sure what to get in response to my message. I waited anxiously picking the skin from my fingertips on the other hand than I had before.

Thirty minutes passed by and I got increasingly more anxious checking my phone for a response, anything. My stomach turned as I felt my skin start to bleed. I managed to sit up and retrieve a bandaid from my nightstand drawer. I carefully wrapped it around my finger and sat cross-legged on my bed rocking slightly with skating breaths from my anxiety. I found a new sense of determination and courage. *Fuck it,*

I'm calling him. I listened to the phone dialing and got two rings before the other line opened up.

"Hello?" said a voice that didn't belong to Marshal. I wracked my brain for who the voice could belong to, who would be with him right now *I thought he wanted to be alone.* I thought with a sour face.

"Hello? Who is this and why do you have Marshal's phone?" I demanded

"Chill K it's KJ," he laughed on the other end.

"Don't call me K first of all, and second you didn't answer my question. Why do you have Marsh's phone?"

"But Marsh calls you K? Why can't I?"

"Because that's *Marsh's* nickname for me, not yours!" I said defensively, "Now for the last time KJ why do you have Marsh's phone?"

"Oh yeah, I'm over at his palace right now."

"So you just answer personal phone calls for other people?"

"Yeah I guess," he laughed again, "Well I figured he would want to talk to you so I didn't want him to miss your call, he's pissing right now so I'll give the phone to him when he comes back."

"Why are you over at Marsh's house anyway?" I felt my heart break a little knowing he'd rather have KJ there than his boyfriend or whatever we were now.

"He called me and asked me to come over he sounded pretty bad, he's all messed up because he's in love with some guy and-"

"He's in love with some guy?" I said interrupting KJ my face becoming more rosey.

"Yeah, but that little shithead wouldn't tell me who, he said he didn't want to talk about it," KJ said, sounding annoyed. I breathed a sigh of relief knowing that he hadn't told KJ that I was that 'some guy'.

"Oh- uh, I didn't know Marsh liked boys," I lied trying to act like this was all new information I wanted to test the waters and see how KJ felt.

"It's not that surprising to me."

"So you're okay with it?"

"Jesus Kia, I get I'm kind of an asshole but I'm not *that* big of an asshole," he sighed heavily. I felt like a weight was lifted off my chest knowing I would have the support of Benji, KJ, and my brother behind me once I was ready to start being openly out and in a same-sex relationship.

"Sorry, I interrupted but yeah uh that's cool, go back to what you were saying."

"He also said he had some fight with you and he felt like overall garbage. Again that's why I picked up the phone and figured he'd want to talk to you he seems miserable," KJ explained. *He feels bad?* My heart fluttered a little now knowing that maybe he didn't mean everything he said and that maybe we were okay. He told KJ he was in love with some guy, some guy being me.

"I'm coming over," I said hanging up before I could get a response. I checked myself in my bedroom mirror about to head out my door and I realized I was still wearing Marsh's shirt and the shorts I picked up in my panic were his as well. I quickly changed into some of my own clothes that were better fitting, I didn't want KJ to think anything was happening now he knew Marshal was into guys. Before I left I stopped by Ike's room. I knocked on the door before pushing it open and he sat at his computer playing Minecraft.

"Hey Peter," I said clearing my throat to get his attention.

"Huh?"

"You're right everything is going to be fine! I'm going over to Marsh's now," I couldn't help but smile.

"Kia?" he said as I was turning away.

"Yeah?"

"Is Marshal like your boyfriend or something?"

"W-what? Why would you even ask that?" I stuttered out trying to hide my shock and embarrassment.

"Because you like boys and Thatcher always calls you 'super best boyfriends'"

"Never quote Thatcher again," I said deadpan, "and uh- It's complicated okay?"

"It is?" he gave me a skeptical look and with a red face I slammed the door. I raced downstairs and out the door speed walking in the direction of Marsh's house, eventually breaking into a full sprint. My heartbeat was thudding in my ear accompanied by my heavy pants of breathlessness. I wasn't out of shape I was on the varsity basketball team, I just wasn't built for distance running.

Heavily wheezing now I pounded my fist against Marsh's front door, I waited before slamming my arm into the door yet again. I raised my fist to knock again when the door was pulled open.

"Kia?" Marsh said looking as if he'd just seen a ghost. He threw his arms over me and brought me tight against his body nuzzling his head into my neck, giving it a quick kiss. "I- but- you- and-," I let him continue stuttering before I pulled out of our hug. KJ crept up behind Marshal and I gave him a small wave.

"Move it," he pushed Marshal out of the way and gave me the weird 'bro' side hug.

"What are you doing here?" Marsh asked still looking shocked.

"I told KJ?" I looked at KJ with a questioning look wordlessly promoting an explanation.

"Yeah he did call you but you were in the bathroom so I picked it up," he said innocently.

"KJ, what have I told you about answering my phone?" Marshal sighed pinching the bridge of his nose.

"It was Kia dude, not a big deal," KJ groaned. The last time KJ had answered the phone for Marshal, it was his sister calling and KJ proceeded to answer the phone with, 'You've reached the hot twink hotline. Stay on the line and I'll connect you to a dark-haired mysterious twink,". Shelby was pissed, and Marsh was even more pissed.

"But still K, why are you here?"

"Do you not want me to be since you kicked me out and have KJ now?" I snapped. Marsh's expression changed from shock now replaced with minor annoyance and frustration.

"Kia- don't fucking start this shit, look I'm sorry, and I was drinking and just-"

"Marshal you hurt me, I came over here because we need to talk about it, we need to talk about us, and preferably without KJ!" I slightly raised my voice still being defensive, "No offense KJ I love you dude but this is personal," I turned to him softening my expression.

"You stormed out and I was upset, obviously I couldn't call you so I called KJ," Marshal said snarkily. I took a deep breath.

"Marshal you hurt me," I began, "and we both were upset but I need you and I don't want to be without you," I sighed and turned back to KJ raising my eyebrows hoping he would understand the look I was giving him.

"Oh- *oh!* Yeah, I'll see you guys inside," KJ said going back in the door and leaving Marshal and me alone on the porch.

"Marshal, look okay?" I said digging my toe into the porch. "I'm not just hurt, I'm brokenhearted and actually really pissed," I felt all the self-pitying emotions being replaced by a wave of new anger that came with seeing him. "You pushed me away and rather than talking to me you started drinking! You didn't give me any reason and just started falling apart!"

"K?"

"I am NOT done!"

"Kia,"

"Marshal!" he pressed his lips onto mine before I could continue speaking, my anger melting away into our kiss.

"Can I talk now?" he asked and I looked at him with a new compassion. I nodded my head hesitantly.

"I feel like... I don't deserve you, I left you guys all of you for Winnie, and now that I realize how much you loved me and for how long you've loved me I feel guilty. I feel like you pulled away because you didn't feel comfortable with me anymore and I don't deserve your love and to have these feelings about you. I love you K and I really *really* like you, I just feel like a dickhead. Listen this morning I did something and- fuck this is kind of embarrassing. I'm really attracted to you and like I just don't think it's fair I can like you so much so fast and how not that long ago I was obsessing over some girl. I was obsessing with some girl and you, you were hurting. Why should I get to be with you." he said breathless now.

"W-why? What? Marsh? " I said holding his face. I leaned down to plant a kiss on his forehead. "It's okay, Marshal I love you and I've always loved you and what hurt me was how you didn't just tell me this all to begin with. Why do you think you don't deserver me?"

"Because I was such a shitty person to you, no wonder you pulled away from me," he said with glossy eyes.

"I was hurting but I wanted you to be happy, and now I'm happier than ever and nothing can hurt me anymore. You Marshal Langdon, deserve the world."

"Well, Kia Shwartz, you are my world. You are the sun to my moon, and the world revolves around you." I pulled his lips onto my and kissed him again.

"So what happened."

"I'm just mad at myself, I made you have a fucking panic attack and I felt too guilty and angry. I love you I don't want to be the reason you hurt, and I thought about all that time you spent away from me, and in some fucked up way my stupid brain told me you didn't want me and I just wanted you to remember it all, I wanted to hurt you, and just- Christ I'm fucked up."

"I love you," he whispered, leaning in, his forehead against mine, our lips mere centimeters apart.

"I don't understand why."

"You don't have to," and with that, he pressed his lips into mine. We talked more about our relationship and setting some boundaries, I was going to do this right, I wasn't going to fuck this up.

MARSHAL

I opened the front door, let Kia back into the house, and stepped in after him, closing the door behind me. The inside of the house was almost as hot as it was outside, from standing out on the porch talking to Kia my shirt began to stick to my back due to the humidity but inside was almost worse. We had no air conditioning and the air was heavy.

"Oh, hey, gaywads," KJ greeted, craning his neck to look at us. I rolled my eyes and jumped over the back of the couch to join him. Kia walked over after I took a seat. The three of us sighed, almost in sync.

"Marsh it's so ungodly hot in your house," Kia groaned. KJ had even ditched his iconic hoodie in favor of a NASCAR t-shirt I'm assuming was a hand-me-down from Jason, with the sleeves ripped off.

"I know it's a fucking problem," I groaned, this was the one thing I hated most about summer, the insufferable heat. The humidity inside and outside made everything feel heavy and my clothes and hair stuck close to me damp with sweat. Despite the heat, I still wore jeans all year round because I hated shorts.

We all sat around sweating, watching TV. Kia's text notification went off and I watched his face light up, *I wonder if he smiles like that when I text him or if it's everybody.*

"Guys, Benji is ungrounded, he asked if I wanted to meet up with him and Thatcher at the arcade, you guys down?" he beamed.

"Count me in you can only watch so much shitty tv before it becomes annoying," KJ said blandly.

"Come on, not you too!" I protested throwing my hands up in the air, "It's not *that* bad." KJ had never before watched The Walking Dead and I took it upon myself to introduce my best friend to my favorite show despite the protests from both him and Kia. KJ was a firm believer and stood with Kia that the show was stupid and full of plotholes and said he had no interest in watching it.

I watched Kia excitedly type back a response to Benji settling a plan with him and telling him that KJ and I would be coming as well.

We met up with Benji and Thatcher outside the arcade the summer heat making my shirt stick to my back damp with sweat.

"Finally, you queer-os are here," Thatcher scoffed.

"Takes one to know one," KJ retorted quickly with a sly grin.

"Guys! I told you I'm not gay!" Thatcher whined while Benji stifled a laugh while KJ, Kia, and I all let ours out.

I separated KJ still giggling and Thatcher who was a cherry red before anything more could be said or done to result in a fight. Benji led us inside and we were all hit by the cool refreshing air of the well-air-conditioned arcade. The sudden change in temperature made Kia shiver a small bit and I put my arm around him giving him a squeeze. His shoulders tensed up and I remembered our conversation at the carnival and let go. Thatcher, KJ, and Benji had all run off and Kia looked at me shoulders still tense, and interlocked his fingers with mine, his face glowing a rosy red and I felt the warmth spread to my face as well. I squeezed his hand and was relieved to receive two squeezes back before Kia took his hand away as we caught up with the guys. Inside my chest felt warm and there were butterflies as they put money into a change machine.

"Kia wanna play Dance Dance Revolution?" KJ grinned.

"Oh, come one dude that games so lame! Come one play Guitar Hero with me," I said giving a fake pout.

"Shut up Marsh you can actually play the guitar," KJ laughed as he took Kia by the hand over to the game he wanted to play. Kia and I were legends at Guitar Hero, playing with Kia was like breathing. Everything we did together was as easy as breathing. I shook my head laughing a little as KJ and Kia got ready to play.

"Marsh I bet I can get a higher score on the boxing machine than you," Thatcher said with a smirk.

"Yeah, right, you fat piece of shit," I scoffed.

"You're just scared!" Thatcher teased and began to cluck like a chick.

"I'm not scared I just want to watch KJ and Kia make ass out of themselves playing Dance Dance Revolution," I chuckled.

"Whatever that's so gay," Thatcher rolled his eyes, "Benji wanna play a racing game?" he called over to Benji who was happily playing PacMan.

"Sure, Thatcher!" he said back with a wide smile walking over to the racing games with Thatcher. I watched as Kia clumsily stepped between arrows, and KJ was red in the face laughing.

"You know Thatcher might be right! Jews have no rhythm," he cackled.

"Don't ever say Thatcher is right about anything ever," Kia said irritated and I couldn't help but join in on KJ's laughter. The game finished showing a score that crowned KJ the winner who whipped small beads of sweat from his forehead while Kia wheezed. I giggled at how tired Kia was.

"Damn, I thought you were in better shape than this," KJ said playfully punching Kia's arm.

"Yeah Mr. varsity basketball," I joined in, "You got your ass handed to you by a scrawny stoner."

"You know what!" Kia huffed. "I'll beat your ass at Street Fighter then!" he challenged with a smile.

"You're so on!" I said slapping his hand and accepting his challenge.

"You lamos do that I'm hitting up pinball," KJ said, slapping our backs and walking away. Kia loaded in the quarters to the game and gave me a devious grin that I couldn't help but find attractive. We each chose our fighters and began frantically mashing buttons as I struggled to keep a higher score than Kia. I threw my hands up and pumped my fists when the game ended, breaking into a victory dance.

"Eat it, babe!" I danced around Kia, hooting. I stopped when I noticed how red in the face Kia was, "What's wrong?"

"You called me babe," he said in a hushed voice with a shadow of a smile creeping onto his lips. My eyes grew wider when I realized what I said. "No, no! Marsh doing worry!" Kia said frantically waving his hands at me picking up on my sudden horror, " I uh- I kind of like the pet name," he continued as he rocked back on his heels blushing intently. I smiled at him with admiration. I reached my hand out and placed it

160

delicately on his cheek. Kia placed his hand over mine and leaned his face into my hand. At that moment nothing mattered, I didn't care where we were or what was happening around us it was all a blur the only thing I was focused on was Kia's beautiful face. I watched as Kia's face turned from the loving look he was giving me to slight panic as his eyes drifted away from mine and fixed on something behind me.

I turned around and saw Craig playing with the claw machine hovering over Theo who smiled and stared at us giving a small wave. I found the height difference between the two, it kind of comical and most of the difference between them. Craig and Theo were so vastly different yet fit together perfectly, a cold tall dark-haired boy with his significantly shorter bright blonde boyfriend. Theo taught on Craig's t-shirt sleeve breaking his intent and focusing on his attempt at winning one of the stuffed animals and pointed in our direction with a wide grin. I looked back to Kias whose face was now engraved with panic and red as a nervous sweat broke out on his forehead.

"Oh shit," Kia said under his breath, "I think he saw that," his voice more panicked now, knowing that someone we knew might have seen our demonstration of the couple's affection. Theo turned to Craig and tugged on his sleeve, drawing his attention to Kia and me.

· XXXVII ·

KIA

I felt my stomach turn as Theo and Craig approached Marshal and me. His hand quickly dropped from my face and into his pocket. Out of a nervous habit I had developed in elementary school, I brushed his hand with my pinky, signaling I wanted his hand. We intertwined our pinkies loosely behind our backs. Even though it was an everyday habit for us, something small we always seemed to do for each other for comfort, it felt wrong to do it in public now.

"Hey, guys!" Theo said, giggling as he pulled Craig over by his hand.

"Hey Theo," I waved, trying to breathe through my panic, "Craig," I gave a nod acknowledging him. Craig's eyes narrowed at Marshal.

"So Landgon?" he began, "guess you figured it out," he said with a sly grin.

"Figured it out?" I asked, throwing a confused look at an embarrassed-looking Marshal.

"Craig! Shush, that was a private conversation," he nervously fidgeted with the hem of his shirt.

"Private conversation?" I said still confused as hell looking to Marsh for answers. Craig chuckled at the deep red of Marsh's face from embarrassment enjoying the discomfort he had put Marshal in.

"Lover boy had to be told he was in love with you," Craig teased and revived a swift kick to the shin from Theo, "Ouch! Theo!" he said hopping grabbing his shin where Theo's foot ha connected to it. Theo pulled Craig down to his eye level by his ear.

"Stop instigating!" he demanded.

"He's not- We're not-!" I stammered.

"Listen, Kia, we know," Theo said calmly.

162

"You- You know?" I looked to Marshal for an explanation.

"Well- I started to realize kind of when I was around you, I'd get all nauseous and my heart would start pounding and my hands would get all sweaty, and I kind of didn't realize what those feelings for you were," Marshal explained still kind of red with a loving expression.

"Yeah, he came over asking about how we knew we liked each other, and now it makes perfect sense!" Theo cheered. He pulled Marshal and me into a hug, "Oh my god guys! I'm so happy for you!" he pulled away smiling.

"Theo? Listen I don't really want people to know, okay?" I said shyly. His expression changed but I knew he understood.

"Come on babe, I don't want to spend my date with Langdon and Shwartz," Craig said pulling Theo by his hips back to him and resting his chin on Theo's head while interlocking one of his hands with one of Tweak's. "Come on you said your hello's," Craig urged.

"Okay, okay, bye guys," Theo smiled being led away by his boyfriend.

"So," I said, smiling at Marsh, "Someone had to tell you that you like me?" I giggled a little.

"Yeah I guess not wanting to like cuddle your best friend and kiss him isn't platonic," he said giving me a quick peck on the cheek.

"To be fair, Benji had to pull me out of my denial," I laughed. We looked at each other with a slight blush on each of our cheeks and started laughing.

"I think we're stupid," Marshal said with a wide smile laughing at the obliviousness of our feelings towards each other.

"Yeah, I think you're a little more stupid if you didn't realize wanting to kiss your best friend isn't normal," I agreed, still grinning.

"Okay but in my defense I thought every pair of best friends were occasionally gay for each other," he said dramatically. "That's why you say no, homo!" he further defended himself.

"I love you, Marsh... Full homo," I said and took a deep breath before kissing him trying to ignore my slight fear of kissing him in public. Marshal pulled away from our short kiss with a look of pleasant surprise.

"Don't you care if people see us?"

"Only a little, right now I just want to let you know that I love my idiotic boyfriend."

"I love my idiot boyfriend too, come on let's go find the guys and we can continue this later," he said kissing my forehead. We wandered around the arcade for a minute or two before finding KJ at the pinball machine with Thatcher and Benji on his sides cheering him on. Marshal walked over to join them, and I trailed closely behind.

"He's going to do it!" Benji exclaimed.

"Go, poor boy!" Thatcher cheered.

"Shit KJ why are you so good at this?" Marshal laughed. I joined the rest of the guys and saw that KJ's score was now nearing the current high score, which was his own already. KJ mumbled something in response, not breaking his focus from his game. We all stood around KJ with growing excitement with each point KJ gained. Our excitement quickly was shut down when KJ failed to block the ball from falling and his game ended.

"God damn it, KJ! Poor people are useless!" Thatcher side stomping.

"Aw Kenneth James, You'll get it next time," Benji said rubbing his back.

"Guys, I don't really care about it that much; it's just a game," KJ said, walking oddly to find something else to entertain him. We were all extremely bothered by the fact he wouldn't beat the high score but he truly seemed to not care.

"Buttercup! Come here," KJ said, waving over Benji. *Buttercup? That's new.* KJ had all sorts of little nicknames for Benji and each one of them made Benji's face turn a light pink and give him a wide grin whenever KJ called them out. Benji skipped over to the game KJ was at and I watched as they loaded quarters into the game and began to play. Benji stuck his tongue out in concentration, and I couldn't help but laugh when he did that. KJ and Benji laughed while they played, and I redirected my attention back to Marshal and Thatcher.

"Now that Kia's done with his faggy game, I bet I can beat you on the boxing machine," Thatcher said raising his eyebrows at Marshal.

"You know what, fine because it's better to punch something that's meant to be punched rather than your flat pug-looking face," Marshal said, annoyed.

"Marshal! You can't say that about me! You're just jealous because I'm hotter and get more girls!" Thatcher yelled, stomping and waving his arms around in response to Marsh's comment.

"God, I love pissing off Thatcher," Marshal said with a sigh of relief I couldn't help but laugh as we made our way over to the boxing machine. Thatcher went first, the bag swung down after he inserted the quarters and he took a step back. Thatcher planted his foot stepping with the other taking a hard swing and the punching bag quickly snapped back up into the machine with a loud thud, and we watched as the number climbed higher and higher.

"Wow, didn't think fatass had it in him," I whispered to Marsh, who let out a small laugh. Thatcher snapped his head back to our stifled laughter as we tried to cover it up with coughs.

"I know you gaywads are making fun of me! Stop it I swear to god or I'll tell my mom on you!" he whined.

"Oh nOoOo," said said mocklingly dramatically throwing his hands up, "I'm so scared of your mom Thatcher," he said blankly. Marshal stepped up to the machine and inserted the amount of quarters needed to make the punching bag swing back down. I watched intently as Marshal got ready to punch the bag. He steed back and bent his slightly before winding back his arm. With one powerful twist of his torso propelling his fist into the bag, I watched in amazement as the score of the machine began to climb higher and higher. The resulting number was significantly bigger than Thatcher's and I watched as his jaw dropped. Marshal turned around and threw a middle finger up at Thatcher who still looked dumbfounded. He quickly snapped his jaw back shut, looking as frustrated as ever.

"So yeah, I'm sorry, Thatcher, what were you saying about beating me?" Marsh said with a proud grin that only earned an annoyed grunt from Thatcher.

"Whatever this is so gay, I'm going to find KJ and Benji," Thatcher said huffing shoving his hands deep into his pockets.

"Marshal?" I said, stopping him from further walking after Thatcher.

"Hmm?"

"That was actually kind of impressive, dude you should like to do sports or something," I encouraged.

"I think I'll leave that to you. Just because I can throw a punch doesn't mean I can play a sport. I just have a lot of pent-up anger and plus I hate running," he quickly jumped to defense.

"Sports are a great way to let out all the pent-up anger!"

"I'm not really built for sports dude. I tried and failed."

"Yeah, in like the fifth grade, for a week, you played basketball with me," I rolled my eyes, but he was resistant.

"No, it was freshman year, and it was awful, so I'll just stick with what I know," he shrugged

I gave up on trying to convince him as he protested every further point I tried to push. We all gathered together as a group again in the middle of the arcade.

"We should play Ski Ball!" Benji said excitedly pointing at the adjacent wall lined with several ski ball lanes.

· XXXVIII ·

MARSHAL

We were surrounded by the sounds of ski balls flying up the lanes with a ding signifying points had been one followed by the sounds of tickets being dispensed. Kia was still bugging me about sports, we both knew I was no good at basketball so he suggested things like football or lacrosse. I shot down every sport he offered, feeling more secure in my musical abilities than my athletic ability. I watched Kia fling the game balls up his lane and my stomach started to grumble. I walked between him and Benji and tapped them both on the shoulders.

"Dude I'm getting hungry you guys want to leave and go get something to eat?" we had been in the Arcade for a couple of hours and now the signs of early evening were starting to show.

"Oh jeez it has been a while," Benji said checking his phone.

"Yeah I could eat," Kia said counting his tickets from all the games he had played today.

"Fatass! Come one, we're leaving to go eat!" I called out to Thatcher.

"Can we get KFC?" KJ yelled over the impending response from Thatcher.

"Yeah as long as I actually get some of the chicken skins this time!" Kia spat at Thatcher.

We left the arcade and made our way to the KFC location each ordering a different chicken meal and eating without saying much, being too busy chewing to talk anyway.

"What's the plan for tonight then?" Kia said breaking our silence.

"Well I have to be getting home soon fellas," Benji started. "My folks are still a bit sore so they said I'm not allowed to stay out for a little while yet."

"I got a girl's number at the arcade so I'm going to try and get some," KJ said with a mischievous grin biting his knuckles.

"Gross KJ!" Kia hissed.

"Well I have a hot date with my toilet I believe after this," Thatcher added on.

"So I guess it's just you and me K," I smiled and allied my fingers to find him under the table. I brushed my pinky over the back of his hand that he had placed on his thigh. He spread his fingers allowing me to slide mine in between his and we both smiled slightly while we finished our meals. We each said our goodbyes and split into our separate ways except Kia and me.

"So now what?" I asked as we walked down the street side by side our shoulders brushing against each other. Each brush gave me butterflies any physical contact with him made my heart jump.

"Well my ma kind of complained about me being out all the time so I think I should go home," he said with a hint of disappointment.

"Oh, can I stay over?"

"I'd love that but I think Ma wants me to take a break," his eyes looked sad.

"Can I stay just a little?" I whined at Kia stealing a kiss. I felt a smile form on his lips as he kissed me back.

"You have to go home," he whispered pulling away from my lips slightly. I pulled him back to me and pressed my lips on his, not wanting to let him go.

"Marshal really you should go, and I won't want anyone to see us making out it's not like we're hidden on my front porch."

"Oh okay yeah I get that," I tried to hide the bitterness in my voice. Since we had made up Kia hadn't left my side and I didn't like the idea of being separated from him even for a few hours after our last fight especially. It was weird feeling all these things I didn't feel before the jealousy, loneliness, and just how much I missed him just after he walked away from me. Kia and I were inseparable and I had always been a little bit clingy to him we did everything together and rarely were apart but now more than ever it was like I wanted to be a part of him. I had definitely felt them before but never as strongly. I usually wasn't the jealous type especially but when it came to Kia it somehow became different, I didn't want to admit I was jealous when Donovan and K got close but still, deep down it hurt but now seeing how easily it bothered me the way he just simply interacted with Benji it made me feel stupid.

I shook my head trying to clear my mind and began the long walk home. My dad's truck was parked in the driveway for the first time in several days and I raised a surprised eyebrow to myself. I opened the door and the house was still quiet.

"Marshal?" my dad's voice called out from the kitchen.

"Yeah, who else would be walking into your house?" I rolled my eyes.

"Come here Marshal I need to talk to you." His voice had an odd amount of seriousness in it. I slowly crept my way into the kitchen where my dad was seated at the table. When he saw me he pointed his hand to the seat across from him urging me to sit down. I hesitantly took a seat. *His eyes are red and he looks... sober, and he smells sober too. He smells clean?*

"What's this about?" I nervously laughed, trying to break the awkward tension.

"Your mom," when he said that, it was while making a 'your mom joke,' but right now, that wasn't the case, and my stomach twisted into knots. My dad and I locked eyes, "She's staying in Califonia," his words ripped through my ears my chest pounding with a deep ache. I felt like he had just leaped over the table, shoving his hand down my throat to rip out part of my soul.

"W-what?" I squeaked out.

"She's staying in California, she said she really likes it out there and being close to your sister," there seemed to be more that he wasn't telling me balancing on the tip of his tongue.

"Well, what about me?! Why the fuck does she always fucking drop everything for fucking Shelly!" I yelled pounding my hands on the table.

"Marshal, can you calm down. I want to have a civil conversation," he said.

"Calm down?! Yeah sure *Dad* let me just try to forget the fact that my mother is abandoning me!" I angrily yelled with heavy sarcasm.

"It's not like that Marshal, you knew she was unhappy-"

"I'm unhappy Dad! What about me!" I cut him off. I shoved back the chair and stormed off with hot tears in my eyes. Once I slammed my bedroom door I slid down onto the floor and hugged my knees as I began to cry. *Why doesn't my mom love me as much as my stupid fucking sister?*

I sat on the floor longer feeling the knees of my jeans starting to get damp from my crying and I raised my head looking around my room dimly lit by the golden hour glow. My eyes focus on the edge of my bed frame. Tucked beneath my headboard and between my mattress and boxspring, was a small thin silver flask. I weakly crawled over to my bed and lifted the mattress retrieving the flask. I listened breathing lightly at the swish of the liquid the flask held. Unscrewing the cap met with the musky smell of whiskey.

I took a large sip slightly grimacing at the sweet taste of the burning liquor as it passed through my lips. I took a deep breath before continuing to empty my flask, it didn't take long and it felt like I was trying to drown myself with the alcohol.

I need more.

This isn't enough.

I need more.

I sat curled up on my floor clutching tightly my now empty craving for more ways to ease the pain and started crying again. There was that feeling again, the feeling of missing my mom, feeling nine years old and missing my mom, crying, and wanting nothing but my mom to make me feel better. I was mourning her loss but soon the mourning turned into anger. The anger built in my chest feeling higher and I couldn't breathe, I was so mad that she left me but I was even more mad that I was so upset about it.

I scanned my room, under my mattress wasn't the only place I had alcohol hidden about, it was just the easiest to get to. My body felt weak like all of my bones had turned to silicon and I couldn't move, all of my feelings psychically manifesting and weighing me down. There was a full bottle of whiskey in my closet and I found the strength to get up and retrieve it. I rolled over and sat up with a sway trying to get my body to move despite the weight on my chest and the lucidity of my bones. Shaking slightly, I stood up and walked over to the closest and I reached up and fell around blindly on the shelf until I felt the cool glass in my grasp. I plugged my nose and threw back my head quickly letting it pass through my lips and smoothly down my throat. I wanted to be numb, I didn't want to hurt.

· XXXIX ·

KIA

It had only been a couple of hours since Marsh had dropped me off but I weirdly missed him, the way his hand fit perfectly into mine and his slightly chapped lips against mine. I was alone for the first time it felt like in a while. My family was glad to have me back home for a little while, especially my mother seeming pleased I picked up on her hint to have some time without my friends. Despite just having eaten, I sat down and picked at a plate of the dinner my mother made. We ate dinner together and I helped my dad do the dishes.

"So Kia? I haven't really seen you that much lately, always running off," he chuckled.

"Well it's summer break isn't that what I'm supposed to do?"

"Well yeah it is you're just being a kid," he smiled giving me an awkward side hug. "Still since your mom and I got back I haven't really had a chance to catch up with you buddy. How are things going?"

"Pretty good, Marsh's been sating over a lot or I've been staying with him, it's nice we haven't hung out like this in a while."

"I see you haven't gotten into any more fights," he said scanning my face.

"Oh yeah, that was just over something stupid. It's all okay now," I quickly returned to the dish I was washing.

"Ever going to tell me what that whole mess was about?"

"Dad really it's nothing, it was some stupid fight and it's not going to happen again."

"I hope not Kia violence is never the answer and I hope I taught you well enough that you know that," my dad said sternly. "How is Marshal by the way? You boys were also attached at the hip and then weren't."

"Marsh's really good! Yeah, we kind of had a weird phase going into high school and whatnot but now we're back together better than before," I laughed to myself. *Not only are we back together, but we are also together together.*

"Well that's good, I'm glad to hear it! Marshal's always been such a good kid," my dad smiled fondly. It was interesting the different view my father had on my friends compared to my mom, maybe it was because he was friends with all their dads but he seemed to like them all, and a lot more than my mother.

I started to wonder what my parents would think when I eventually told them that Marshal and I were more than friends. I thought back to how in elementary school, our dad had said to us that we needed to be less friendly with each other. Marshal and I had always been close and super touchy, we would intertwine our pinkies for comfort, and there were frequent hugs and even hand-holding. Our dads warned us how people might think we were 'funny' with each other or 'swinging for the same team.' *Ironic now.* After some time downstairs with my family watching TV, talking, and enjoying each other's company I retreated back to my room as it started to get late and prepared for bed.

My bed felt much bigger, more empty, and less warm without Marsh in it. Before, I always missed Marsh when he wasn't around but this was a new type of missing him, I wasn't just missing my best friend I was missing my *boyfriend.* For some reason, the word still gave me chills. I never saw myself describing Marshal as my *boyfriend.* I never saw myself in general having a boyfriend. I smiled at the way the word made me feel, a warmth spreading across my chest thinking about it over and over again. *I have a* boyfriend *and my* boyfriend *is Marshal Langdon* I giggled like some kind of middle school girl.

My phone started ringing, and I looked to see Marsh's name scrolling across my screen, his contact picture one I had taken several years ago that I had been lucky enough to get in time as he was being hit in the face by a frisbee. When I had taken the picture, we were at the park and he had been throwing a frisbee around with Benji. At that moment I thought he looked so breathtakingly beautiful so I wanted to remember that moment and pulled up my phone to take a picture. Marshal noticed out of the corner of his eye what I was doing and turned to face me right as Benji had thrown the frisbee. I snapped the picture before he could ask what I was doing and right at that moment, the frisbees connected to the side of his face. I couldn't help but giggle at the picture before answering his call.

"K-Kia?" he said in a slurred hushed voice. My heart slightly fluttered hearing his voice.

"Hey, are you okay? What's up?"

"I just- I love you s- so - s'much," his words were slurred together and the fluttering of my heart stopped and it sunk.

"Marshal, are you drunk right now?"

"But I- Love you," he hiccuped. "I- love you to t-the m-m-moon and back."

"Marsh, I love you too, but seriously, what the fuck?"

"K- I love you, I just wanted to hear your voice K."

"Well you heard it," I said annoyed, "Go to bed talk to me when your sober, goodbye."

"No! K please I need you!" he protested before I could hang up.

"Marshal I don't like it when you drink it solves nothing!"

"But I need to tell you- tell y-you what's wrong, cuz you said, you wanted me to tell you."

"Yeah, Marsh, I wanted you to tell me *instead* and not get fucked up."

"Kia, my sweet, sweet redhead boy with the pretty, pretty hair, it's so pretty, babe."

"Marsh, I'm going to hang up the phone now. I'll talk to you when you're sober."

"My mom's gone," he blurted out.

"Yes, Marshal, I know."

"No you don't she's never coming back," he sniffled on the other end of the phone line.

"What?" I asked softly.

"She's gone, not coming back; she wants to stay with FUCKING SHELBY!" he screamed the last part. I dropped my annoyance and now felt bad and wanting nothing more but to confront him.

"Marshal, Im so fucking sorry, dude." It was all I could think to say.

"Kia, please don't leave me, not ever." His voice was soft and quiet he yawned like the screaming had tired him out. He sounded so vulnerable and soft; he was just a kid again.

"Not ever, Marshal." The line went silent, and I got a bit worried.

"Kia, I'm not ever going to leave you," he finally said. "I don't ever want to lose you K, and you are the center of my solar system K. You hear that?"

"Yes, Marsh, I do."

"You're the everything in my nothing." He yawned again and the line went quiet again this time longer and I figured he had probably tired himself out and passed out. As much as I hated it when Marshal would drink and even more so call me drunk or drunk text me it was hard to be upset with him. *At least he told me what was wrong and he wrapped it up with all those sweet things, I can't be mad at that.*

• XL •

MARSHAL

I woke up on my floor, still wearing my clothes and soaked in sweat. I sat up ignoring the searing pain in my head and looked around my room, squinting my eyes at how bright my room was. I could feel the dried tears down my cheeks and my eyes felt crusty and still puffy from crying. My mom wasn't coming back, and my chest still hurt. The pain from last night was still rampant throughout my body. It hit me all again at once like a title wave. I crawled over to the trash can and heaved until I threw up.

It was a heavy aching pain that was deep in my chest. My stomach turned, and I started to regret the rapid alcohol consumption. I laid back down flat on my back, covering my face with my hands, and slightly dug my nails into my temples like I was trying to rip out the pain behind my eyes. I just wanted Kia right now.

I remembered I called Kia last night crying. Hearing his voice made everything hurt less, it made me feel like the world wasn't as bad as it was because as much as it hurt me there was his sweet voice to tell me it was okay and pick up the pieces. I wanted him to hold me and I wanted him to comfort me right now because it still hurt. I looked around on my floor for my phone, and it was tossed slightly aside. I rolled over on my side, reaching my arm out, struggling to pull my phone closer with my fingertips that barely reached. I wanted to hear his voice again, last night just his 'hey' made everything feel better.

His voice was like a drug that sent me an instant wave of relief. I unlocked my phone and stared at my home screen, a picture I had taken of Kia sleeping. He was curled up on my chest and looking more than perfect. His beautiful red hair with curls sticking out at odd angles, his arms wrapped around me, and I just wanted to remember how perfect he looked, how perfectly sweet and innocent. Kia's contact picture was less adorable but still perfect for him. I knew his contact picture for me was a picture of me getting hit in the face by a frisbee so in retaliation I got a picture from one of Kia's games where he was red and sweaty, out of breath, and looking terrible all around. As awful as he looked mid-game, it was still kind of attractive. I called him again, listening to the dial tone as it rang over and over. I got no response and was greeted with his voicemail message, *'You've reached Kia Schwartz, I couldn't make it to the phone so leave your name and a message along with a good number to reach you at.'* I laughed a little at how professional his voicemail message was.

"Hey K, uh, it's Marshal; you probably know that, though because, like caller ID and whatnot. I just wanted to hear your voice again, I had a bad night and I just want you right now because you make me feel better I guess. Sorry I know you are probably still sleeping, I actually have no idea what time it is but I woke up and you were my first thought, and- and- I just love you K and I need you, dude. Call me back or come over or something and if you don't know my phone number by now I think you have some issues," I ended my messages with s deep breath, still lying on the floor. Why did everything have to suck except for Kia? Everything sucked and everything hurt, my head throbbed and my chest ached, and the aching reached all over my body down my arms and legs. It was six a.m.

The early summer sun was messing up my sleep schedule. The curtains in my room were blackout curtains but I had left them open letting in the golden rays. Any amount of light change in my room was enough to wake me up, and I wouldn't be able to get back to sleep. It was something obnoxious that I hated about myself that I couldn't help. I sat upright and began to remove my damp shirt and jeans, feeling the intense heat in my room. The air was so heavy and dragged everything down all the time. I was so tired of my hair constantly sticking to the back of my neck. I cut my hair hoping to be able to cool myself down and keep the hair from sticking to my neck too severely.

I loved Kia's house for so many reasons but being back in my room reminded me of what I loved the most, *his air-conditioned room.* Kia's house was welcoming his parents loved each other and loved their sons, they had family dinners and talked to each other, but Kia loved to sleep in the cold. His parents had several air conditioners around their house but Kia's room was freezing. I missed him more than ever. I missed not only him but his room. His room was cold and comforting. His room was light and cold, the opposite of mine, dark and hot. Kia's room was painted a light green, and his walls were a little bare. He had some fairy lights hanging around his bed and a couple of anime posters from middle school. He had some shelves with a couple of academic awards and the accomplishment he was most proud of; the medal he got for winning the championship game.

My room was painted a dark blue and filled with clutter. I had my walls covered in posters for bands and movies I liked. My desk was shoved in a corner half hazard stacks with books, clothes, and other things I didn't know what to do with, along with my dresser top. I had a shelf that held a small trophy I won from the Boy Scouts pinewood derby and a couple of Lego sets I had built and kept. I wanted so badly to bask in the light atmosphere of Kia's room, shivering in the cold but warm in his arms. If I could find it in me to get off the floor, I wanted to go over and lay on his floor. My phone rang, and I jumped at it fumbling to pick it up, expecting it was Kia. I quickly pressed the answer call button without really looking at who was calling.

"Kia?" I asked in a shaking voice.

"No? Marshal baby, it's Mom," my heart sank with disappointment.

"I don't want to talk to you, *Shannon!*"

"Marshal! What have I told you about calling me by my first name?" she said angrily.

"I do not give a rat's ass!"

"Langage! Marshal stop being difficult," my mom sighed on the other end of the line.

"Remember when I called you crying? Remember it was because you left me? Remember how you said you were sorry about leaving me?"

"Marshal, please-"

"Mom, you left me here with dad! I don't want to hear what you have to say," I was getting angry now.

"Marshal, just please! Listen! Marshal, I-"

"I'm tired mom, I didn't sleep well, and I don't want to listen anymore," I removed the phone from my ear, and my thumb hovered over the end call button. I faintly heard my mom's protests. All my thoughts swam around, and my head felt heavy. I wanted to drink again, my snobs were empty, but I had a bottle of whiskey hidden snuggly in my dresser drawer.

I dug out the bottle and began the vicious circle of couping. Due to my headache, I didn't want to get wasted again so for a couple of hours I nursed the whiskey bottle taking it slow so as to not get totally messed up. It had been a couple of hours before there was a sharp quick knock on my bedroom door.

"What?" I snapped, not wanting to deal with my dad.

"Oh- uh, hey, Marshal?" Kia stepped in. My demeanor instantly changed at the sight of the person I wanted most in the world. The whiskey had made me a bit more peppy my thought a little less coherent but I was still decently sober. I smiled at Kia and beckoned him to sit on the floor next to me.

"K, I'm so fucking glad to see you," I wrapped an arm around him, thudding my head onto his shoulder.

"Marshal have you been drinking?" he fidgets with his fingers, I looked down at how red they were the dried blood around his nail bed concerned me. I took his hand and kissed each one of his fingertips.

"K don't hurt yourself your so beautiful," I put down his hand and reached for the other and kissed each of his other fingers.

"Yeah, you have been drinking," he sighed, disappointed. I held up the half-full bottle shaking it and listening to the lovely swish of the liquid.

"Yeah, just a little, I just- my mom..." I trailed off and eyed his neck, without much thought I pressed my lips into his soft pale skin and kissed his neck feeling the warmth of his body against my lips. Kia flinched a little at my sudden action.

"Marsh, please," he protested but I pulled him back a little bit kissing his neck more. His breath shook slightly, and he hummed, enjoying the feeling. I began now to suck a little, biting down.

"Marshal dude stop. We need to talk about this," he slightly pushed me off, and I looked at him with disappointment deep in my face. I smiled slightly at the now-forming dark mark from where my lips were. He wiped away my silvia and faced me with compassion.

"I'm tired of talking!" I grunted in protest.

"You can't drink your feelings away Marsh," he cooed softly and kissed my forehead slightly.

"I don't want to feel anything," my face was hot, and my vision started to blur with tears. I used the back of my hands to wipe them away furiously. "Can't we just kiss or something?" I said in a low whisper that was more of a whine the way it came out.

"I know you're hurting but need to deal with it, you can't just shut out the world."

"Kia- I- I don't know how to stop," I choked out. I had to force the words out like they were stuck to my throat and were holding on for dear life.

"I love you, Marshal Xavier Langdon," he breathed out, my stomach jumped at the usage of my full name, it felt somehow intimate. He continued, "And I want to help you but you need to want help," he said softly.

I nodded vigorously, and Kia traced his thumb over my cheek, wiping away a stray tear. I loved the way he said my name. I kissed him innocently this time and I felt Kia smile against our kiss and he pulled away from it, foreheads resting together, the moment was soft and I wanted to live in it forever.

"I love you too, Kia Mathew Schwartz," I mumbled.

◆ XLI ◆

KAI

Marshal was asleep on the floor, wrapped in my arm. His hair was stuck to his forehead with sweat, his small upper body shook with each breath. He was still drunk and had cried himself to sleep after I told him he needed help, and he had to want the help. I watched him carefully as he slept, when Marshal was asleep he looked younger at peace, and less disturbed by the world, whenever he was drunkenly passed out such as now, his face was pinched tightly and marked heavily with discomfort. I hated seeing him like this. For the past five years, everyone in the group watched Marshal slip further into what he is now.

Marshal had started drinking after freshman year, and we all sort of pulled away from him. Everything was shitty to him, and being the selfish, awkward, self-obsessed teenagers we were. We didn't want to deal with him acting like that. We all got older and it looked like Marsh got better, things started to go back to the way they were. It was the four of us against the world until things all went to shit again. It was getting harder to repress feelings, and Marshal got worse with his parent's divorce. I blamed not wanting to be around him on his mood and drinking but in reality, it hurt to see him like that all I wanted to do was help but all he wanted was someone else. Marsh frequently called me drunk crying because he needed someone or a place to stay or some other bullshit and I always dealt with him. Marsh was an emotional drunk he either balled his eyes out or was over the moon happy both could be switched interchangeably. I always picked up the drunken phone calls but left him with KJ to deal with.

KJ understood what it was like, he understood Marshal. As we got older, Marshal and KJ got closer like he was replacing me but I knew just by the look in his eyes. Marshal could never replace me. We were dumb and we still are to consider this normal. It was just one of those things that were always around and no one said anything because when you did he got angry about it and super defensive and we got too tired to argue. There was a far too familiar pang of guilt in my chest. I was too wrapped up in my own self-indulgent bullshit to see Winnie was right, as much as I hated to say it, she was. He was destroying himself and I was already a shitty friend for waving it off as normal but I'd be an even shitter boyfriend for continuing to wave it off. Since we had gotten together he'd been fine but for the first time, it all came crashing down. All it took was for one big emotional outburst to see, he was hurting someone; himself, and I was an idiot for ignoring it.

I put my hand over his hair, ignoring the greasy texture. *When was the last time he showered?* I studied his face while he slept it usually relaxed, making him look younger and at peace, but right now, it was pitched tightly in discomfort, and a shiver ran through his body, making him shake his entire.

"I'm so fucking sorry Marshal, what the fuck is wrong with us," I whispered softly continuing to pet his hair. He eased into my touch, a small sleepy whimper escaping his lips as he shuttered again. It was all so fucked up, why didn't anyone else think it was fucked up?

"Marsh, are you awake dude?" I asked getting close to his ear, downstairs I heard the front door open and heavy footsteps downstairs.

"Nooo," Marshal whined in a sleepy tone.

"Marsh I think your dad's home you need to get up and clean yourself up."

"Why should I-" he was interrupted by a yawn and he stretched out rolling onto his back reaching his hands above his head and forcing himself into a sitting position. "Why should I do that, he doesn't care?"

"Because Marshal, you're rank, you smell and you look like shit," I glared.

"Love you too babe," he smirked at me hosting himself off the floor. He offered his hand out to me and I took it allowing myself to be assisted off the ground. For being so skinny Marshal was relatively strong it was slightly surprising.

"When was the last time you showered dude?" I rolled my eyes. He looked about to argue but his hesitation told us both everything we needed to know.

"Touche."

"Marsh?"

"Hmm?" he was stripping out of his clothes and I awkwardly avoided looking at his bare body now only wearing boxer briefs. I knew it was an insecurity of his, he hated his body. He said he didn't care about his appearance, he said nothing bothered him but I knew how bad the dysphoria really was.

"Do you remember what I said?"

"About?"

"Uh... look, Marsh, I-" I paused thinking carefully how to proceed with this conversation. "I said you needed help, and you agreed with me." Marshal stopped what he was doing, I looked up from the ground when I heard his sharp inhale of breath, his back was turned to me, and his mussels were tense.

"Kia, I don't need help dude. I don't have a problem I just," he paused and turned around looking me in the eyes, a desperate look etched on his face. "I don't have a problem, I nodded because I love you, I wasn't agreeing or disagreeing just understanding. See I don't have a problem, I remember." I huffed, why does he have to be so goddamn stubborn.

"Yeah whatever Marsh, put some clothes on dude," I huffed embarrassed to be standing in his room while he was basically naked.

"Under your suggestion, I'm going to go shower," he narrowed his eyes at me his lips pressed into a thin line. I met his eyes and his gaze softened, "Hey K?"

I didn't give him any verbal response just some kind of throat grumble. "I love you and, I'm sorry I'm kind of dysfunctional," he slipped out of his room with a bundle of clothes in his hands.

I was still awkwardly standing in the middle of the room so I moved to the bed and sat on the edge, taking in the atmosphere around me. The air in Marsh's room was stale, hot, and stiff with despair. It was dark so I struggled behind me to open the curtains watching as dust flew as I opened them further allowing the light to reach into the depths of Marsh's dark room. It was genuinely depressing in here. I opened the window as well basking in the resheshing new air that circulated into the room helping air out the mildewy smell of dirty laundry and B.O.

The room seemed so bleak, void of joy or any reminisce of the old Marshal. I shuddered at the thought, *the old Marshal.* He really had changed over the last few years. In my bedroom, Thatchers, even KJ's a little bit, you could still find remnants of the kids we used to be. There was still a variety of remainders from our childhoods. There was a certain brightness that Marsh's room lacked. Ever since he moved out here, it was like there was part of him that never moved with him. I don't know how long I just sat there, staring into my boyfriend's room taking in the depressing atmosphere but the door opened and Marshal reappeared smiling weakly shutting the door behind him quietly.

I bit the inside of my cheek, Marshl looked handsome fresh out of the shower. His hair now clung to his face, still damp, the messy layers framing his face in a fitting way, there was a dark shadow of his roots showing. He was beautiful.

"What are you staring at?"

"You," I answered without missing a beat, no hesitation in my answer but I started to feel my face heat up and Marsh's face started to get a little pink as well.

"Oh," was all he said smiling snapping his head down not wanting to make eye contact.

"Dude... we are like so gay for each other it's sicking," I joked, earning a chuckle.

"Didn't we say no, homo?" he joked back.

"Absolutely not, I think you're remembering that wrong because if I recall correctly, I said full homo."

"Oh right!" Our eyes met for a moment and we both burst out laughing. It was moments like this that I loved the most, times where it was just Marshal and me, where nothing else mattered in the world, it was just us together a light in the dark twisted world around us.

• XLII •

MARSHAL

Kia made me get up because he heard my dad come home, and yes he was home but when I crept downstairs I noticed he was passed out on the couch, so as I had predicted it didn't really matter if I got up to look presentable or not he'd never notice a difference.

"Dude, he's passed out cold," I yelled up the stairs. Kia came downstairs, not wanting to bother my dad, but I initiated it would be fine he crept down the stairs quietly. "K, you're not going to wake him up I swear," I laughed in spite of myself, it was sweet how caring and careful he was trying to be to everyone around him, even if it was someone who didn't deserve his compassion. Kia told me he was hungry, so I told him I'd make us some breakfast, and by making something that probably meant putting something in the toaster.

"So as expected..." I said opening the cabinets, "We have no food. There's like... canned beats?" I grimaced and so did Kia. "fucking Spam, beefaroni, granola bars.... and cereal I don't remember the last time we bought so it's probably stale. What a selection, huh?" I said sarcastically. At the very least, my mom could have gone food shopping before she left, knowing my dad was basically a man-baby.

Kia frowned at our lack of food options, I wasn't one to eat a lot and he knew it. In middle school, Kia suspected I had some kind of eating disorder when in reality it was just the medications I was on that made me not want to eat. My dad mostly went out to eat without me and since food shopping was something my mom did, it hadn't really been done since she left. Kia was always urging me to eat still even if I didn't feel like it, he didn't care it was cute how he worried about me.

184

It didn't bother me not having much food other than snacks and frozen junk I preferred to drink my calories anyway. Back when Kia thought I had some kind of eating disorder he'd always bring me some sort of stupid nutrition shakes and I wasn't opposed to drinking them, drinking was a lot easier than eating, and along with my medication and the amount of alcohol, I drank I didn't really feel like I needed or wanted to eat. KJ understood it, he also hated to eat he felt like he shouldn't eat until everyone else in the house did, always giving his portions of dinner to his brother or sister when he was getting high with Craig it was Craig who always provided the snacks and only then would KJ indulge himself.

"How about some peanut butter toast?" Kia suggested

"Yeah that's doable," I smiled at him. Peanut butter was a stable on my house something we always had on hand and there was still a loaf of Bread in the cabinet I put the bread slices in the toaster and Kia got some plates out of the cabinet, struggling a bit with the clinking dishes accidentally setting them down heavily making a loud sound of the ceramic plates against the countertops. He looked horrified at the loud sounds and I just brushed it off.

"Marshal? Is that you fucking around in there?" My dad called out in a half-awake voice and I heard Kia curse under his breath.

"Yeah, I'm making breakfast... or brunch I guess," I said looking at the clock.

"Jesus keep it down my head is killing me," he responded back with a groan. Kia sucked in his breath looking worried but I mouthed to him, *It's fine he's being dramatic.* Heavy footsteps led my disheveled father into the kitchen doorway.

"Oh, hey Kia... You're here... again," he said narrowing his eyes and looking almost annoyed.

"Hello, Mr. Langdon," Kia waved politely. My dad just grunted and turned to me.

"You know, people are going to start to think things about you boys."

"Think things?" I echoed.

185

"Yeah, you know like you're funny with each other or something. The way you're constantly with each other and people are going to start talking, Marshal," he shrugged, continuing on with his explanation.

"Dad, what the fuck?"

"I just don't want people thinking you boys are... how should I put this?" he paused to think, "I don't want people thinking you're playing for the team, you know?" I looked at Kia who looked horrified and was red in the face

Kia leaned in close to my ear, "Marsh I think I'm going to go upstairs." I nodded and he gave me a last fearful look before disappearing out of sight. Once Kia was gone my dad continued what he was saying.

"Marshal, you know I let it go when you boys were younger, but now it's just weird. It was better when you boys were around each other less it looked less faggy," he said so casually it made my blood boil.

"Dad!"

"I'm just saying!" he waved his hands up defensively. "Marshal I think you need to hear this," he said calmly. "I'd expect it out of the Schwartz boy I mean he's always been kind of soft but if you keep up this attached at-the-hip bullshit-"

"Leave Kia out of this, Dad!"

"See? There you go again, defending your queero boyfriend!" My dad grunted out in frustration.

"And what if he is?!" I spat back angrily.

"What?" his voice was low.

"You fucking hear me, Jerry, what if?" I said between gritted teeth.

"No Marshal there's no what-if, your just confused," he said angrily.

"No, I'm not, Dad!"

"No you are confused Marshal we all feel like this about our best friends at some point but you grow out of it! What happened to that nice girl you were dating?"

"No, Dad I'm not growing out of this feeling, goddamn it! I was confused because of that girl but I'm not anymore because this boy helped me figure my shit all out!"

"You don't like boys Marshal," he said sternly but annoyed. He was starting to get frustrated. I was past frustrated. "that fag just has you thinking you do!" he finished and that was all it took to let the rage blind me.

"You're right I like one boy and don't you dare fucking call him or me a fucking fag again!" I yelled angrily I was done with his bullshit I wasn't going to stand here any longer and take it. I pushed past him into the living room, Kia was sitting on the stairs teary-eyed.

"Common K, get your stuff we're leaving," I said ushering him upstairs. Once we were in my bedroom I closed the door and Kia wrapped two lanky arms around my neck and buried his face into my shoulder. "I'm sorry Kia I really fucking am, you shouldn't have to hear any of that shit," I said hugging him back.

"I'm sorry," he mumbled into my shoulder. I put my hands on his shoulders pushing him away a little so he could look me in the eyes.

"Don't ever apologize for that Kia it's not your fault, " I said sternly he gave me a simple nod, I gave him a light kiss on the forehead and started wiping at his eyes with the backs of his hands. Both of us quickly grabbed the things we needed before going back downstairs without fingers interlocking with each other meeting my dad by the door.

"Marshal we need to talk about this I'm not going to have some fairy for a son!"

"Too late, Dad!" I yelled pushing past him. I texted KJ to see where he was and he replied by telling me that he was at Thatcher's house with Benji and a girl I knew from school, Craig's cousin Amara. I raised an eyebrow that Amara was there but still sped walked down the road with Kia in tow. My fists were tightened tightly with my nails digging into my palms I was fuming, I needed a smoke hopefully KJ would have some.

"Marshal? Where are we going?" Kia pulled me from my thoughts with the rage building inside my chest.

"Thatcher's."

"What? Why?" Kia sounded visibly disgusted, reasonably so.

"That's where KJ is and Benji too," I responded cooly, I was angry still and trying my best to not let it come out the last thing I needed was to snap at Kia. I wasn't mad at him. I wasn't going to take this out on him, I'd done that enough. I'd done enough damage, I couldn't let myself do anymore.

"Oh okay cool," he said. I walked at a quick pace, my entire body was fine. Red-hot rage pricked at my skin as we walked to Thatcher's palace in comfortable silence, it was heavy, so many things left unsaid but I didn't want to talk about them or deal with any of them so it felt better to say nothing. I usually hated silences like this but it was comfortable with neither of us being able to really say anything to each other. I could tell he was hurting and I was in a rage. There wouldn't have been any kind of productive conversation.

· XLIII ·

KIA

Marshal was boiling with rage, I could tell. The way he walked, the way his face was resting, he had a look like he was about to hit someone. He dealt with it horribly but I wasn't dealing with it much better. My parents were going to find out, this was it, I wasn't fucking ready for this.

"Marsh?" I forced out his name from between my lips, it was strained and laced with a panic I couldn't suppress despite my efforts. My voice sounded odd and not like mine, Marshal jumped back at the sudden break from the silence.

"K?" he responded softly his voice was smooth and sent a wave of relief and comfort over me. I loved how he called me 'K' it was a name only he called me, his special nickname for me, and it always made me feel a sense of feeling better the way he said it so smoothly and comforting.

"I love you, Marsh," he turned around, we stopped walking and he pulled me tightly into an embrace.

"Oh god, this is bad, isn't it?" Marshal said into my shoulder.

"I-"

I couldn't think, I couldn't speak, there was nothing but panic starting to build. I wasn't ready for this. This wasn't how I wanted it to happen. What if they were mad at me? I couldn't handle it. My chest started to burn with the heat creeping up my throat and behind my eyes.

"It's going to be okay Marsh," I finally said. We stood there hugging each other wallowing in panic and regret on the sidewalk for what felt like ever before we continued our venture to Thatcher's house. All I could think about was how they would react and when my mom knew it was over, everyone in town would know. Marsh didn't mean to do it this way but when I pictured coming out as gay to anyone, let alone in a gay relationship, I imagined it would be how I wanted, not against my will forcing me out into the open under a spotlight when I wasn't ready.

We were now standing on the front porch of Thatcher's house Marsh pounded his fist into the door before it swung open.

"Hiya, guys!" Benji cheered and wrapped his arms around me in a tight hug, the Xbox controller still in his hand, to which I returned. He squeezed me tight, differently than when Marshal held me tight. When Benji squeezed me it was like he was trying to break me but with all his love and admiration for me.

"Hey, Benji," I smiled, and he led us inside. Thatcher was on the floor in front of the TV playing some video game, controller in hand, while KJ and Amara were sprawled out on the couch.

"Sup Jew," Thatcher grunted not taking his attention from the game.

"Yeah, hey dude," I waved at KJ, "uh, nice to see you, Amara?" she waved, giving a small smile.

"Yep," KJ scoffed, "Real nice indeed," he groaned and she laughed a barky unattractive but genuine laugh.

"He's mad because he's losing," she said as her laugh died down.

"So, what's up with you," KJ asked, sitting up now.

"I just had a shitty fight with my dad and needed to get out of there with K," Marshal answered.

"You guys fight all the time, so how's this any different?" Thatcher asked, now more interested in the conversation.

"He just said some shitty stuff, and shitty stuff specifically about Kia."

"Okay yeah whatever ever gaywads," Thatcher mumbled turning his attention back to the game.

"Stop with the fucking gay stuff," Marsh grumbled but nothing else was said about it.

Marshal and everyone started making small talk but it sounded like everyone was underwater. All the things flying threw my head about how I was going to explain everything to my parents and what they would say, I had forgotten slightly about the guys and what they would say. I wanted them to hear it from me, and I couldn't hold it back anymore.

190

"We're dating!" I blurted out. I wanted to feel in control and this was the only way I knew how, everyone was going to know sooner or later and I wanted someone to be told under my circumstances. I would have preferred it to be only between Benji, KJ, and Thatcher, but I couldn't help Amara being there, which still didn't make any sense to me.

"What?" Thatcher coughed out holding evident astonishment in his voice.

"Kia, do you really want to do this now?" Marshal whispered to me.

"Yes, okay I just-" I took a deep breath feeling a heaving start in my chest, "*I* want to be the ones they hear it from and I wanted to say it, you know?" I said at a normal volume instead of whispering. Marshal nodded in understanding.

"I'm gay, and Marshal was fighting with his dad because he was being a dick, and Marshal just snapped. He was defending me and our relationship and yelling, and it just came out! He told Jerry about us and just," I paused, pinching the bridge of my nose trying to calm myself down. Somewhere in the room, there was a stifled, 'ha, coming out.'

"Schwartz, please, we already knew you guys were totally gay for each other. Isn't that right, Kenneth James?" Thatcher laughed. KJ smiled, nodding.

"Yeah, I just feel stupid now. When Marshy boy told me he liked some boy I should have figured he was talking about you. You guys are terrible at hiding your feelings from each other. God, how did I miss this??" KJ attributed to the conversation. I gave a pleading look to Marshal who was sporting his own shocked expression.

"Now you guys owe me some money," Benji stated proudly.

"Benji?" I squeaked out in utter shock.

"I didn't tell nobody Kia, I swear, scouts honor, but come on fellas it was only a matter of time," he responded.

"Yeah, our oh-so-very sweet and innocent, Benjamin Junior here bet us both fifty dollars you'd get together before high school ended," KJ snickered.

"Dude!" Marshal said in surprise.

"What the fuck guys? When?- How long?" I stammered out.

"Freshman year," Thatcher said.

191

"I said it was going to be after graduation when you idiots realized it, now I'm out 50 bucks," KJ said rolling his eyes.

"You, me, Donovan, and Theo are all out twenty bucks Conwell you're not special," Thatcher retorted.

"Kia, I could just tell Marshal was as head over heels as you said you were for him," Benji smiled at me.

"Wait, did you tell Benji?" Marshal asked, gasping in a fake shock.

"You told KJ, jackass," I laughed. There was a sort of awkward tension in the room, and Marshal was trying to light the mood, which sort of worked.

"But I didn't tell him who it was," he grinned at me, our faces pulling towards each other.

"Ew gross, are you guys going to get all gay with each other in my fucking living room?" Thatcher yelled out.

"No fatass!" I snapped back.

"It's been fun, guys but I think my cue to leave was a while ago," Amara said, looking uncomfortable pushing herself off the couch and heading to grab her shoes. When she finally walked out the door, I looked at the guys. Everyone was silent like we were all holding our breath until she left. Everyone let out a collective sigh of relief when the door closed.

"Okay, now spill, why the hell was Amara here? She doesn't even like Thatcher, and none of us are friends with her? Right?" I said.

"Oh, you aren't the only one Cupid got to," Thatcher teased, giving a smirk at KJ.

"Was that your date??" I asked, shocked. "How? When? Why?" all the questions tumbled out. KJ didn't say anything just looked down with a stupid grin.

"Now, are you two idiots just going to stand awkwardly or join us?" KJ asked, patting the couch next to him. Marshal and, I awkwardly laughed before taking a seat.

"Now spill dumb and dumber," KJ said, giving a different grin. "This is *way* more important," he said dramatically.

I got red in the face a little."Yeah, we always knew you were gay wads, but when did you become mega gay wads?" Addie chirped up.

"Addie!" Benji hissed, and he only shrugged, rolling his eyes. I couldn't help but laugh. This seemed like something that would happen at some chick's sleepover. I gave in, telling the guys about everything that happened, Marsh occasionally adding things or making commentary. They were all way too intrigued adding on their own commentary. We fell into a content lull.

"Say, Kia, it's been a while since we had a sleepover, can I stay over?"

"Well, actually, I just... there's a lot of stuff going on at home; I really don't want to be there..."

"Oh, well, okay, maybe another time," he sounded so defeated. I felt like I was lying to him, there wasn't a lot going on, I was just scared to go home, that was the only thing. The overwhelming fear of my mother's impending wrath felt like a lot of things and Benji looked disappointed but that kind of disappointment you're used to.

"But wait! Maybe the four of us, you, me, KJ, Marshal, can stay over at Thatcher's house?" The defeated look in his eye vanished, replaced by new hope.

I felt my phone vibrate in my pocket. I pulled it out, and horror overcame my body, a paralyzing fear spread throughout me as I stared at the screen.

INCOMING CALL: MOM

The ringing stopped bringing me back to reality.

"Kia?"

"Uh huh?"

"You okay?" Benji asked, the concern in his voice genuine.

"Yeah, sorry," I shook my head as if I was trying to shake out the thoughts of my impending demise.

"Who was calling you? You look worried?" he noted.

"It was just a spam call," I lied. "Sometimes I like to answer them and say stupid shit," I tacked on quickly.

KJ and Marsh were now comfortably situated back on the couch, slouched down lying and occasionally kicking at each other, demanding more leg room. KJ and Thatcher played some racing game against each other, I didn't pay much attention, just sitting with immense panic and fear building up.

"Oh yeah, I was gonna ask that too. I don't feel like dealing with my dad," Marsh asked.

"Oh yeah me too," KJ added with a fake sweetness to his voice.

"Goddamn hippies, every time my mom leaves to on a longer trip, you guys always have to crash it." Thatcher's mom was a flight attendant, meaning his house was the prime hang-out spot due to how he spent most of his time home alone without a dad here either. Part of the reason Thatcher was still here was because of KJ, they had almost the same depth of bond that Marshal and I had.

KJ came from a house of addicts, where his parents hated him for pretty much existing. Thatcher's mom, for most of our childhood, was deep in addiction, meaning at least once a month, he had to go live with his grandma. Thatcher's dad wasn't in the picture because, like KJ, his mother had no clue who his dad was and never really wanted to bother with it. It was a sore subject for both Addie and his mom but for different reasons. Lana Thatcher didn't think it was important and even though she loved Addie more than anything, she'd get extremely angry when he brought it up.

"Please?"

"Pretty please?" Both Marsh and KJ added still fake sweet.

"Yeah, whatever, guess it beats being alone anyway," Thatcher sighed giving in.

"Aw, Thatcher, I'm touched," KJ whipped away a fake tear placing a hand on his chest being his over-dramatic self. "It's almost like- like you like us," he broke out into a wide grin.

"Whatever feeds your ego," Thatcher snipped back and KJ and I just laughed.

· XLIV ·

MARSHAL

"Common Marshy, I need a smoke," KJ groaned pushing himself into an upright position. I noticed the jitteriness of his presence while he was sitting, he moved almost too quickly as he led himself through the living room and made his way to the back door. I got up, following KJ's route outside.

KJ's fingers fumbled with the lighter and he let out a frustrated grunt finally managing to get the lighter to work. He tossed it to me before taking a sharp, quick inhale, blowing smoke out his nose as he breathed out just as heavily as he breathed in. The tension in his body had him strung high, almost like Kia was constantly a rare way to see KJ however

"So Amara?" it was all I could come up with to say.

"Yeah?"

"Craig's cousin?"

"Yeah? Your point?" he smiled that stupid smile that made him look almost punchable. I had managed to light my own cigarette with a lot more ease than he had, letting it dangle from my lips as KJ furiously sucked in air shortening the cigarette significantly faster than mine.

"Really?"

"Oh my god, yes, *ja, si, oui,* that's all the languages I know how to say yes in," he laughed.

"Huh," I let out, not being much for conversation.

"So, what were you guys playing before K and I came in?"

"GTA, and I got to admit, Amara was actually kicking ass," he cringed.

"You're a sore-ass loser, you know that KJ?" we both laughed, smoke flowing from our mouths.

"Like you're *sooo* much better- Oh! And another thing? Why are you the only one allowed to call Kia K?" KJ asked his hands on his hips like a middle school girl about to start a 'fight'.

"I don't know?"

"I called him that and he yelled at me dude, said it was only your name for him," KJ elbowed me wiggling his eyebrows in a joking manner and I couldn't help but get red in the face. *He only wants me to call him K because that's my special nickname for him.* I liked the idea of calling him by a name that no one else would use, it was mine, just mine, like him. KJ and I finished our smokes heading back inside. I hadn't realized how pent up I was the slight buzz of nicotine sliding my nervous system was a welcome sensation as I resituated myself on the couch.

Kia was on the floor but when I sat down he got up and walked over looking defeated and more anxious than before. I sat up making room for him next to me which he sat down in thumping his head onto my shoulder. I put my arm around him gently rubbing his shoulder.

"Ew, are you two going to be all gay with each other?" Thatcher snorted, "It was one thing when you were fucking each other with your eyes, now you're going to be drooling all over each other."

"Shut it fatass you're just jealous it's not you drooling all over Kia," KJ teased getting a glare from Thatcher. Kia visibly gagged at the implication.

"God, KJ, what the fuck is wrong with you?" Kia asked, face twisted.

"I swear I'm the only one here who's not all gay for each other," Thatcher grunted, KJ returned the glare now.

"Nope, just jealous you get no bitches," KJ snipped back snidely.

"I get bitches," Thatcher retorted, "I could have whoever I wanted I just choose not to!"

"Liar, liar, liar," KJ teased in a sing-song voice.

"You aren't getting any either!" Thatcher's voice started to raise and he and KJ continued bickering back and forth but I looked to Kia. His eyes were dull, the kind of dullness that came from when he was thinking too much and not in a good way.

"You okay?" I asked rubbing circles on his bicep with my thumb.

"Nothing," he mumbled but I could tell it was a lie, anxiety radiated off him. His whole body was tense, shoulders and knees squeezed together, his hands folded in his lap, but he was holding onto his hands hard enough that his knuckles were white.

"I call bullshit," I said in a low voice next to his ear, "What's wrong K?"

"Really nothing, I'm just kind of tired," he shrugged—another lie.

"Come on dude, talk to me, you get all pissed when I don't talk to you."

"That's different, you don't talk and instead get shitfaced," he replied with a sigh.

"So how's this different?"

"My liver won't fail," a ghost of a smile on his lips, but his eyes said it was a genuine concern.

"Okay yeah say what you want, I'm fine but you're not. seriously spit it out," I said skipping over his concern.

"Just leave it Marshal please?" he almost begged me. "Let's just be stupid guys tonight, everything feels like it's too heavy. Life feels like it's crushing me and I want to step away before it does crush me and my chest collapses."

"Wow, where is this all coming from?" now it was my turn to be concerned.

"Just leave it alone!" Kia said harshly with a bite to his words. He sighed pinching his nose and inhaled deeply, exhaling like he had been holding his breath, "Sorry, we can talk about it later right now I want to forget I'm totally fucked."

"You're not fucked, dude," I tried to reassure him, not entirely sure what he meant but still wanted to make him feel better. The bickering between KJ and Thatcher had died down a while ago, and the two, including Benji now scrolling threw Netflix.

"let's watch something scary," Thatcher urged.

"Netflix's horror movies suck plus I've seen them all already," KJ groaned.

"You can't afford heating but you can fucking pay for Netflix??" Thatcher breathed out in both annoyance and shock. "God I hate poor people," he added.

197

"No you fuck! I borrow Craig's account," KJ replied matter of factly. "and if you hate poor people so much, then why do you keep me around, huh?" he now smirked at Thatcher.

"Because like true scum, you. won't. go. away." Thatcher said punctuating his words with a clap of his hands.

"Why don't we watch a show then?" Benji suggests.

"What can we watch in a day Benji?" Thatcher huffed turning his annoyance from KJ to Benji now.

"I don't know, we could find something with just a season or two there's a couple of good shows that got canceled," Benji rubbed his knuckles together like he always had since we were kids. It was weird to me how we could grow up but still keep small habits like that. We could change into a completely different person and still, when it boiled down to our core; there were parts of our former selves we could never get rid of.

I felt Kia's phone vibrate against my thigh from his pocket. He flinched but otherwise remained unbothered by the sensation.

"You going to get that?" I asked nudging him.

"It's probably spam," he responded dully.

"Ooh! Can I answer it? Please? I have a good one ready and everything," I asked excitedly. Usually answering spam calls with dumb bullshit was something the four of us all got a kick out of, Kia would jump at the opportunity and usually got a good laugh from it, but now he just shook his head 'no'.

"Oh okay," I said a bit put off by his lack of reasons but otherwise shrugged it off. There was an odd guilt pooling in my chest, tugging at me, saying that I should continue to intervene, I needed to get to the bottom of what was bothering him, but Kia was stubborn and short-tempered. He would resist and resist until he snapped like a rubber band.

· XLV ·

KIA

It felt odd being in an atmosphere like the one around me. The air felt thick and suffocating with the joy surrounding my wallowing misery like I was a singular dark cloud floating in an otherwise brilliantly bright blue sky. My stomach turned at the thought of my mother's messages and voicemails, probably screaming ones, she was leaving. My phone continued to ring and vibrate. After the first call, I switched it just to vibrate, not wanting everyone to be annoyed with the constant bombardment from my ringer.

The guys ended up not being able to pick a movie or show, so as we always did when we couldn't agree, we turned on a kids' cartoon. It was weirdly indulgent of us to all be teenagers on the verge of adulthood watching shows that were meant for age groups younger than my brother. I watched with vague interest but not really paying attention to the animated show that was supposed to mirror a reality TV show. I secretly still liked watching most cartoons because it was like a break from reality, cleansing our minds with something bright and light that didn't require much attention and was just childish enough that it could help turn off your brain but still adult enough that it wasn't annoying or stupid. I hated the stuff my brother watched but enjoyed things from when I was younger or even before that. Kid's shows were like my guilty pleasure, normally the TV I watched was something plot-heavy with deep characterization and heavy topics, but sometimes I just needed to watch a show about a kid with a talking dog and two genius sisters that used him as a lab rat.

"I'd hit that," KJ said, breaking me from my deep trance-like state, reflecting on aspects of my childhood I missed the most; when the world didn't feel like it was on my shoulders. I missed days when I wasn't overthinking my life plan, worried about what I would do after high school, or planning every detail of my life because that's what everyone wants from you at a certain point. Of course, I was still an anxious kid but less so now.

"Kenneth James, what-ever-your-middle-name- is Conwell..." Thatcher sighed, breathing deeply. "That is a two-dimensional animated character on a kid's show."

"Okay and? It may be a kid's show, but she's also sixteen with a RACK!"

"That's not a rack dude, that's a fucking shelf," Marshal interjected, laughing and getting a chuckle out of everyone else.

"True, but still, *if* she were real, her tits would be like..." KJ placed his hand on his chin, trying to find the right words to describe the girl. "eh, doesn't matter, but point in case, she'd have big 'ol titties, and I'd totally hit."

"Like you'd even have a chance, hot shot," Marsh grinned stupidly.

"Oh, I'd totally have a chance," KJ replied, wiggling his eyebrows, "I'd work my magic, and kablam, she's in my bed naked," he grinned.

"Sick dude!"

"Ew, KJ!" Benji and I both let out protests grimacing.

"I could and would hit that; that's all I'm saying," KJ shrugged.

"You say that about everyone, KJ you're a whore," Thatcher said blankly.

"Not as big of one as your mom," KJ snipped back, sticking his tongue out.

"Stop talking about my mom like that!" he squealed in response.

The stupid teasing fights contained. I was lost in my own world, only being brought out by the sense I'd just witnessed between the other three people in the room, but now I was more aware of what was happening. I felt the warmth of Marsh's body pressed against my side, his arm still snaked around me, his hand resting on my bicep. Thatcher squealed about his mom and dropped me back into my own personal hellscape, the vibrating in my pocket yet again persistent as always, announcing that I was a dead man walking.

"Okay, seriously, dude, who is blowing up you're phone? No one gets this many spam calls," Marsh said clearly getting annoyed with the situation.

"I'm sure it's nothing," I tried to dismiss him.

"It could be, or it could be something important, Kia. It's not like you to ignore this many messages." Marshal had a point. I never turned off my ringer in case someone needed to contact me for something important like a family emergency but I knew the messages being left had nothing to do with anything important. Usually, this many calls and texts from my mother would give me a heart attack from the panic it caused, but I already knew. I *knew* what was waiting for me, and the anxiety that ignoring the calls gave me was much more bearable than the anxiety it gave me to think about answering.

"It's nothing important, I promise," I said after I realized my lack of response was probably suspicious.

"How could you be so sure?" *because I know it's my mom blowing up my phone, and I know exactly what she wants and I know exactly what's going to happen, and this is all your fault!* I wanted to snap at him but retained my composure.

"I'm trying to spend time with you guys. I don't need to answer my phone right now. Whoever it is can wait," I said, my tone boarding on annoyed.

"You know something," his eyes narrowed at me in suspicion.

"No, I don't," I started to peel away at my fingers, basking at the familiar sting.

"That's the only reason you don't care."

"Marsh, just stop. It's annoying that you can't let this go," my voice carried a warry tone to try and serve as a warning.

"Why don't you want to tell me?" he pressed further sternly. "Is it like another dude, and you don't want me to get all jealous?"

"Yes, it's another dude," I replied sarcastically, "his name is Langdon Marsh, he's your evil twin from a different dimension," I said flat and deadpan.

"It's not funny, Kia, common tell me."

"There's nothing to tell!" My voice rose.

Until now, we had been decently quiet, enabling us to be ignored by the other three allowing them to focus on the TV, but Benji and KJ both turned their heads, throwing confused and concerned looks. I waved my hands up to say without the words 'everything fine,' and with that, they emerged themselves into the animated reality show.

"Fine, if you don't know, and you don't want to know, at least let me check your phone I'll tell them to shut up and go away," Marshal crossed his arms in an almost pout. I had to stop myself from laughing. He was the one pouting right now? He was the one who was going to huff at me with crossed arms as if I wasn't the one who was totally fucked. I should be pouting at him for putting me into this position. I didn't want to blame him, but the longer I sat with it, him outting me, accident or not, the more it bothered me. The anger was deep routed and slow to come to the surface but with each buzz of my phone, it slowly began to come up.

"Marshal, I said fucking stop! You're such a fucking asshole!" I said in an angry harsh whisper.

"Can you two fucking shut up, Jesus Marsh go to the corner store and get your flaming hot Cheeto some tampons to stop the bleeding out of his vagina," Thatcher snapped, turning around.

"I am not bleeding out my vagina! I don't even have one!" I full-on yelled, voice cracking a little bit. There was a stillness over us encased by the silence, the only sounds coming from the TV as the fake reality show host announced who was staying on the show. Suddenly Benji started to giggle quickly, slapping his hands over his mouth and quieting the noise, but not long before it spread to KJ. Marshal looked at KJ and it was;t long before the three of them all burst out in a chorus of full-on laughter.

"What the fuck is wrong with you nut jobs?" Thatcher asked, a smile tugging at the concerns of his lips as he tried to resist the temptation to laugh along with them. I felt it build in my chest as well, bubbling up my throat as I looked at Thatcher, sharing his confusion but slowly began to lose control. Maybe it was some kind of hysteria caused by my intense anxiety or some other psychological effect but now I was doubled over laughing.

"What is so funny you ass hats?" Thatcher asked again, resisting the smile forming on his lips.

"Kia!" Benji wheezed out, "Just the way he said it! 'I don't even have one!'" Benji repeated but in a mocking tone causing him and Marsh to cackle even harder; finally, Thatcher lost his battle to resistance and joined in.

"Yeah yeah! and- and- Benji started to laugh and he looked at me-" KJ squeezed words out between breaths.

"And the way he looked at me!" Marsh added. we all sat there until our laughing fizzled out to a chorus of sharp breathing like we had all just run a matron. Most everyone had caught their breath except for Marsh who continued to breathe hard until it morphed into a wheeze and into a coughing fit.

"Jesus Christ!" he exclaimed pounding on his chest, his eyes started to water as his breath still refused to go back to a normal rhythm, instead becoming more ragged. Anytime he had an asthma attack, his eyes blew open wide, filled with fear and panic as if he was dying, but having an asthma attack was like suffocating.

"FucK!" he yelled out again in pure panic, now beating around his pants pockets, desperate to find the familiar bulge of his inhaler. His hands busied themselves now trying to stifle his coughing but also pound into his chest as if that would help, I wasn't sure if it would, but he always did it when he had an asthma attack.

"Fuck," KJ and I echoed together, now feeling Marsh's panic as his wheezing and coughing intensified. I helped to pull Marsh up so he was sitting up straight raising his arms above his head as KJ now emptied Marsh's pockets.

"Sorry dude, not to be all handsy with your ass," KJ remarked before shoving his hand into Marsh's back pocket.

"'s.. fine," Marshal wheezed. KJ pulled out a lighter and Marsh's wallet before diving into his other pocket coming up empty.

"Deep breaths, dude," I said, trying to lead him by example of some breathing exercises he had used before.

"No... shit.." he snipped with an annoyed look before coughing roughly, his face turning a deep red. KJ fished around in Marsh's front pockets, pulling out a pack of cigarettes, he was unable to see my disapproving scowl, but now was not the time to dig into that. His eyes screamed that he was in full panic now, only making his breathing worse, his watery eyes looking as if they were making a pleading deal with the grim reaper. In the opposing front pocket, KJ finally pulled out the object of our panicked search.

"AHA!" he tipped before uncapping the inhaler, Marsh's arms dropping and clumsily grabbing it, bringing it to his mouth and releasing the trigger.

"Holy fuck, dude, that was scary," KJ said, letting out a long withheld breath.

"You have no fucking clue," Marshal shook his head with a weak smile.

"Yeah, smoking really isn't good for asthmatic people," I said, rolling my eyes.

"Honestly... I have no clue how those even got in there," he shrugged, looking at me, his lips pressed into a tight line.

"You're awful," I said, breaking my scowl.

"Seriously, dude, I have no clue where those came from," he waved his hands at me as if the motions would magically make me believe his blatant attempt at playing dumb.

"You may be blonde but you're not a dumb blonde, Marsh," I smirked.

"Hey!" Both Thatcher and KJ yelped, looking at each other and then laughing again.

"Sorry Kia...That's on me, I offered him the rest of my pack," KJ shrugged.

"Both of you are going to die before you're twenty-seven," I sighed deeply.

"Cool, I'll be just like Kurt Cobain in the twenty-seven club," Marshal smiled.

"Absolutely not! Don't deliberately kill yourself, it's bad enough you guys are doing all this self-destructive shit that's probably going to kill you in the end.

"Everyday occurrence," KJ mumbled, and the room all turned to him.

"Every time you hit a bong, you lose brain cells, and you're already a drug baby, so you can't afford to lose much more. The more you lose, the more weird shit you say," Thatcher said with narrowed eyes as if to give off a warning that was lost on KJ.

"I'm invincible," he simply replied.

"No, you're fucked in the head," Thatcher retorted.

"Why can't you two just be nice, KJ's not messed up in the head he's just a bit...different," Benji waved his hands around his head, drawing a smile out from KJ.

"You know that's one of my favorite movies, right?" KJ asked, sounding fond and Benji just nodded, and we all seemed content with the situation.

· XLVI ·

MARSHAL

Our afternoon had been almost completely consumed, the hours melted away with each episode of the show Thatcher had put on his TV. Time seemed to go on slowly, and I felt drained. Almost dying has a habit of taking a lot out of you. Kia was right smoking was making it worse, I had noticed that over the years as I began to go threw more and more smokes on a regular basis. I had been dealt a shitty hand in life with my shitty lungs, but why not exploit that? So with no regard for that contained on with the habit. I had picked up the habit briefly in elementary school but only started to keep it around the time I was thirteen. I didn't have any intentions of stopping, even if it killed me. I looked at Kia and mulled over the question in my head, *would it really be that bad if my self-destructive behaviors were what did me in?* It wasn't like this was my first time ever thinking about it.

I used to think about it a lot and maybe that's why I was like this. I didn't like to plan ahead for my future, I honestly didn't see myself having one. I couldn't picture myself growing up or being around for long. The chats about colleges and careers just overwhelmed me filling me with dread that I didn't know what I wanted, I didn't even know if I would be here, I could barely get threw now how was I supposed to know how I wanted the next five years of my life to go? I would start to think, and the thinking would lead me to questions I didn't want to answer but would take up a large part of my mind anyway, like; would the world be better without me? would my parents be happier without me holding them together like a piece of scotch tape? Is that what I wanted? To disappear into the inky blackness, the numbness taking over my body as I drifted away forever?

Instead of thinking about it much further than that, not wanting to explore those dark cascades afraid of where they may lead me, I drank. When I drank, it was like I could turn them all off, letting the lowly buzz of alcohol take me away from the scary shadows that made up my darkest thoughts. The warmth of whatever drink I had would carry me away, almost like I was floating down a river of pure bliss. I used to not mind the idea of dying, nothing intentional, but I would be upset if I died in a car accident or got stabbed by a homeless guy, or even drank myself to death. I almost welcomed the idea but now? I looked at Kia, my bright, shining Kia, and the idea of leaving the world with him still in it hurt. He was a bright ray of sunshine, and I needed him close he helped fend off the horrible stuff I drank to get away from, and I couldn't leave him. I still didn't want to think of knocking smoking, but at least cut down on it to appease him and lengthen my life span, something I had never considered at any other point.

I was staring at Kia, and if he noticed, he didn't say anything or let on any sign that he did and I took him all in. He was still on edge, his body tense and radiating an anxious aura. His brow was slightly furrowed, eyes shifting back and forth, unable to focus on anything, his cuticles and fingertips were red-stained with blood. His phone would vibrate and he would flinch a pang of horror washed over him for a brief second before he regained his composure. It was so brief I think I'm the only one in the world who could really see it.

"Okay, I know we've all seen this show enough times to have it memorized, but like, I'm still rooting for Gwen to win," Thatcher sighed out with disappointment, knowing that wouldn't be the outcome. Throughout the day, we had all moved around the room various times to various positions leading KJ and Thatcher to now be sitting cross-legged in front of the TV while Kia and I lay on our stomached next to each other propped up on our elbows in between each other. Benji was lazily sprawled out on the couch, no matter where we moved, Kia was always right by my side, seeking out my touch after each disturbance from his phone.

"Really, I would have figured you an Owen stand, I mean, you're like the same person," KJ said in a teasing way, eliciting a giggle from Benji and Kia.

"You guys are such assholes! I'm nothing like that gassy tub of lard," he whined.

"Yeah, totally," I laughed along with the other three, Thatcher just scowled.

"I'm with him, though, she's hot, and I love a goth chick," KJ added, voice filled with the same disappointment.

"Damn straight, big tittie goth girl supramcy," Thatcher hummed in agreement.

"Since when do you like 'big tittie goth' girls?" Kia asked cocking an eyebrow in curiosity.

"Yeah, dude, the fuck? Didn't think that was your thing?" I added on.

"Everyones aloud have a weird preference, you like Kosher dick," Thatcher said smugly. We all looked at him dumbfounded before continuing on. Yet again, the babble of our conversation was interrupted We all stopped when my phone rang out loudly.

"Dude," I looked at the screen in surprise, seeing the name flash across my screen;

Ruth Schwartz (Kia's ma).

"What?" Kia asked, turning his head to the side in curiosity.

"It's your mom," I slid the bar to answer the call, and Kia's face turned white, ghostly pale as all the blood seemed to drain from his body.

"Hello, Mrs. Shw-"

"Where is he?!" I cringed at her shrill yelling. The room went quiet, including the TV and all eyes turned to me, staring intently. Kia's mom was a loud woman, and on the phone was no exception, regularly the person next to you could hear everything she said, but when she screamed, the whole group could hear her voice.

"Weak," Thatcher said, staring with vague interest.

"Who?" I crocked out.

"Marshal, you aren't dumb you know exactly who! Where is Kia?"

"Kia who?" I asked dumbly and immediately wanted to slap myself KJ and Benji cringed, Thatcher's face palmed on my behalf and Kia remained frozen in terror his eyes getting glassy from the water building up in the waterline.

"Listen here, your father may be a four cents short of a nickel but you are certainly not! So if you know what's good for me you are going to tell me exactly where my son is! I know he's with you! I was at your house and you weren't there, I checked with Conwells, Rabbi Adler's house, and the Danials's, he's not at any of their houses, so he has to be with you somewhere!" I could feel her wrath radiating from the phone. I envisioned Ruth, eyes on fire with smoke coming out of her ears, in any other circumstance, it would be funny, but not now. I lowered the phone into my shoulder and looked around, wide-panicked eyes meeting wide-panicked eyes.

"What do I do?" I said in a loud whisper.

"Fuck if I know, I don't want that crazy bitch to come to my house," Thatcher said, matching my tone.

"Come on, Kia, snap out of it," KJ urged and Kia slowly met his gaze, still looking stunned and groggy like someone just woke him up from a deep sleep. "Come on, dude what do we do?" KJ asked. I could hear Ruth shrinking into my shoulder and I cringed, putting the phone back up to my ear.

"Yes- Yes, I'm still here, and despite what you may think, I'm not with Kia he got mad at me and stormed out," I lied, trying to hide the shaking in my voice.

"I would be furious too if my so-called best friend accused me of something so horrific!"

"What?"

"You better believe that once I find Kia, I'm coming for you, next young man! How DARE you even think up such awful things like that!"

"L-like what?" I asked my stomach dropped, and I swallowed hard.

"You said my son, my Kia, my sweet Kia was..." her voice sunk unnaturally low for her, "a homosexual." Her voice raised back up, filled with rage, as ever, "We already have one gay couple, and that's just fine, but my son will be no part of that nonsense!" I looked, feeling appalled at what I was hearing.

"Always a pleasure, Mrs. Shwartz," I said, hanging up and ignoring her screaming protests and demands to know where Kia was. I put my phone down, and Kia collapsed into me, bursting out into tears, choking out fragments of sentences and incomplete thoughts.

'What the fuck,' KJ mouthed at me, all exchanging looks of horror. My dad's reaction was one thing, it could be dismissed as being both stupid and drunk, but Ruth was one hundred percent sober and nothing like my father in the slightest. As infuriating as he was to deal with the few and far times between when he was sober and able to form coherent thoughts, he always expressed his support for the LGBTQ+ community leading me to believe he'd be supportive of me.

I think he was just projecting some unresolved issues onto me, I know my dad had a couple... instances of things he had overshared with me while he was walking the tightrope between sober and drunken blackout. He'd come around I just needed to give him the credit, even if I didn't want to, even if I wanted to hold on to his outburst this morning for dear life and use it to fuel my resentment, I knew he'd come to his senses. Ruthann, however, was a whole other nightmare.

· XLVII ·

KIA

When Marsh said those words, *'It's your mom,'* my whole world went dark. All sounds faded into background noise, a senseless babble, I couldn't see. The room I was standing in fell away from me. I was no longer in Thatcher's living room I was floating. I wasn't there anymore, I was gone, lost in the downward spiral that came with the inevitable wrath of Ruthann Schwartz. Being her son, it was something I was familiar with but still hearing her shrill voice demand to know where I was made my blood stop pumping, everything froze, and despite the summer heat, and the sticky humidity of Thatchers's house, it was all gone, replaced with the cold chill that came with the mere mention of my mother's wrath.

A hand on my shoulder, warm against the still blood that was struggling to continue to course through my body. I focused my vision again retaking in my surroundings, slowly floating back to myself to the moment I was in and my horrible harsh reality. The humidity of the room returned, the slick sweat on my back keeping my shirt stuck to my back, my body was no longer cold but too hot. The sounds weren't back yet it all combined into a whirlwind of panic, voices talking, words being spoken, none of them hitting me. I looked down at the hand on my shoulder, KJ's.

There were other hands, I was in Marsh's arms, tucked safely in the comfort and safety of his arms, untainted. Marshal, for as long as I could remember, had always been my safety and comfort. The many other times things had gone wrong at home, the many other times my mother, as much as she loved me, had unleashed her wrath upon me. I was her crown jewel of the family, her prodigal son but there was so much pressure to do it all right, presues that I would crumble under in the safety of Marshal. Everything would be alright if I had Marshal, it would all be okay. I swallowed hard, my safe haven was tainted the panic spreading and thoughts being entertained about what would happen. The possibility of losing my safety, my haven, my Marsh. *My Marshal.*

I looked around to the panicked eyes and concerned looks, meeting each of them and returning them without my own wide-eyed blank look. "I need to go," the words came out of my mouth, clumsily spilling out from my lips in a voice that didn't sound like my own. I was crying; *when did I start crying?* I weakly fumbled out of the grasp holding me and stood up drunkenly, swaying in my panic.

"Dude, wait, stop," Marsh's voice, the first to finally break through to me, called out. I turned and looked at him, his eyes glassy, was he crying?

"W-what are you going to do?" to my surprise Thatcher asked. I shifted my gaze, raising my eyebrows at his question, him of all people. Thatcher's face turned taking in my confusion and poorly attempting to hide his own concern. As much as we fought it had gotten better, *he* had gotten better, enough now that his general sense of empathy allowed us to be actually considered friends, despite the act he tries to put on of hating me and not caring about anyone but himself.

"W-well, it's just... you know?" he rubbed the back of his head backwardly. "You're moms' a huge bitch, and like, she sounds pissed and well, I'm scared of her, and you live with her," he said something under his breath, and I wanted to laugh my suspicion of what he had uttered, something about the whole situation seemed comical almost.

"What was that uh- last part?" I asked, my voice still shaking as I was coming down my outburst of tears.

"Don't make me say it again," he said in a warning tone.

"Did I hear what I think I heard?" KJ asked with a small smile, the concern for me still on his face.

"Kenneth James shut up, you're poor, and poor people should never laugh," he said in the same tone he had addressed me in.

"Oh come on Thatcher," Benji piped in patting on his broad shoulder.

"Fine!" he snapped, "I'm worried about the jew! Happy? We all good now? I said, 'I'm worried for you Kia!'" he put extra emphasis on the last couple of words.

"Thanks, Thatcher," I tried to force a smile one that was lost on the guys.

"Wait K," Marshal stood up off the floor and took my hand in his, "I should go with you."

"No, no just don't" I pulled my hand away waving my hands in a dismissing matter, "You'd just probably make it… worse…" his face turned he looked hurt but nodded his head with understanding.

Marsh was rather well-tempered, except when it came to my mother. All those times I had come to take refuge in Marsh, *my Marshal*, left him with a strong haterade of my mother. He wanted to put her in her place, rip her a new one, in his words. He cared, he wanted nothing more than to protect me and the biggest threat to me in Marsh's option was the emotional turmoil of my mother. I turned to leave again but was quickly pulled back into a tight embrace.

The arms of love, safety, and comfort, wrapped around me. The arms of my love, Marsh's arms, *my Marsh. Mine, mine, mine, mine, mine, my Marsh.*

· XLVIII ·

MARSHAL

It was quiet, the soft shutting of the front door and the cuttable tension between the remaining four. "And then there were four...." KJ finally spoke, awkwardly. I glared at him his face dusted a light pink from some kind of embarrassment, realizing this was not the time for his stupidity. There was something so cold that he marched out of the house. I swallowed hard biting back my urge to go run after him. I wanted to hold him, protect him from his mother and her stupid stupid unjust fucking judgment. I just still couldn't fathom what the hell her problem was, there was a subtle and dangerous type of rage building.

It was completely different from the anger my dad caused there was always a special kind of nerve that Ruth managed to hit and I hated it. Kia's mom was someone I merely tolerated for his sake, he knew, KJ knew, Thatcher knew, and *everyone* knew how much I didn't like her. Maybe I was just biased Kia being my boyfriend and all but whenever it came to the relationship between him and his mother, it always left me with an uncomfortable lump in my throat that I painfully swallowed and tried to ignore. Everyone knew exactly how I felt about Ruthann Schwartz.

When we were younger things were different, we were just kids but when we started getting older Ruth started to change. It was very clear how she felt about Kia's place in the world, both his parents made it subtable but still very clear they thought that themselves and their children were better than most. The Schwartzs had always liked me, I was always the parent pleaser of the group, and compared to the other options, KJ and Thatcher, I was the best company they could hope for Kia. I basically lived at their house during breaks to get away from my own shitty family trading it for another type of shitty family. While Kia's family welcomed me with open arms they still made it clear that there were invisible lines I needed to stay behind.

Both his parents wanted so much from him and pushed him so hard and it didn't help that Peter was some kind of kid genius, They made it clear to all his friends and Ike's friends too, that no one would hold back their sons. Kia is so fucking brilliant but still, I cringe physically whenever I hear Ruth say some bullshit like, "But *Peter* is doing this..." or "*Peter* is doing that..." almost like she was trying to put them against each other. Kia loved Peter and Peter loved Kia so they never saw each other as competition but still, it almost seemed like that's what Ruthann wanted. Ruth had some type of perfect plan for her son and the disgust in her tone made it sound like being gay, let alone gay with the kid that lives on a weed farm was no part of that plan, and she would do everything to keep it that way.

"Do you fellas think he'll be okay?" Benji asked anxiously rubbing together his knuckles together, the sound of the skin on his slim fingers rubbing together dully filling the background.

"He'll be... I don't-" I stuttered, My heart dropped to my stomach and suddenly my rage was gone, the weight uncomfortably sitting while my stomach turned.

"Yeah, he'll be fine, he always is," Thatcher said in a dismissive tone covering any genuine concern.

"Yeah, he always is," I mimicked in the way of agreeance. "he's going to be fine," I said again more to myself.

"This is all so totally weird," KJ hummed and I found myself nodding. This wasn't how it was supposed to go

"What's weird?" Butter's asked with a cocked eyebrow.

"You know we're all so scared of his mom but he acts so much like her I think we should be more scared of him," KJ laughed to himself, and Benji followed suit with a closed-lip smile.

"He's a ginger and jew. There's nothing to be scared of," Thatcher scoffed.

"Tell me that again next time he gives you a black eye and split lip," I nodded. Thatcher and Kia had always been at each other's throats, yeah they got better with age but still, it often escalated quickly and got physical. Thatcher just grumbled something under his breath and I let out a breath I didn't realize I was holding in.

"He'll be fine guys because he's basically just a smaller copy of Ruth, he's just as angry and just as rude," KJ said and we all hummed in agreement, he did make some valid points. As much as Kia complained about her and as much as he resented a good part of her, it was clear who he took after.

"So you losers still staying over?" Thatcher asked changing the topic, The thoughts of Kia and my worry still lingered but I needed to get my mind off it.

"Yeah, why the hell wouldn't I be," KJ asked, stretching out on the floor now.

"Ditto," I replied and Benji nodded his head.

"Your mom got anything to drink, fatass?" KJ asked, it was almost like he was reading my mind, *I need a drink.*

"Goddamn it! I'm not fat!" he squawked, "I'm pleasantly plump you ass holes just don't know the difference apparently AND I've been losing weight," he scoffed, "But yeah, there's the liquor cabinet above the microwave and fireball in her nightstand, she won't notice if any of it goes missing," he sighed answering KJ's question.

"You guys down?" I asked, looking around the room with raised eyebrows.

"Just because I said she wouldn't notice doesn't mean you get to get shitfaced and cry like you always do you alcoholic little bitch," he stated so matter of factly.

"Shut up, your fetal alcohol syndrome doesn't go unnoticed," I scowled.

"Now that was just uncalled for!" he yelled.

"Can you two shut up? Just because Kia's not here doesn't mean we need someone else in place to fight Thatcher," KJ groaned flinging himself into an upright sitting position. "I'm down, so I'll be mixing myself a drink if you need me," he made his way off the food heading to the kitchen. "Marshal I know what you like, Thatcher?"

"Just grab me a beer out of the fridge."

"Mhm'k what about you Benji Babes?" KJ asked, but the moment the words left his mouth his eyes went wide and face a deep crimson.

"Benji babes? What the fuck?" Thatcher started laughing. I looked over at Benji who looked like a deer in the headlights.

"It's- it's cute, KJ," he nervously laughed, "but uh- I think I'm good for right now," he smiled. KJ fled to the kitchen and Thatcher was still giggling on the floor like a hyena. KJ came back a moment later drinks in hand and handed them out to each of us refusing to look Benji in the eye.

"Goddamn this is not how I excepted today to go at fucking all," I said with a drawn-out sigh.

"I just want one normal day," KJ grumbled in agreeance.

"Well, I think it's kind of fun. I mean, sure, this town is pretty fucked up, but at least it's never boring," Benji added.

"But boring is good, the alcoholics over there make a good point our lives are like some shitty loosely related cartoon adventure that probably isn't going to end until we move out of this shit hole," Thatcher interjected, another hum of agreement. KJ disappeared into the kitchen only to reappear momentarily, drinks in hand.

The argument between Benji and Thatcher long forgotten as we contently sat together, resuming the show we had paused before Kia left. My stomach twisted thinking of him and how he was doing. I took a large gulp trying to cover the cough resulting from my unprepaed sip. I basically outed him to his mom and it was pretty much my fault he was about to get beheaded by his mom. I quickly fished my drink.

"KJ? Another, please?" I asked, shaking the empty glass.

"Yeah yeah, I got you," he took the glass and headed to the kitchen.

"Wait, just bring me the bottle. Fuck glasses," KJ turned his head to the side squinting at me but shrugged anyway returning with a mostly full bottle of whiskey. It was the cheap stuff that tasted like ass but I wasn't going to complain about it, alcohol was alcohol, and cheap or expensive it would still give me the warm buzz that would make life feel a little fuzzier. The deeper I drank the worse I felt, how could I have been so fucking stupid? He didn't deserve this. *I'm such a goddamn fuck up, I can't keep a fucking relationship. My mom left because she fucking hates my dad and me, Winnie hates me, and now Kia's going to fucking hate me. I'm just fucking like him goddamn it.*

• XLIX •

KIA

My eyes fixed on my house. Thirty-nine feet. The was the distance roughly between each side of the neighborhood. I stood on the edge of the sidewalk. Thirty-nine feet. That distance had always seemed so insignificant, so short, and I had always taken it for granted. For fifteen years, almost every day, I walked that thirty-nine feet thinking nothing of it, across the street, the brief distance between my house and the other's. Thirty-nine feet. It wasn't enough, the short distance seemingly impossible short.

I stood on the edge of the sidewalk for what felt like an eternity, contemplating walking out into the street without looking. Hopefully maybe if I was lucky if god and mosses were on my side, and in situations like this they often weren't, maybe some dumbass on his phone would run me down. The walk I had taken for granted, running across the street to meet up with the guys, playing with the neighborhood kids in elementary school, chasing each other around the streets playing superheroes or police, where we set up street hockey, now it all felt like a walk of fucking shame.

Not only did I straight up ignore my mother, but forty-seven also missed calls and over one hundred text messages enough to already sentence me to death, she now knew the deep-seated secret I kept so close to myself that I had only come to realize it recently. Thoughts of conversations with my mother concerning my future ran through my head. Get good grades, join clubs, sports, and activities, create an impressive resume, get into a good college, get a degree, become a doctor, get married to a nice Jewish woman, have a couple of kids, and carry on the family name.

Marry a woman. *A woman.* Not a man. Have kids, give my mother maybe a couple of grandsons or daughters. She made it very clear she didn't have a preference and despite only being a child she talked an obsessive amount about having a daughter-in-law that she would bond with, go wedding dress shopping with, and do all the things she wanted to do that she didn't get to do with her two sons. The idea of having grandchildren, a son to carry on the family name, that she would spoil and fawn over passing on some kind of motherly knowledge to my wife in this whole overwhelming fantasy. Of course, this all applied to Peter as well, but she made it painfully apparent to me, the first born how she was excited that *I* would be the one to give it all to her.

Would she be mad? Would she yell and scream at me for ruining her perfect world? Would they do everything in their power to try and get me away from Marshal? From any boy?

My chest tightened, my breathing becoming almost irractice I continued turning around and running back Into Thatcher's house hiding there for probably the rest of my natural life, It would be the last place my mom would look for me but in reality, she would end up checking there. I laughed to myself, the sound coming out as a surprise to me barking almost, loud disrupting my thoughts. Never in my life did I think that Thatcher's house, Addison fucking Thatcher, never in my life would I have thought that his house would be my safety. It was truly laughable. *God, I'm fucked.*

I didn't turn around fighting every instinct I had and instead took a deep breath and stepped one foot onto the street. A second foot. The first in front of the other. Each step closed the distance between my refuge in the Thatcher's residence and whatever hellfire was awaiting me at home—thirty-nine feet, not long enough of a distance. I stood on my front doorstep like I had done a million times beforehand, a million times I reached out to open that door but now it was like I was stuck. My arm wouldn't move and my heart pounded in my chest surely loud enough that everyone could hear it. The house I had called home for the entirety of my life, now suddenly didn't feel like home.

I made a move to reach for the doorknob, my arm heavy like it was made out of lead, my hand gripped clumsily onto the door handle; *how the fuck do you open a door again??* musscule memory kicked in and my wrist made a turning motion and the door slowly creaked open I forced one leg into the threshold and then the other.

"Hello?" I cracked out surprised my mother wasn't standing in the doorway with steam coming out of her ears waiting for me.

"Kia?!" a shirke from the kitchen responded. within what could only be an inhumane amount of time, my mother was staring me down; *how did she even get here that fast I didn't even blink and she just appeared.*

"H-hi Ma," I tried to say casually, breathing evenly, trying to make it look like I wasn't literary about to piss my pants. Her pudgy face was twisted into a look that could only be described as motherly rage. Her eyes squinted narrowing in at me attempting to make eye contact that I couldn't hold, green eyes burning on green eyes. Her frown lines are deep and visible her cheeks are angry red.

I closed my eyes and leaned my head up, *God? Are you there? It's me Kia Schwartz and I'm sure you're a nice guy and all but I don't want to meet you yet give me a couple of years then you can strike me down or whatever but for now, just don't let her kill me okay?* I uttered by silent prayer if it could even be considered that.

"Kia Mathew Schwartz!" she yelled, snapping my attention back to the current situation.

"Yeah, Ma?" I attempted to cough, clear my throat to make my words come out less drenched in fear but it failed as my voice still came out small and shirll.

"Yeah, Ma?" she said mockingly, "That's all you have to say for yourself?! Where have you been?! What is the matter with you, young man!?" she started yelling I slightly cringed at the shrillness of her voice.

She grabbed me by the ear continuing her tangent and dragged me to the kitchen where my dad sat at the table reading a paper.

"Do you have any idea what you've put me through?! Put *us* through?! You didn't answer my messages or my calls! What is the point of you having a phone if you're just going to blow me off hanging around with those good-for-nothing social security moochers in that making?! At least Marshal had the decency to answer his phone even if he didn't for his own mother! Is that where you get it? Thinking ignoring your mother is okay because Marshal does it?!"

"Ow! Ow! Ow!" I muttered as she sat me into a chair releasing my ear. I rubbed gently at my ear with the heel of my hand, she hadn't taken me by the ear since I was like nine at the most.

"I got a very awful phone call today from Mrs. Langdon today Kia, anything you want to say about that?" She sat crossed from me. My dad folded his paper putting it down now looking at me his expression calm as ever compared to my mother who was fuming and vibrating with anger. Rather than answer, I looked down my hands neatly folded in my lap and I started to scrape the nail of my index finger against my thumbnail cutital trying to peel back at it.

"Kia, your mother asked you a question," he said in a stern but even-toned voice.

"No," I mumbled before clearing my throat to speak up again, "No, ma'am what about it?"

"God, I hate when you mumble, Kia but I hate it even more when you play dumb. You're a very smart boy with a bright future ahead of you, and you need to start acting like it," his voice was eerily calm now I looked up meeting her eyes, but they still burned with rage. "I don't want you to be around that boy anymore it seems everywhere you two go, trouble always follows, and Marshal is at the center of it."

"BUT MA-"

"Kia, what have I told you about interrupting your mother?" My dad intervened and I closed my mouth still hanging open and looked down at my hands once again, my nails continuing to scrape at loose skin. My cheeks felt red and my throat was starting to burn a little.

"I see how that boy treats his parents and now how you've treated me today? Kia this morning Mrs. Langdon called me or rather she'd be Ms. Kern now, all that besides. She called me today to tell me about a fight Marshal and Jerry had. She had said that Marshal yelled at Jerry, which first of all is appalling enough; the boy would even talk to his father like that even if his father is Jerry Langdon, but he yelled at him that you two boys were in a homosexual relationship and do you have any idea how upsetting that was to hear? And then you didn't answer the phone?"

"Ma, I-"

"Kia enough! I wasn't done talking!" she huffed at me, and I swallowed the lump in my throat, wishing I could sink down into my chair so far that I could just disappear. "The phone is a whole other issue but right now we need to focus on the bigger issues," she deeply inhaled steadying herself. "Now Kia I know that boy has issues, and I know he always has to rebel in some way but that rebelling shouldn't be taking you down with him. The audacity of that boy for dragging your name down in the dirt! The way he just accused you of that! You know it's a sin, Kia have we taught you nothing?!" she threw her hands up in frustration.

"Mother!" I yelled firmly, pounding my fist on the table. My dad's eyes widened slightly with his surprise.

"Kia Ma-" I cut her off quickly.

"No Mama it's my turn to talk!" my voice shook, I don't know what had come over me but I grew the balls I lacked to stand up for myself against my mother. Both my parents looked beyond shocked at my random outburst. "First of all, you have no idea what you're talking about! Marshal is going through a lot and he's not a bad person he's just hurting because his entire family is being torn apart and now you want to tear away the only person who's constantly been there for him for the entirety of his life?! What's wrong with *you*?! I've always been there for him, and I always will be! You can't take us away from each other no matter what you think or how bad of an influence you think he is! Marshal is smart, and caring and kind, he's so sweet and he's handsome, and a nice guy, he's nice to me and damn it he needs me! I need him!" Tears welled in my eyes my voice getting caught in my throat the words suddenly became scrambled and fuzzy.

"Kia, that's enough," my father said sternly.

"No! I'm not done! He isn't just 'rebelling,' and he's not dragging me down with him. What the hell is that even supposed to mean? I was so scared to tell you guys because this is exactly how you'd react I knew it! I was in denial for so long about being gay that it took me years to even accept that all because you guys are insane and try to micro-manage my life! and god forbid I do anything that doesn't fit into the perfect little life you've made for me! I'm still me, guys! I'm still Kia! Why does it fucking matter if I like a guy?" My voice was horace and I was crying now. "What the fuck is wrong with you guys?" I uttered breathlessly before falling back onto my chair, wiping at my eyes. The room was silent; nothing else was said until a couple of moments later.

"You know I don't like that language, Kia," my mother said deadpan. I looked up threw blurry eyes the rage my mother once was gone, blank, unreadable. My father's even expression was now something softer and concerned. I wanted to laugh out of everything I had just yelled. She picks the fact that I said 'fuck' to respond to?

"Do you really feel that way?" my dad asked my mom, and I both turned in surprise.

"What? Gay?" I asked annoyed crossing my arms across my chest.

"Do you actually feel like that or is Marshal telling you to feel like that?" my father reworded his question and I couldn't help the almost psychotic laugh that escaped between my lips.

"I have loved Marshal since we were like ten, and I tried not to I really did. I tried to like girls because Ma over here always talking about how I'll be the first one to give her a daughter-in-law and how being gay is a sin, so I tried too hard for everyone just to stop," the wetness in my eyes started to come back only this time not out of anger. "So yes, I do fucking feel like this and no, it's not because Marshal feels it too, which he does. It's not just a way to rebel, Mamma."

"I already told you once about the language Kia," she glared.

"I think it's more important to focus on the literal identity crisis I was having for years that took a serious toll on my mental health rather than what words I say," I grunted in frustration.

"How long have you felt that Kia?" my mother asked, still stone cold. Her sudden shift in tone made me want to start screaming at her. It wasn't fair that she could just do that. It gave me emotional whiplash to be around that woman.

"I don't know! Okay? and don't even try to say 'oOh YoU cOuLd HaVe jUsT tAlkEd To Us' because no I couldn't have!"

"Kia your mother and I ar-" my dad started but I made a motion with my hand to science him.

"Don't even start because look at us! I was terrified to talk to you guys about this! I barely started understanding it myself and if It wasn't for Jerry being such a piece of shit drunken idiot then we wouldn't be here. Coming out is a hard prosses and it took forever for Marshal and I to figure it out ourselves but thank god we had each other because neither of our parents would have been good support," I sighed pinching the bridge of my nose and inhaling before continuing. "Do you even know what the fight was about?" I paused, and neither parent made a motion. "Jerry was blubbering some hateful shit and Marshal wanted to defend me because everything we feel is genuine! This isn't a phase. He isn't using me. He loved me, and I love him! And he didn't mean to out me but he did and this is how you guys reacted? This is why I was so scared to tell you guys! I don't think if it wasn't for today I would have ever done it!"

"Kia... *Beibi* we're sorry," My mother began but I just rolled my eyes and muttered a 'whatever' under my breath not in the mood.

"I was terrified, Mom, terrified of you and you're reaction," I pointed an accusatory finger and my mom looked genuinely hurt but I didn't care I could have relished in that feeling.

"Kia we still need to talk about how unacceptable it was for you to just ignore your phone like you did," My father spoke up in a stern voice yet again.

"Yeah let's talk about how I was terrified to answer the phone because I knew this is what was waiting for me! Yeah, let's talk about it!"

"Kia you made your point enough of the adutide. This is childish, Kia really."

"I don't think I did, though, Dad! I didn't want to go home or answer my phone because I was scared of my parents reacting to a fundamental part of me! I was so scared to be myself because I thought it was wrong! I thought there was something wrong with me and now that I finally FINALLY have come to accept that my biggest fear was my parents not accepting that and that fear isn't too far out because look how you two reacted? I was scared because I honestly thought my life was over! Don't you realize how fucked that is?! I'm not sitting here any longer and I'm not going to deal with whatever bullshit punishment you're going to deal out!" I declared and stood up out of the kitchen chair, storming away. It had been a while, the sky started to darken and was patined with the colors of the setting sun.

I stormed back across the street that thirty-nine feet feeling more bearable but still not long enough. There still wasn't enough distance between my parents and myself, I wasn't scared anymore, just angry. Maybe they'll get their shit together and it'll all be okay but until they can get the sticks out of their asses I'm staying the fuck away from them. My body was shaking as I was coming down from the high of standing up against my parents. As I knocked on the door the wave of aftermath washed over me, realizing that I yelled at my parents, cursed at them, and stormed out. I didn't regret anything I said or did but I absolutely could have handled it better and now they actually had a reason to be mad at me.

· L ·

MARSHAL

"Yeah, he does kind of look funny?"

"Oh god! I know that face! He's going to puke!"

Voices were talking around me pully me from my dreamy state of mind

"Marsh! Marshal, I swear to god if you throw up on my couch!" Thatcher was yelling at me. I had zoned out with a bottle on the couch slumped over being held upright by three sets of hands.

"Kia?" I mumbled out, why was he mad at me again?

"No dumbass it's Thatcher! Now get up and go sit in the bathroom so it's easier to clean up after you!"

"Clean up?" My train of thought wasn't staying and comprehending what they were saying to me was taking too much effort. The sudden swirl of nausea hit me, bile from my stomach jumping up my throat and both my hands flew over my mouth in an attempt to stop what was happening. The bile reached my mouth I had calmed shut effectively preventing it from spewing everywhere and I heavily swallowed grimacing.

"Ew! Get him out of here!" Thatcher squealed.

"Sh-shut up Thatcher, you sound like a little girl screaming," I slurred out. Thatcher was sitting directly in front of me, large hands planted firmly on my chest, and KJ and Benji were on each side of me each gripping an arm. I shook my head back and forth between the three of them making myself dizzy. Wide-eyed I looked at KJ Right now he seemed like the only person I could trust. I pulled away from the other two sets of hands and latched onto him.

"Why's he mad?" I slurred out gripping onto his sweatshirt.

226

"Who buddy?" KJ asked softly.

"K, he's mad at me, he fucking hates me," tears brimmed in my eyes.

"No Marsh, Kia doesn't hate you," Benji's voice answered from behind me a hand reaching out to gently rub my back but I arched away from it like his touch was burning.

"Little B, just let me take care of him, he gets all weird when he's like this okay?" KJ asked an apologetic look on his face. KJ reached his arm around me so his hand was under my arm and he lifted us off the couch, my body heavily leaning on his. "Let's get you some fresh air dude," he said leading me to the back door. I groaned swaying into KJ heavily and he mumbled something under his breath I didn't catch probably some curses as he struggled to drag me along with him. The sun was setting. When did it get so late? The fog in my brain leaves me without a sense of time. I leaned into KJ tightly squeezing my eyes shut.

"He's gonna be so mad," I blubbered again more words came out almost incoherent.

"Marsh he doesn't hate you he loves you and you dumbasses have loved each other far longer than either of you is going to admit to," he sighed with his supporting arm still around me giving a reassuring squeeze.

"He won't love me anymore," I mumbled, my words feeling heavy caught in my throat.

"Yeah, he will."

"No KJ he'll fucking hate me and you don't get it because look at the example you have, you don't even know your actual dad and your dad hates you because your mom cheated and she hates him and you," My words came out slurred but confident.

"Dude shut up," his face tightened into a displeased scowl.

"You'll never get it because everyone says you'll be just like them! And you'll be a fuck up like me you won't get it." KJ sucked in his cheeks pulling in a sharp breath before he let it out slowly closing his eyes like he was trying to center himself.

"Marshal, dude, chill the fuck out this isn't about me, this is about you and I promise Kia doesn't hate you." I pulled away from his support almost stumbling over my own feet as I tried to find my balance.

Standing still wasn't working for me so I settled for shifting back and forth between my footing.

"You don't want to be a fuck up like me because he does hate me and I fucked up and I lost my best friend and the guy I love because I can't think before I fucking open my big fat mouth." KJ just rolled his eyes but I thought of something making my lips curl upward into a smile broad and toothy with lidded eyes the kind that only comes from someone with as much alcohol in their bloodstream as me.

"Dude talk to Kia so maybe he can fucking tell you what I've been telling you all along," KJ said annoyance heavy in his tone.

"Yeah, whatever," I was dizzy and wanted to go back inside, it was too hot the air thick and sticky. I stumbled slightly before less than gracefully sat down next to Benji. There was plenty of room on the couch, Thatcher having situated himself on the floor but I sat close enough to Benji that our thighs were touching.

"You feel better after having a smoke?" Addie asked and I just groaned.

"K-KJ's stupid, he doesn't get it. Just because my daddy issues aren't as bad as his doesn't mean it's not fucked up."

"What are you on about now?" Thatcher scowled.

"KJs' never gonna understand, he doesn't know what he's talking about. He's too stupid to get it because he's going to be just like them."

"My ears were burning, missed me?" KJ said announcing his reappearance with a smug smile.

"Fuck off you white trash wife beater in the making," I groaned. His face dropped, void of emotion but his fist clenched tightly and he clenched his jaw.

"He's just drunk ignore him," Benji intervened, but that didn't stop KJ from storming over to me, grabbing a fist full of my shirt and bringing us face to face, my smug smile never once wavering.

"That's it! That's fucking it, Marshal! I'm tired of your shit! What the fuck is wrong with you?!" KJ yelled, breath hot on my face. I cringed at the volume.

"Me? Wake up, KJ, and smell the fucking roses!"

"Jesus fucking Christ you're intolerable when you drink," KJ threw me back against the couch.

"KJ?" Benji reached out for KJ, gripping his bicep and he instantly relaxed into the touch. "He's just spouting off nonsense no need to get so defensive, he's drunk and I'm sure he doesn't mean it." KJ's body tenseed the rage coming back in full swing.

"Drunk words are sober fucking thought," He said between gritted teeth to Benji whose eyes widened like he was about to cry.

"God Benji," I laughed. "Are you going to fucking cry? This isn't even about you, like if you want it to be then fine! I got a lot of shit I can say about you!"

"I'm going to fucking kill you! What the fuck is wrong with you!" KJ barked between his teeth. He shoved hard against my chest making me almost fall backward onto the ground but I steadied myself.

"Well he's right about one thing," Thatcher mumbled.

"I'm going to fucking kill both of you!" the rage reanimated KJ now, "Addison Theodore Thatcher I'm going to knock your fucking teeth in for encouraging this shit! You don't know what the fuck you're talking about and shouldn't be encouraging this drunken idiot! God fucking damn it!"

"Whoa dude chill," I slurred.

"Don't fucking tell me to chill Marshal!" KJ balled his hand into a fist making to draw it back. Before he could do anything, however, a loud pounding on the door drew everyone's attention to the door now, Thatcher groaned lifting himself from the groan to open the door.

Kia stormed into the house, face red, seeming to be holding back tears. He pointed a stern finger at me, making a B-line to where I was standing.

"You!"

"Me?" I pointed to myself the fog suddenly whipped from my brain with the sudden shock of Kia's seemingly almost angry words. or word. But that fear was quickly melted away when he grabbed me by my cheek pulling me into a soft kiss. our lips parted and our foreheads rested against each other.

"I love you," he said in a small whisper. My breath caught in my throat as I felt the warm feeling of his words crawling up my throat. I smiled and kissed him back. It was sloppy but it was the best form of 'I love you' I could muster at the time. Kia leaned back whipping his mouth suddenly returning to the moment and his face lit up with the glow of an embarrassed blush.

"Sorry that was really dramatic, I'm just pissed off with my parents and I don't know what came over me," he mumbled looking at the ground.

"Well, you can always use me to take out your pent-up rage if you're going to do that, "I stupidly smiled, laughing as Kia's face got darker.

"Whoa," Kia stepped back and looked around, catching onto the room's high tension, " What's uh going on guys?"

"Control you're alcoholic little shit of a boyfriend," KJ grumbled giving Kia a harsh shoulder check and leaving out the front door, still dramatically thrown open from when Kia had burst through.

"Hey don't fucking take it out on him!" I yelled after KJ. Kia held his hands on my shoulders as if to hold me back or maybe hold me up, not like I would go after KJ anyway, but something about how coldly he treated Kia made me see nothing but red.

"KJ?? What? Marshal?" he turned a confused head between me and KJ leaving obviously raging still.

"Oh, *farshiltn!* KJ wait!" Benji scampered out the door after him slamming the door shut.

KIA

No one said anything, and I continued to whip my head between Marshal and the now-closed door, that KJ and Benji had just run out of.

"Dude! What the fuck was that?" I asked breaking the heavy silence.

"What just happened with KJ and Benji? And- godman it, Marshal! Why do you smell like a bar? Are you fucking real right now?" I huffed suddenly angry all over again but now it was all at Marshal. *Why can't you just have standard coping mechanisms?* I wanted to yell at him. I wanted to scream, be mad, why was he like this?

"All good questions...." Marshal said dumbly, his voice quiet and seemingly stuck in his throat as he forced out the words. The unfocused look in his eyes was almost hidden behind the shiny gleam of tears.

"Marshal, seriously, what the fuck did you do?" he sniffed, and the tears started falling. I pushed him away from me, the smell of cheap booze wafting off him, but Marshal quickly latched back onto me.

"I knew it! I knew it! I knew it! you fucking hate me!" Marshal gripped onto my arms sinking down to the floor and taking me with him.

"God damn drama queens, screw you guys, I'm going upstairs while you homos figure you're shit out," Thatcher groaned thudding up the stairs with dramatic thumps.

"Marsh," I brushed back his hair from over his forehead where it stuck, trying to hush him. "Marshal honey what? I don't hate you... I could never dude, you're like my best friend, you're like my other part dude, you're my boyfriend, I love you."

"But I fucked up!" he wailed before thudding his face into my chest heaving.

231

"You didn't fuck up..." I gently rubbed his back while his shoulder continued to rise and fall shakily with his ragged heaves.

"I did! I outed you and now you're mad at you're parents and they're mad at you! And KJ hates me too!" He choked into my shirt the cries getting louder. I had been here too many times before. Marshal sobbing on the floor into my chest, Dunkley claiming that he's a fuck up and/or he fucked up and everyone hates him.

"What happened with KJ?"

"I was- god Kia, I'm a terrible person. I fucking brought up his family," he sobbed

I rubbed his back therapeutically, "Yeah dude that's really fucked up, and we've fucking talked about this Marshal, drinking isn't a fucking solution. You need to stop."

"I'm sorry, I'm sorry, I'm sorry," he muttered between sobs. We sat there in Thatcher's living room, him clenching onto me like if he loosened his grip I'd disappear and I gently rubbed his back, sometimes running my fingers threw his hair until his sobbs slowed down, his uneven choppy breathing evening out and like many times before he had drunkenly cried himself to sleep. I stood up on shaking legs having fallen asleep while Marsh's body weight was passed into me on the floor stuck in a less than ideal position for who knows how long. I hoisted his limp body up with me, dropping him on the couch. If it wasn't for the slight groan that escaped his lips you might have thought he was dead, but at last, he shifted to get comfortable, an unpleasant frown plastered on his lips. I made my way upstairs to Thatcher's room. The day's events finally settled in and I was exhausted, drained from such an eventful day and it was a type of exhaustion that was deep in my bones rooted into my body that sleep wouldn't fix.

"Hey? Thatcher?" I tapped on his door.

"What's up, khoser boy?"

"Stop calling me that would you?" I groaned with annoyance fully opening the door. Thatcher sat at his desk in front of his computer headset playing World Of Warcraft, it'd been a long while since we all got together and played that game and I smiled at the memories it provoked.

"Sorry, what I meant to say was; Why are you still in my house you Cheeto?"

"Why can't anyone around here ever act fucking normal?" I barrier my face in my hands not wanting to deal with Thatcher's shit.

Thatcher snorted, "That's hilarious, really Kia. Maybe Jews are funny, when has anything about anyone living in this fucked up town been normal?" Unfortunately, he had a point.

"I'm still here because my boyfriend is passed out on your couch and well both of our parents are being dicks this is..." What I was about to say made my eye twitch as I struggled to say, "This is the safest place right now." It came out gurgled and quiet not wanting to admit it out loud.

"I'm sorry, could you repeat that one more time?" he asked with a smug look.

"You heard what I said, I'm not saying it again, and I never will, don't gloat."

"Oh come on!" he protested.

"Thatcher!"

"Fine, whatever fucking fire crotch," he mumbled.

"For the love of god! Stop with the name-calling! God how old are you fucking nine?!?" I snapped. Thatcher's only response was a snarky laugh at my expense seeing how upset I got.

"So lover boys staying over obviously, and I guess you are too?"

"...Yeah."

"Just don't fuck in my house, if not for me think of the children," Thatcher glared at me.

"The children- the fuck?"

"Bow Tie the cat, you dense moron."

"God you and that fucking cat," I sighed smiling and Thatcher's lips morphed into his own smile.

"So what happened with your mom? I take it shit didn't go well?" it was weird hearing Thatcher being concerned. Sure it was hidden under a thick layer of insults and sarcasm but he did genuinely care deep down.

"No, it- uh it didn't. I'm gonna lay low for a couple of days, I turned my phone off sure my parents are probably blowing it up, I kinda stormed out on them after I cussed at them, threw a fucking tantrum, and just yeah..."

"Holy shit... You yelled back? The world is coming to an end! Kia fucking Shwartz went head to head with the world's biggest bitch!" Thatcher shouted. I elbowed him in the ribs swiftly.

"Ow! You fucking sneaky ass little bitch boy!"

"Don't call my mom a bitch Thatcher!"

"Whatever I do what I want!"

"Shut up!" our yelling quickly turned into sizing each other up and some shoving but we soon lost interest before it could really break out into a fight. Thatcher and I played some games together upstairs online for a while, it was getting late, and the day just seemed to never end.

"How you heard from Benji?" he asked me.

"No, have you?"

"Why do you think I'm asking you?"

"So I take that as a no?"

"Look at that, you're learning," he gave a stupid grin and I flicked him on the forehead.

"So what went down? I didn't get much out of Marshal."

"Oh yeah, he got all fucked up, yelling you hated him and you know Marshal, everything shit and everyone's shit so he has to drag them down to his level."

"Oh..." it was all I could muster to say, scratching my brain for any kind of response. "Thatcher?"

"Yeah?"

"Do you think Marshal needs help?"

"*Pfft*, remember the last time you suggested he get help?"

"Yeah, he almost knocked my fucking teeth out?"

"He's in denial dude, wait for something to really go to shit before he realizes it's a problem, let him figure it out himself."

"But... isn't that kind of cruel?"

"He literally beat the shit out of you, no letting his own actions bite him in the ass isn't cruel," Thatcher responded, his face pinched into an expression that said, 'duh'.

· LII ·

MARSHAL

My head pounded, as to be expected. I dragged the back of my hand across my forehead wiping away the sweat that had accumulated. It was a restless sleep, tossing and turning, my body too hot and my mind scattered trying to process the events of yesterday coming out in the form of weird dreams. My body felt heavy, my chest hurt like someone was standing on it but it was just me alone, on Thatcher's couch, drenched in sweat. I didn't sleep well, tossing and turning, and now being awake there was a weird pain in my neck and back I'll blame on sleeping on the couch.

The pressure in my chest slightly decreased as I sat up looking around. From the kitchen, I could hear the back and forth between two voices. I rubbed my temples trying to dig up a coherent thought. Yesterday; I yelled at my dad, K and I went to Thatcher's, his mom had been calling him nonstop, and he left to go talk to her, I started drinking, and then KJ was upset with me. *Where was KJ?* The thought accrued to me now realizing neither of the murmuring voices flowing in from the kitchen belonged to the scrawny blonde. The voices I was hearing belonged to Thatchers and when I focused more on listening, Kia? *He was still here?* The voices were quiet enough that I wasn't able to hear what they were saying so at least that meant for once fatass and Kia were getting along which was a relief, for the sake of my throbbing headache at least.

But where's KJ? Why was he mad? I did something, I don't remember. I was drinking. Kia had left, and I was drinking because Kia left so why did KJ get mad? I sat on the couch head in my hands almost on my knees with my eyes scrunched tightly trying to wrack my brain for any kind of answer.

"Pennywise! Sleeping beauty's up!" Addie's thick voice cut through my thoughts. I cringed at his volume.

"Can you stop fucking calling me that! I swear to fuck I'm going to knock your teeth in Thatcher!" I heard him before I saw him as Kias's higher voice rang out from the kitchen.

"Morning princess, how's that head?" Thatcher asked with an artificially sweet voice and mocking tone.

"Shut up dude, that's how," I scowled as Thatcher burst out laughing and began his regularly scheduled tyrant of teasing.

"Ha! You're hungover you alcoholic!"

I smacked him in the thigh, " it's too early for your bullshit Thatcher," I grumbled.

"Early? Marshal, it's fucking 3 pm," Kia now stood in front of me, hands on his hips giving me a look my mom would give me.

"Shit, okay," I steadily raised myself up off the couch stretching. I stood up on my toes cracking my ankles stretching my hands high above my head scrunching my eyes shut in the process. When I opened my eyes Kia was staring at me with a goofy smile.

"What?" I asked cocking my head to the side confused.

"Nothing you're just really cute," he smiled and leaned in close to kiss the tip of my nose. We leaned against each other foreheads touching, and Kia's eyes fluttered shut. His face relaxed and for the first time in the last couple of days, he looked utterly one hundred percent at peace.

"Aye! I said you homos could stay over if you didn't start fucking in my house!" Thatchers interrupted the moment drawing us away from each other. Kia's face scrunched into an annoyed scowl directing his firey gaze to Thatcher.

"Would you fucking shut up!"

"Would you fucking stop being gay?!" Thatcher replied in a mocking tone. Kia grunted, balling his hands into fists by his side but before he could do much else I grabbed his shoulder and gave him a gentle squeeze. He turned around eyes softening.

"You guys made it like almost the entire day without killing each other how is it now that I'm awake, you're on the verge?" I asked with a soft smile on my lips.

"You're the common factor," Kia teased back giving a slight smirk. He started to lean into me again most likely for a kiss but I put my palm out to his face generally pushing him away laughing at his response to my action.

"Now we don't want to upset our host do we?" I laughed.

"Yeah I'll throw up if I have to watch any more of this," Thatcher rolled his eyes.

"I'm surprised you're still here," my statement was directed to Kia who raised an auburn eyebrow.

"Well yeah? I mean you were still here and I really don't want to go home. I turned off my phone because after I yelled at my parents and stormed out I just didn't want to deal with anything, you know?" he shrugged.

"Oh yeah that makes sense," I shrugged alongside him. I pulled Kia by the waist to me and fell back onto the couch, he let out a surprised squeak and I just laughed into his shoulder.

"Gay wads," Thatcher rolled his eyes sitting on the other side of Kia and me. We fell into a comfortable science the three of us, Thatcher scrolling on his phone, Kia and I leaning into each other pressed firmly into one another.

"So you yelled at your parents?" I was the first to break the silence we'd fallen into.

"Yeah, I came over and told you all what happened?" He turned to face me with a puzzled face until it looked like a lightbulb went off in his head before a saddened expression took over his face. "That's right you were drunk," he sighed.

"Yeah..." I swallowed, it was awkward now.

"Marsh you seriously have some issues, at least when KJ gets drunk he's funny. But you? You act like an ass and shit, or you start crying," Thatcher chimed in. I turned to face him now shooting a disapproving look.

"Fuck off you son of a crack whore," I shot back, Kia's brow furrowed. Thatcher's response was a sharp "aye!"

"No, Marshal seriously, I- I needed you, dude and you were drunk," he readjusted himself, shimming off my lap, sitting next to me now. Both he and Thatcher had turned to face me, and I looked between the two of them; this conversation had obviously been premeditated.

"Guys seriously, I'm fine," I folded my arms sinking down hoping the couch would just swallow me or something, anything but this.

"Marsh, you made KJ storm out," Thatcher reminded me.

"You know what? That's his issue then!"

"Yeah, it's his issues you basically told him he was human garbage, sure. You fucking told him he was going to end up just like his parents? That's cruel man," Thatcher raised an eyebrow crossing his arms.

"Wait- whAT?" K and I both said at the same time. Was that what upset him?

"Oh fuck, I knew- I knew he was upset but I couldn't- fuck!" I searched my pants pockets for my phone pulling it out quickly trying to turn it on only to be met with the dead battery symbol.

"Fuck!" I yelled again slamming my phone down. Internally I cringed, I didn't hear a crack but the force I threw it down with would still probably be enough to crack my screen even on Thatcher's thick living room carpet.

"Marsh," Kia used his hand to lift my chin up and make me face him. "Breath dude." I hadn't realized when my breath started to pick up, but my chest heaved. Kia led me through a breathing exercise until my chest heaving went down significantly.

"Okay, what's wrong?" he asked, his eyes soft and gentle.

"I- I should call him, but my fucking phone died," My throat burned as the panicked words flooded out. My brain was still foggy and with each word, it was like a throb of my head was being used to punchate. "K I need to use yours." Wordlessly Kia handed over his phone, powering it back on before handing it over to me. I didn't need him to put the password in, I knew it already. His phone's password had never changed since he had gotten his first phone in fourth grade. I carefully typed in my birthdate and was berated with an unholy amount of notifications, text messages, and missed calls from, his mom, dad, and even a couple from Peter.

I scrolled through his contacts smashing the call button, next to KJ's name. *One ring, two rings, three rings.* On and on until it stopped.

"Hey it's KJ, speak if you must," his curt voicemail message.

"Damn it," I sighed opting to text him. Quickly I typed out a message;

dude it's Marshal I'm srry, I fucked up call me or Kia, I'm srry. Please

It wasn't even a minute when the message read 'opened' and the three little typing dots came up, they quickly disappeared only to return again. It went on like this for a while before finally a message came through;

drunk words = sober thoughts

Another message.

better start groveling bitch

My fingers flew across the keyboard but ultimately I decided to hit the call button. The phone only rang once before it was denied and I got another message on Kia's phone

busy now ttyl.

I breathed out a heavy sigh of relief at least he was willing to talk to me.

"You good?" Kia asked.

"Yeah he said he'd call me later," I said in a breathy voice.

"So now that's all sorted out," Thatcher began.

"What Thatcher is trying to say," Kia cut him off and was given an offended look.

"Bitch I didn't even start let alone say anything," he folded his arms and gave a frustrated grunt.

"Marshal, you have a problem, and it's a problem because it's affecting other people. You managed to piss off KJ and that's not something easy to do," Thatcher nodded in agreement as Kia contained to speak. "He might be okay with you now but how many more times do you think he'll forgive you? How many times and I going to have to pick you up off the floor?"

"For the love of god Kia! It's fucking fine! I was just having a bad time!"

"You're always having a bad time," it was Thatcher's turn to speak now as he reentered the conversation. "Kia and I talked about this okay, because after last night when you passed out, it was just the two of us, and like dude, seriously. You're not even a fun drunk, at least KJ gets all stupid, and so does Cade when he's wasted but when I'm with you, it's like a mega bummer. You kind of kill the vibe Marshal and if you're 'just having a bad day' when you get like that then you have a whole other issue because it's like this all the fucking time."

I clenched my jaw tightly, my lips into a thin line of annoyance, *how many times was I going to have to defend myself like this in these half-assed interventions?* "How many other ways can I say it guys? I don't speak any other language!" I let out a forced laugh trying to ease the tension. "You're both fucking overreacting."

"No we're not dude, and I bet KJ would agree if only someone didn't fucking CHASE HIM AWAY!" Thatcher's voice rang out.

"You know what? I'm done with this, I don't have to listen to you guys bash me like this and try to convince me of something that's not even real!"

"God you're impossible!" Kia scolded. Thatcher just rolled his eyes and brought his phone back up to continue reading or watching whatever it was he had been originally doing before this 'intervention'.

"You know I didn't really think this would work but now you can't yell at me I never did anything for Marshy boy," Thatcher muttered. His voice was just loud enough that Kia caught it.

"And so are you! You're both impossible!" he yelled lunging over me to grab at Thatcher's shirt getting two big handfuls of fabric balled up into his fists and dragging Thatcher down, I was stuck in the middle of it all.

"Guys, guys, guys!" I yelled trying to use myself as a wedge between the two of them preventing an all-out brawl. "Fucking cool it!"

"Or what, Marsh? Huh? Are you going to fuck me up again? Like the last time I tried to talk to you out of genuine concern and you just fucking attacked me?!" Kia's voice quivered, and his eyes began to get glossy as they welled with tears threatening to overflow.

"Kia-" I reached out but he shrugged off my hand quickly standing up off the couch to get away from me.

"No Marshal, just forget it, destroy yourself or whatever," he huffed. The room was overtaken by a deafening silence. heavily words unspoken hung in the air between the three of us but mainly between Kia and me. *I don't have a fucking problem.* But seeing Kia standing turned away from me like that made me question myself a little bit, bringing back all that guilt from the night of the bonfire.

The only sound that broke out in the room was Kia's quiet sniffling until his phone rang out. I quickly shot up hoping it was KJ, eager to get the phone and speak to him. Kia pulled the phone from his pocket and wiped his nose on the back of his hand.

"It's not KJ, but I need to take it," he sighed and began to head out to the backyard through the kitchen.

· LIII ·

KIA

The conversation with Marshal left me feeling deflated, emptied out almost like our conversation had taken out part of my chest. My phone lit up the screen being overtaken by an incoming Facetime call from Peter. Talking to him was probably my least taxing option, between, Marshal and the countless missed calls from my parents I needed to talk to someone who wouldn't make me want to blow my brains out. I couldn't avoid it forever and Peter didn't really even know what was going on, he didn't deserve to be ignored, he deserved answers.

I swiped to answer the call, "Dude what the fuck! Ma's losing her mind what did you do?!"

"Well hi to you too Peter, I'm doing peachy thanks for asking," I rolled my eyes with a sly smile, "also don't say fuck."

"But seriously what the fuck happened? Wait- sorry sorry- what the fart's happened?" I couldn't help but burst out laughing.

"No, no please don't say that again 'What the farts?' Stop, fuck was better, say fuck please," I wheezed out

"Make up your mind Kia," he huffed but there was t much malice behind it. "You're dodging the question though."

I took a deep breath letting out a drawn-out sigh, "Yeah I kinda came out to ma? It really wasn't a coming out it was- you know what it doesn't matter how it happened it just matters that it happened. I've been avoiding them since our 'talk'," I put "talk" in air quotes as it seemed more like an interrogation and defense trial.

"So they know?"

"Yeah"

"Guess it didn't go great?"

242

"No, 'iTs A sIn'" I said in a tone mimicking my mothers high pitched voice.

"Oh, Jesus Christ on a bike and Mary on the handlebars!"

"Dude-" I sputtered out laughing trying to speak through it, "you say... the weirdest shit! What the hell was that?! Mary on the handlebars?! Oh fuck I think I'm going to piss myself!" I grabbed at my side the painful side stitch from laughing forming. It was so stupid but it was what I needed. Too much heavy shit had gone down and it's like Peter knew I needed this. God I love the kid.

"I don't think mom meant it tho, Kia you should really talk to her she's like super upset," Peter's voice had a hint of pleading to it.

Hearing that made my mood shift the fast it's ever changed, "yeah whenever she apologizes to me," I rolled my eyes.

"Dude you know she gets all heated and says a bunch of crazy shit she doesn't mean," Peter tried to defend. "She's been acting all moody Kia, like last night she was like crying? I mean Ma cries a lot but I think she felt bad. I knew you guys fought, shit I heard it but didn't really hear what it was about. I think she knows she was wrong, I don't know she and Dad are all whispery with each other." he said in a questioning tone before continuing on.

"It's freaking me out they don't act like this, all secret. You know how dad is, he wants to be upfront with us about everything, he wants us to grow up adapted and he thinks we should know everything, so you could understand why him not telling me shit is freaking me out!"

It was laughable, Mom being wrong? The Ruthann Schwartz? Wrong? It was in fact so ridiculous that I couldn't help the giggles that did end up escaping my throat. "I'll believe it when I see it," I grumbled after I killed my slight giggles. "Peter they're probably talking about disowning me or something I doubt she feels bad, just listen I'm sorry they aren't telling you things but what you need to know is they know I'm gay, they know I'm in a relationship with Marshal, and they think I'm just being 'influenced' by him! Whatever the hell that means!" I huffed in frustration.

"Kia I just- wait! Hold up! Back the fuck up dude! Marshal and you?" His mouth hung open in shock. It took a minute for the shock to wear off he blinked dumbly, "You can't just drop something like that on me! ...Damn I own Craig money now," he murmured but loud enough that I could still hear it.

"Wait! Craig?! Like Craig Martinez?!" It was my turn to have my mouth hung open in shock.

"Well yeah, what other Craigs do we know?" He shrugged so causally.

"Why do you owe Craig money?!"

"Because he said you were gay and would end up with Marshal, I said you'd end up with KJ, felt like he'd be the one to pull you out of the closet, you know with some experimentation," he wiggled his eyebrows at me.

"Oh my god! Peter Issac Schwartz! That's so fucking- UGH!"

He just shrugged while I continued to make an assortment of baffled noises. The fucking audacity of this kid!

"When did- you and Craig?! When? Why? Fucking how?!" I couldn't form a coherent sentence.

"I went over to Dezzie's house, you know his sister? for a social studies project and he said, 'Are you Schwartz's little brother?' So I said yeah and he said, 'You know; gay know gay and man does Kia look familiar, guess it's not a family trait,' and then I told him I don't think you'd come out until KJ tired to fuck around and find out. He said no way, it'd be Marsh you've been pining so hard," Ike just shrugged.

"Oh my fucking god! This shit is unbelievable!"

"Yeah it's only 20 bucks but still I could have used that!"

"No the fact you bet against me with Craig fucking Martienz! Oh my god!" I got over my initial shock and started to laugh, "fuck it I'm never coming home now," I laughed.

"Oh come on that's no fair!" Ike laughed with me. We both died down and settled catching our breath. "So you and Marshal hun? I mean I guess I can see it makes sense."

"Yeah he makes a lot of sense to me," I smiled dumbly thinking about Marshal, he was perfection, and he completed me. For a moment I forgot about everything that happened that morning. I forgot about the conversation Thatcher and I had planned to talk to him about his drinking, I forgot about how mad he god, how defensive he got, and only thought about those beautiful ocean eyes. I could only think about the way his face crinkled so perfectly when he smiled wide, a toothy off-white smile that was so genuine it made my heart jump. "He's just... he's my world, like the oxygen I breathe I don't think I'd be able to survive without him," I said dreamily. "He's always been there and we've always been us but like now it's different... it's just so much more."

"... Ew that's hella gay," Peter rolled his eyes dramatically.

"Peter!" Leave it to him to ruin my moment, but after all, that's what little shits of brothers are supposed to do, it was on me anyway for getting any form of venerable with him.

"Ki-" Peter was cut off by a high-pitched voice.

"PETER!" A shrillness and volume that could only be achieved by my mom, "Who are you talking to? I asked you to put the laundry away twenty minutes ago!"

"Sorry ma! I was just getting to it."

"No, you weren't you little delinquent! It's like that thing is super glued to your hand! Turn it off! Right now!" She demanded and before I could even say anything the screen went dark.

"...Bye" I mumbled to no one.

⋆ LIV ⋆

MARSHAL

"Duuuuudeeeee," I groaned laying flat on the floor, hands coving my face with my fingers tugging at my hair slightly. "God I'm a fucking idiot! I was such a dick head."

"Goddamn it Marshal, I really don't want to hear you wallow in self-pity right now," Thatcher grunted on the couch. He was taking up most of the sofa and I had sunk down to the floor, so I was physically almost as low as I felt emotionally.

"Why am I like this? God Kia probably does actually hate me now," I groaned again. "Wait!" I shot up into an upright position, tugging at my hair, "what if he breaks up with me? God, I'd fucking deserve it."

"Marshal! Get a fucking grip, Jesus," he hissed at me. "Your Marshal and Kia, you guys, whether you admit it or not, have been super boyfriends since like the beginning of times trust me when I say Kia wouldn't dump you. Trust me I've tried to convince him to get rid of your alcoholic ass. Which brings me to my next point; you fucking ARE an alcoholic, and your 'like this', because of every minor inconvenience you throw yourself a pity party and drink yourself into early liver failure. I'm all for watching people's downfalls but yours isn't fun or my doing, it's just sad and gross."

"Goddamn it! I'm not an alcoholic!" I yelled my head throbbing at the effort to raise my voice.

"Whatever Marshal, the jew rat isn't going to leave you that's all I'm saying, actually for some reason he cares so much about your twink ass it's disgusting."

"Ew never call me a twink again," I grimaced. "And Hey! Don't call my boyfriend a 'jew rat' you tub of lard!"

246

"Just calling them like I see them no need to attack me!" he shrugged in defiance.

"I really hate you," I said deadpan to him.

"Yeah yeah love you too or whatever," he just leaned forward to flick me in the head.

"Oh fuck off," I shook my head, "your such an ass Thatcher."

"It's my job," he snuggly smiled. I smiled and got up off the floor making my way to the kitchen.

"Where are you going?"

"Kitchen, need something?"

"Yeah, there's a bag of cheesy poofs in the cabinet I'm gonna turn something on to watch and I feel weird if I'm not eating when I'm watching TV."

"Then damn if not eating makes you feel weird you must feel weird all the time you fat fuck," I chuckled.

"AYE! Don't fucking call me fat!" He whined but I continued laughing making my way to the kitchen. Above the skin were two windows that looked out onto Thatcher's back patio where Kia was on FaceTime pacing back and forth, I watched as he grabbed at his side laughing. God, I'd kill to hear him laugh just all the time, it is the sweetest sound in the world. I opened the fridge and took a beer from a twelve-pack in the refrigerator before taking Thatcher his snacks. I cracked the can open with my teeth and took a long gulp. I needed something to distract me, give me a comfortable fog, and lift me up slightly from all the tensions around me. Everything had been so heavy recently why can't we just have some light-hearted fun, no drama or threats of inillation against us?

"What are we watching?" I asked when I came back into the kitchen.

"Dunno yet, haven't decided," Thatcher mumbled clicking threw Netflix. He gave a side glance before snapping his head back to me.

"What?"

"Dude.... You have got to be shitting me," his face blank and eyes narrowed.

"*What?*" I asked again.

"Marsh, you are unbelievable," he scoffed.

"Do I look like a mind reader?" I scoffed back, plopping down next to him on the couch.

"Never mind you dense moron, have you heard from KJ?"

"No... he said he'd call me later."

"Oh..." an unsteady silence formed between us the only sound just the clicking of remote buttons as Thatcher searched for something to watch. For once in our lives, Addison Thatcher seemed to have nothing left to say.

"We could watch The Walking Dead?" I suggested, unnerved by the quiet. Silence like this made my skin itch.

"Fuck no, that shows hella lame, and so are you for watching it," Thatcher groaned but with a trace of a smile on his lips. I threw a light elbow at him.

"Shut up, I don't see you making up your mind any time soon," he threw an elbow back.

"Here," he stopped on a show, "how about hoarders? I've watched it all already, but It's a show all about you. I've fucking seen your room. *Unlike* you, I don't watch the same shows over and over again," Thatcher laughed.

"You suck Thatcher like so much," I laughed.

"Okay but seriously, is this okay?" Thatcher had clicked on a show.

"What is it?"

"Exactly what the title says, Two-sentence horror stories," Thatcher rolled his eyes.

"They made a show based on a Reddit threat?"

"Fuck off, dude," he shoved me over on the couch, and we both just laughed before he hit play. With the sound of the TV playing it was more comfortable to not be talking. Neither of us really paid attention to the show. It was precisely as Thatcher had described it, a sentence would come up, and then some kind of 'horror' story is played before seeing the last part of the sentence. Thatcher kept sneaking glances at me as if he wanted to say something but never did.

"I'm getting another beer, want anything else while I'm up?' I asked, rising from the couch where I'd been plastered on my side somewhere between laying down and sitting up, never moving from when Thatcher shoved me over.

"Wait, dude, stop, okay?" he exhaled deeply. I didn't respond, just paused to give him a confused look. "Christ, I can't believe I'm about to say this. This is so fucking gay," he pinched the bridge of his nose.

"Spit it out dude, you've looked like you've had something to say for a while," I scowled.

"Well, obviously, for some reason, Kia's sickinly in love with you, and KJ, for some reason tolerates you meaning he has to care at least a little bit and- and well... you know?"

"..."

"I care about you fuck, head! and Kia and I were talking this morning he's worried about you and so am I! I've never really talked about it seriously with the guys before and Kia and I did actually talk and not just make a passing comment and then totally rip on you. I don't like watching you throw your life away... all for a bottle. I know I'm not like good at this stuff, and- I know I encourage it and I'm a shitty friend and- but you- and well I... just- please Marshal, hear us fucking out?"

"Thatcher..." coming from him, all of this was huge.

"Just please, try to help yourself before it's too late and you end up like my mom or something," he gave a nervous laugh, trying to lighten the mood with the joke about his mom. Thatcher hated being vulnerable like this, so of course, he couldn't have a completely honest and whole moment.

"I'm not- I- Wel... Look, dude, I just..." I stammered out, "It's complicated," I settled on.

"How is it complicated, Marsh?"

I went back to stammering incoherent thoughts trying to string together a coherent thought but ultimately couldn't.

"You need to stop or get help or something, dude. Watching you do this to yourself is tearing Kia apart, and I already can't handle him on a normal day, let alone when he's crying at me," he tried to sound tough but the look on his face conveyed his genuine concern for not just me but Kia too.

"Why do you pretend to hate him so much?" my lip slightly quivered as I tried to smirk.

"Just like how you're Marshal and Kia, we're Kia and Thatcher. We've been doing it so long; we can't stop now," he gave a sad smile. "Trust me, the feelings are mutual," he added, and I let out a sharp laugh, the kind that comes out when you don't know what else to do.

· LV ·

KIA

It was hot, the air heavy and sticky, while it weighed down the curls on the back of my neck. It was hot, but I didn't want to go back inside yet. Inside was another type of heavy. Talking to Peter was like a breath of fresh air, a break from everything else. The heaviness in my chest was now only from trying to swallow the thick air, but the knots in my stomach were starting to form again.

I couldn't hide forever, I couldn't just not go home, I was stuck.

At first, I sat down on the patio, but then I ended up laying flat on my back with an arm over my eyes. I basked in the warm, letting the heat from the rocks beneath my back soak in through my shirt, filling my body with a slightly uncomfortable heat. Laying there, the heavy air weighed down my clothes but soaked up the light heat of the sun, leaving me in a limbo somewhere between comfortably warm and too hot and sticky.

This was a labyrinth, and I didn't know how to get out. I weighed my options much like the heat weight in my thick curls. My hair was damp, clinging to my skin, I hated the feeling. My hair was longer than my liking, unruly, more so than usual. I hadn't had a haircut in a while, leaving the loose ringlets hanging almost below my ears, a neater version of Marsh's shag cut kind of.

My back was damp with sweat, my shirt sticking to the middle of my chest, another feeling that normally would drive me insane, but right now, it was grounding. I hated sweat, I hated the cloth sticking to my skin, weighed down by the moister.

I focused on my breathing, deep and even, focusing on the warmth, how my shirt stuck to my skin, and how my skin felt. I took it all in slowly, letting it seep into my pores. I was just trying to take in 'the human experience,' as my mother had called it. It was an old trick my mom used to calm me down when I was a kid. I was really anxious as a kid. I would spiral into uncontrollable rapid breaths choking on air I couldn't seem to swallow fast enough as my body was wracked in panic.

My mom held me close, forcing my ear against her chest. She'd tell me to listen to the beat of her heart.

'Hear that beibi? Focus on the rhythm; breathe with me. It's all about being human,' she took a deep breath, and I followed suit. Her hands rubbed up and down my back soothingly while she hummed a tune I couldn't quite place. 'All of this beibi is part of what it's like to be human, the good, the bad, all of it honey. Focus on what you feel, my hand on your back, my heart that beats for you. It's all okay, the bad is just part of life, but when it gets bad, honey, your mamma will always be here. Just focus on what's around you, what you're experiencing, the feelings, the sounds, take it in and remind yourself that you're just a boy and everything will be okay,' she muttered into my hair, pressing kisses onto my head.

If this was the human experience, I didn't want to be experiencing it. I took in all the feelings I could but still couldn't shake the rapid rhythm of my heartbeat, the way it made the sticky hotness of the afternoon sun amplified. It was still in the back of my mind, the feeling of fear, then anger, then disgust, and lastly, disappointment that I felt with everyone and everything. No amount of grounding could distract me from this part of the human experience.

I hate the human experience if it's leaving me with this shitty feeling. I don't want to be experiencing it if this was it: heavy air, heavy chest, frustration, and anger.

I don't know how long I laid there, but it was enough that I felt like I had fully melted my shirt now almost wholly soaked on the back. My skin had passed uncomfortably warm and spread into what would probably develop into a nasty sunburn. I peeled myself up and headed back inside, reveling in the cool air that hit me as soon as I opened the door. The house was quiet. The low lull of the TV could be heard coming in through the living room.

Marshal was lounging on the couch on his stomach, legs up on the back of the sofa, head on his folded arms, facing the lazily watching whatever show was playing. Thatcher was on the floor leaning against the couch, not even looking at the TV but rather scrolling on his phone.

I cleared my throat, "Uh... hey," my voice came out hoarse, almost like it hadn't been used in so long, and I was just trying to figure out how it worked again. I hadn't sounded that timid for as long as I could remember. At the sound of my voice, Marshal sprung up immediately, whining and gripping at his head.

"K! Dude! Fuck, I thought you left or something, I- god Kia..."

"Where would I go?" I said numbly strolling over to the couch and sinking into the cushions next to Marsh.

"Well... I don't know, but I just kind of figured- I mean, you were so mad and-" he stopped looking down with sad eyes. My eyes focused on something on the floor, two brown glass bottles with an oh-too-familiar label.

"Marshal Xavier Langdon!" my voice was high and sharp. I sounded like I could be seconds away from tears, and maybe I was. Everything recently had me feeling like some kind of out-of-body experience and I wasn't really here anymore.

"What?" he turned his head eyes suddenly winding when he saw what my gaze had fixed on.

"I can't fucking believe you..." my voice no longer high, now just barely audible.

"Kia untwist your panties. Those are my bottles," Thatcher interjected, and I snapped my eyes down to his position on the floor. He reached over to the half-full bottle taking a long gulp and making an exaggerated 'ah' sound once he had gulped down the rest of the bottle.

"Oh..."

"K? Listen, I talked to Thatcher, and I shouldn't have yelled at you guys," he looked up again, with wide glassy eyes. A unique shade of blue bordering on grey with flecks of green dotted through. His eyes were sunken, dark bags under his eyes, a permanent kind of tired etched into his face. I just stared, taking in every bit of Marsh. I was back in the moment, grounded, back in my body. I remembered that all the panic and frustration and anger was a necessary experience so I could really appreciate the good. So I could really love Marshal.

"I'm listening, dude," I cupped his check in my hand, running a thumb over his sharp bone.

"I want to get better, I don't want to destroy myself, or you know? end up like Thatcher's mom," he smiled that stupid boyish grin. It was contagious, and I mimicked it.

"Aye! Don't say shit about my mom!" Thatcher interjected.

"You know what, Thatcher? I bet the reason you're so fat is because you need all that extra room to keep all your other personalities in there, you goddamn hippicrite!" Marshal laughed.

"I'm not a hippicrite! Do you even know what that word means? It's a pretty big word," he shrugged.

"Yeah, it means you're full of shit!"

"No, I'm not because I'm allowed to say shit like that about my mom, and no one else can!" Thatcher protested.

"Jesus Christ, I can't have a nice moment with you guys, can I?" I shuttered out a laugh.

"No, because gingers don't deserver nice things," Thatcher pipped up in a snarky way.

"You're mom's a hoe, and you're a drug baby. Shut up before I smack you," I said deadpan, but my lips curled upward as I resisted the urge to smile.

"But really, fatass and I were talking, and, god help us all, the earth might start rotating backward after I say this, but I think for once Thatcher... had valid points and made sense."

I couldn't help but snort a little at that. "Shut up. I know the idea's fucked! But just listen to the words," Marshal scolded with a smile.

"Thank you, Marsh," Thatcher said smugly. I quickly pulled Marsh's face in, a sweet, soft, chaste kiss on his lips. I could sense Marshal tensing before he relaxed and kissed me back.

"Thank you," I whispered onto his lips.

"For what?" he said in that innocent but dumb way.

"Everything," I smiled, kissing him again. It was simple and sweet.

"I'm proud of you, Marshal..." Thatcher's voice cut in, low, barely audible, the way he gets when his small shreds of humanity slip out.

"Guys... this is getting kind of gay," Marsh snickered.

"Oh fuck you! Fucking making out with Kia and me saying *I'm proud of you* is where it starts to get gay?" Thatcher's face palmed, shaking his head and laughing. It was comfortable, this was comfortable. I felt like I was home, not in the sense of the building, but here with Marsh, tensions resolved, and even with Thatcher, our regular banter, it was home. There were still so many unspoken things, but they could all be said when the time was right. Everything seemed right.

We stayed like this for a couple of hours, all doing our own thing together, the TV providing ample background noise. Marshal had moved his head onto my lap, and I ran my fingers over his hair, gently coming through it.

"Your hair grows crazy fast, dude," I said more to myself, but Marshal gave a confused hum.

"Just your roots are like really kind of grown out, needs retouching," I said, inspecting his hair. "And washed dude, you're greasy."

"*Humph,*" was what I got out of him; Marsh was half asleep. I just smiled down at him before half paying attention to the TV show Marshal and Thatcher was playing. I jumped a little, as did Marshal when my phone started ringing. He sat up and rubbed at tired eyes.

"KJ?"

"No," I answered, seeing Peter's contact picture on my screen for the incoming Facetime call, "Peter, actually."

"Thought you were radio silence with them?"

"It's Peter, dude," I simply responded, swiping to accept the call, "Hey kid, what's up?"

"Uh... You know, we never really finished our conversation earlier-" he looked nervous.

"You good?"

"Uh yeah, I just..."

"Kia Mathew!" my father's stern, off-screen voice called out. *Oh fuck.*

"I'm sorry, Kia!"

Peter yelped.

"You bastard," I seethed. Marsh and Thatcher were both intently staring at me. "Unbelievable, he ambushed me!" I groaned, looking at Marsh slack-jawed. Thatcher and he shared an uneasy look.

"Give me one good reason not to hang up right now," I grunted.

"Well, since you won't talk to you're own parents but will talk to Peter, we saw this as our only option to contact you," My mother said in that victimizing voice.

"Hmm, wonder why I don't want to talk to you, Ma?" I said sarcastically.

"Hear us out, *beibi!*" she pleaded.

"Kia, please, we understand you're upset, and for good reason, too. Your mother and I have been talking, and we need to revisit that conversation from last night. It definitely should have been handled differently," my dad said with that lawyer's way of talking.

My eyebrows raised, "I'm listening." Phones were put down, and the TV paused, eyes and ears on me.

"Kia, what you said was... shocking, and it caught us off guard," my mother said through the phone, both parents sharing the screen and taking turns talking. "We didn't mean all those things we said."

"Really? Because you seemed pretty damn sure about your stance," I said coldly.

"Kia, you have to understand... your father and I are from a different time," my mother tried to plead.

"Oh, sorry, did I miss the part where you were frozen for the last few decades? That's not an excuse," I tried to remain calm and even, but still, the anger was starting to build low in my chest. My mom's eye twitched, and her mouth started to open.

"And we know that!" it was my dad who spoke this time. "Tensions were.. well high, and your mother and I were upset about a couple of other things, and we just focused on the wrong things. Truth be told, we always sort of... suspected," my dad shrugged. Thatcher's jaw flew open wide-eyed and cackled. I kicked him, and it was Marsh's turn to let out stifled giggles. My parents shared a confused look before continuing on.

"I'm ashamed of myself for trying to weaponize religion against you, Kia. Homosexuality isn't a sin. It's who you are, and god loves you no matter what," my mom said in a sweet, genuine voice that only a mother could have. I hadn't realized how tensed up my body was until my shoulders dropped.

"Both of us love you, no matter who you are or what you do. This is you, Kia, and we want you to be who you are. We want you to be happy and free, *beibi*," she cooed at me. I felt my eyes start to widen slightly.

"I- I uh... I think you owe Marshal an apology, too."

"Is he there?"

"Yeah," I signaled with my hand for Marsh to come closer, and he leaned in to view of the camera.

"Hi, Mr. and Mrs. Schwartz," he said with a slight voice crack that I couldn't help but laugh at.

"Hi Marshal, I'm sure Kia's filled you in, and he's right. We do owe you boys both an apology. We're sorry. You've been a part of Kia's life since you boys were in diapers, and you're almost like our own boy," my mom started, and Marshal just awkwardly smiled.

"We weren't trying to put a blame on you, or anything of that matter. We're glad he has you, and we want to be supportive of not just Kia but you too and your relationship," my dad added.

"Wow, uh, thanks- I mean, actually, that means a lot to me," Marshal stuttered slightly but beamed ear to ear with rosy cheeks.

"I talked to your mother, Marshal, because I guess you boys have a habit of not answering your phone," she sighed with annoyance. "She wants you to call her. She has a lot of things to talk about with you. Both of us smiled at each other.

"Kia, we'd like you home. We have more things we need to talk about, and I'd rather do it in person," my dad added.

"Yeah, sure, I'll be over soon," I agreed. We said our goodbyes and ended the call. My chest was buzzing, my body filled with the static feeling of excitement, and I looked at both Marsh and Addie. My cheeks hurt from the wide smile that broke out over my face, and when I looked at each boy, their faces mirrored my own. Marsh, Thatcher, and I all shot up, dancing around in a celebratory way, yelling. We all pulled each other into a group hug. The moment died, and I quickly pulled away.

"Ew! I got so excited I hugged Thatcher," I pushed him away playfully, laughing while sticking my out in disgust.

"That's it! Out of my house, Jew," he laughed. I lunged at Marsh, interlocking our lips, wrapping my arms around his neck, and pulling him close.

"I love you, dude," he smiled at me once he pulled away.

"I think everything's going to be alright," I smiled.

This was the start of something new, a new stage of life I was ready for. This was a new phase for Marshal and I. Everything was lining up with him by my side, making everything feel right. *The right time and the right place*- that's what this was.

We belonged together like the sun, and the moon go together, and together, stepping forward into this new phase, our worlds were coming together in a perfect way like the stars aligning.